Remember No More

Remember No More

Pamela Reid

a novel

Covenant Communications, Inc.

Cover image by Jeremy Woodhouse, Photodisc Green/Getty Images

Cover design copyrighted 2005 by Covenant Communications, Inc.

Published by Covenant Communications, Inc.
American Fork, Utah

Printed in Canada
First Printing: June 2005

11 10 09 08 07 06 05   10 9 8 7 6 5 4 3 2 1

ISBN 1-59156-858-7

To my family

NORTH ISLAND

Auckland

Hamilton
▲ N.Z. Temple

Wellington

Christchurch

SOUTH ISLAND

Glenorchy
Lake Wakatipu
Queenstown

Dunedin

Location Map

New Zealand

GLOSSARY OF TERMS

General Terms

Car park	Parking lot
Intermediate school	Middle school for 11- through 12-year-olds
Jumper	Sweater
Mate	Good friend or confidante
Nappy	Diaper (a *nappy bag* is a diaper bag)
Kiwi	Nickname for a New Zealander based on the bird, the kiwi, which is a national icon of New Zealand
Pohutukawa	A native tree that flourishes in coastal areas (it has distinctive red flowers that blossom in December, earning it the title of the New Zealand Christmas Tree)
Rimu	A native tree whose wood is a favorite for furniture making
Sheep station	A ranch situated in the more rugged mountain areas of New Zealand
Docket	Supermarket receipt

Pronunciation of vowels in the Maori Language

a – (ar) as in *far*

e – (ea) as in *leather*

i – (ee) as in *me* or *he*

o – (aw) as in *awe*

u – (oo) as in *moon*

Maori Words

Karaitiana	Christian
Koati	Goat
Koro	Grandfather
Pakeha	White-skinned person
Wahine	Woman
Whanau	Family
Whakapapa	Family history/genealogy

Maori Phrases

Aroha mai	I'm sorry
Haere ra	Good-bye
Hiki ake ki tou ake mana	Lift yourself up and realize your potential/strength
Ka haere mua	Move forward in a positive direction
Kia ora	Hello
Mate atua koe e manaki	God be with you
Taku mokopuna	My grandchild

Maori Names

Henare	Henry
Herewini	Selwyn
Hoani	John
Maata	Martha
Petera	Peter

Prologue

It was a strange mixture of sounds and silence that seemed soothing in their monotony. First there was the sea talking from outside—a quiet background whisper that she always thought was too quiet when so much water was being stirred around. Then, from across the room, the sounds blended with the labored intake of air followed by a long pause when the sea noise got louder. A sudden throaty gurgle, and then the waves crashed just as the snore reached its strangled peak.

She almost smiled as her grandfather stirred only enough to move his shoulders and for his chin to settle back onto his chest, ready for the next round. She knew there would be three quieter snores while the waves gained momentum, then both the ocean and he would crescendo together again.

It was chilly in the small room, and her thin shoulders trembled in a sudden shiver as she glanced over at the thin floral sheet that curtained off the pile of thin mattresses she slept on. Getting into bed was an option, but it always felt lonelier now. Lonelier and emptier without the warmth of her mother's body against her back, safe arms wrapped around her, holding her close.

Her grandfather snorted again, so loudly this time that he woke himself up and immediately raised a bushy eyebrow and peered at her across the room.

"Why are you still up?" His voice was muffled as he rubbed his hand over his face and stood up slowly. "Put those crayons away and get to bed, girl." He began to shuffle toward his bedroom, his too-large slippers making slapping noises on the bare floorboards. "Your mother should have taught you better. Little children go to bed early."

She shivered again as she obediently folded the old newspaper with its neatly colored-in advertisements and carefully put what remained of the precious stubs of crayons into their cardboard box. The well-worn top ripped slightly as she closed it, and she tried to suppress the instant tears that threatened.

Sing a song in your heart, my daughter. Where only you can hear it and no one else can stop it.

She didn't know the song she began to hum, but she felt the melody in her narrow chest and the sob stopped beside it. At the same time, she instinctively gave a quick glance toward the closed bedroom door. She knew without asking that there would be no more crayons once these had finished, and her hands trembled as she held the precious paper and crayons in her lap.

Coloring with her crayons had become her evening ritual, but she had already finished every picture on every page in the one coloring book her mother had bought her. There had always been story time before bed each night, but she couldn't read all of the words on her own yet, so coloring filled in the lonely hours.

"The old man gone to bed?"

She looked up and nodded silently as a blast of cold air preceded the stocky figure of her uncle that seemed to fill the doorway. He coughed loudly, and even from across the room she could smell the musty odor of his breath. He always smelled like that after he'd been out with his friends. Usually they would come back and sleep in the chairs or on the floor, but lately he had been coming home on his own.

"Ya want Uncle to tell ya a bedtime story?" When she didn't respond, he cursed under his breath and leaned heavily against the doorjamb. "Not as if your mumsy's going to tell ya one . . . not anymore."

She stood up without speaking and walked to the window. It was a habit she'd gotten into just before she went to bed. If she stood on tiptoe she could see the top of the hill, and the moon would shine a soft light on the three solid headstones silhouetted alongside the waving stems of long grass. She raised two shaking fingers to her lips like her mother had shown her and blew a tiny kiss toward the hilltop before turning to him.

Her mother used to tell her stories and sing her songs. She didn't really remember what they were about . . . only that she loved the sound of her mother's voice as she talked or sang, and the warmth as she was held close. She missed that warmth so much. She missed the stories. She wanted to be cuddled.

Without a word she went and stood in front of him.

"Ya don't say much do ya?"

She felt herself lifted up and instinctively turned her face away from the smell.

"Bit of a strange one—just like your mother. All quiet and thinking she's high and mighty."

His laugh was short and derisive.

"Didn't do her much good, and it won't help you either."

It wasn't the same when her uncle told her stories. He'd laugh about their "special" stories, but she didn't feel like smiling. He cuddled her, but his whiskers hurt her face when he rubbed against her cheek, and his hand didn't hold hers gently like her mother's had. Instead, his large, rough fingers would trace patterns all over her body.

Once she had cried out when she hurt, but he said he'd take her crayons away if she made any noise. She quickly learned to cry inside.

Sing a song, my daughter. Sing a song in your heart.

There was the ocean whisper again, but it was mixing with the other noises now. She tried to put her mind into the ocean and let it get pulled down in the giant mesh of kelp.

Sing a song in your heart.

Chapter 1

"Kiri, wait a second! Can you please, please cover my shift for me tomorrow?"

Tightening her grip on the door handle, Kiri rested her forehead against the edge of the door and paused as the other waitress on duty rushed up to her. Resigned to her fate, she waited for the inevitable reasons why Dolly wouldn't possibly be able to work her set shift the next day.

"Kiri, I've got to go to the doctor's and then he'll probably send me for blood tests. My car's already playing up so I don't know that I'll be able to get anywhere on time." Dolly shook her vibrant, bottled-red curls and pouted equally bright red lips. "Please, Kiri . . . please, please, please. I'll owe you big-time."

Kiri tried to smile, but even that seemed to add to the pain that was throbbing behind her left eye. She lifted her head and winced slightly with the effort.

"I'd like to, Dolly, and I could do with the extra hours but . . ." She shut her eyes briefly. "I'm kind of looking forward to a day off."

"Is it that headache you had earlier?" Dolly patted Kiri's arm consolingly. "I noticed you hadn't been humming as much when you were clearing up. Beats me how you can be cheerful doing the nasty stuff. Anyway . . . I'm sure you'll be fine by tomorrow—you just need to get a good night's rest. So, shall I tell Ben that you'll cover, then? It's just the two-till-eight shift, then you'll have the whole evening free."

She barely paused between thoughts, and Kiri managed a weak smile as Dolly's now familiar high-pitched voice dropped to a tone of desperation.

"Please, Kiri."

"Who is it this time, Dolly? Is he German or Dutch?"

Dolly hesitated for a second, then she giggled and pretended to stamp her foot. "Kiri Karaitiana . . . how can you know me so well after only a few days?" She glanced around quickly as if someone might be listening, then rolled her eyes. "Actually, he's a genuine Frenchman, if you please, and he's absolutely gorgeous!" She hesitated and pouted again. "Besides, now that you're here to take my place, I'll be leaving Queenstown soon. This could be my last opportunity . . ."

For the briefest moment Kiri felt tempted to wish the Frenchman was back in France, but instead she held up her hand and nodded in surrender. "Okay, Dolly. You go and have a good time. Just tell Ben I'll be in tomorrow and that you'll cover for me if I have an 'important' appointment in the next little while."

Dolly giggled again. "I won't have to worry for a while then." She put her finger to her mouth and rolled her eyes again. "Not that I mean that you're . . . I mean . . ." She frowned, then grinned happily. "You know I'd be happy to fix you up with a date, Kiri. There are heaps of foreign guys visiting Queenstown who would love to date a real Maori *wahine* . . . well, half Maori anyway, especially a lovely one like you. I mean, I'd give my teeth to have thick, black wavy hair and that year-round tan . . ."

Kiri shook her head, then grimaced slightly before she finished quietly. "And then you wouldn't be Dolly and life would be so boring you'd die."

"True," Dolly bubbled back. "But I'm serious about getting you a date. Marcel—my Frenchman—has a really fun friend he's traveling with, and they're both university students. You'd have lots in common."

Kiri smiled weakly as she turned toward the door. "Just go . . . before I change my mind."

"Okeydokey," Dolly chuckled, then she hesitated, her head tilted. "Oh . . . and if I don't see you before I leave . . . it's been fun working with you, and you must be rubbing off on me because that big guy left a tip in the middle of his mashed potato and I found myself humming as I picked it out." She leaned forward and gave Kiri a quick hug. "You're a really nice girl."

The evening air was cooled by a fairly brisk breeze flowing straight off Lake Wakatipu, and Kiri pulled her corduroy jacket more tightly around her. A deep breath of fresh air sent her into a spasm of coughing, and she held her head to stop the pounding.

"Hot lemon and honey drink and you'll be fine," she muttered into the collar of her jacket as she set off down the road to the bus stop. She glanced at her watch and saw that she had another ten minutes to wait for the bus that would take her to the one-bedroom apartment she was renting for her stay in Queenstown.

"Times like this, it would be so good to have a car." She pushed the strap of her handbag up onto her shoulder and rested against the support of the bus shelter. She could have bought a car when she'd arrived back in New Zealand from her year spent teaching English in Korea, but she really hadn't seen the need since she was in Queenstown to work, not play. With a car, she knew, it would be easier to go more places and spend the money she'd saved so carefully. After three years at university training as an occupational therapist, it had seemed a good idea to go to Korea for a year and earn twice as much money as she would as a therapist; that way she'd be able to pay off her debts. Now those debts were paid, but there was the future to consider and the need to provide for that.

She briefly toyed with the idea of walking the twenty minutes to her flat, then the wind blew and whipped around her again and she moved quickly inside the shelter as another cough rattled her chest.

"Please, bus, be on time," Kiri murmured at the view of the lake.

"What's that, love?" She turned as an elderly man looked at her intently from the slat-bench seat. "Did you say something to me?"

"Um, no. I was talking to myself." She smiled self-consciously and pointed in the direction the bus would come. "I was hoping the bus would be on time."

"Oh, apparently they're pretty good," the man responded agreeably. "At least the man I called at the depot told me they were. Mind you, he said that it'll get pretty busy soon when the weather warms up. Are you new around here, love?"

Kiri shrugged. "Sort of . . . I used to work down here a few years ago."

"So where are you from? Are you a North Island lass? You don't sound like you're from the South Island."

Kiri hesitated briefly, but the man seemed harmless and genuinely interested, and surprisingly, she felt herself relax. She nodded. "Born and raised in Hawke's Bay, but I've been teaching school in Korea for the last year with Americans."

"Oh . . . do you speak Korean?" The man shook his head. "Amazes me how you young folk can pick up these languages. I spent fifty-five years herding sheep, and I still can't understand them." His perceptivity and humor suddenly appealed to Kiri and she gave a short laugh.

The man looked up and pushed his worn cotton hat farther back on his head.

"You should laugh more, my girl. You've got a beautiful smile and the sun fair shines out of you when you laugh like that. You remind me of my wife in her younger days."

Unaccustomed to direct compliments, Kiri found she was smiling at his obvious sincerity and that her head wasn't hurting so much. She moved inside the shelter and sat down on the seat facing him.

"You know you're very easy to talk to. I don't usually take up conversation with strangers."

The man chuckled. "Believe me, lass . . . I don't usually chat with new people, either." He glanced at her. "You just didn't look very happy when you got here."

Kiri stared at the rough concrete floor, then she shook her head. "Not unhappy . . . just a bit of a headache." She pointed to the bank of shops nearby. "So are you on holiday here?"

"In a way." The man stood up as the bus drew into the stop, and he gestured for Kiri to get on first. They made their way on and sat down before he continued. "My wife says we're on holiday because we're in a different place, but I'm really helping a friend do some building up Glenorchy way."

Kiri noticed the man's wiry frame and leathered skin. He was old but obviously still very agile.

"You said you herded sheep. Do you build as well?"

He chuckled. "When you've lived on a station your whole life, you get to do a bit of everything. I'm no carpenter, but I'm not useless."

He suddenly reminded her of some of the elderly patients she had tended during her training as an occupational therapist, and Kiri found herself enjoying his conversation. She had discovered a natural affinity with older people and now she turned in her seat and instinctively held out her hand. "We'd better introduce ourselves first. I'm Kiri."

The man looked briefly surprised, then he shook her hand warmly. "Kiri . . . I'm Ted," he nodded his head at her hand. "I thought you must be one of those Mormons wanting to shake my hand."

Kiri laughed self-consciously and flexed her fingers. "Actually, you aren't wrong. I am one of those Mormons, but the handshake is just a natural reaction."

Ted turned in his seat and stared hard at her with his eyes slightly squinted. "So you are a Mormon?"

There was more genuine interest than accusation in the tone of his voice, and Kiri nodded.

"Yes, I am."

She fiddled with the handle of her bag, suddenly wondering if she should talk more about the Church. It had been a long time since she'd really talked to anyone about the gospel. The few English-speaking people she'd known in Korea hadn't expressed any interest in religion, and even attending church had been a marathon that she'd only managed twice a month because of her distance from the chapel.

"You might know some friends of mine." Ted indicated to his left. "The Harvey family? They live over in Christchurch."

Kiri shook her head, happy to take his lead. "No, I don't. I'm sorry. I don't really know many members in the South Island. Mainly just some students and a few families in Dunedin I knew at university."

Ted nodded. "So, do you go to church here?"

"Not yet." She patted her chest. "I got a bit sick just after I got here last week, so I haven't made it to church yet."

"You know where they meet?" he asked, shaking his head. "Craziest thing—they hold their meetings in a funeral parlor . . . in the chapel part."

Kiri frowned. "How do you know . . . I mean, I found out . . . but how . . . ?"

Ted scratched his head and adjusted his hat. "The young fellow I work with is a Mormon. That's why I asked you if you knew the

Harvey family. His name is Daniel Harvey and he sort of helps run things down there at the church."

She looked thoughtful. "I only spoke briefly to the branch president to find out where to go. What did you say your friend's name was?"

"Dan . . . Daniel Harvey," Ted began to dig in the pocket of his jacket and produced a supermarket docket and a pen. "Look, why don't you tell me where you're staying, Kiri, and I'll let him know. He might be able to give you a ride to church or something."

* * *

"So you told her I'd pick her up?" Dan studied the address neatly written down the side of the docket.

"Pretty much," Ted chuckled. "I think it'll be worth your while. She's a lovely girl. Reminds me a lot of Winnie when she was young . . . very friendly."

"Are you setting me up, Ted?" Dan tapped the docket against the palm of his hand. "It sort of feels like it."

Ted sipped his cup of tea, then slowly set the cup into its saucer. "Not setting you up, son. I'm just helping you to be a good shepherd. Isn't that what you Mormons are all about?"

Dan laughed outright and turned to Ted's wife. Winnie was standing at the kitchen bench. "You know, my family told me that you two weren't members of the Church, but I think you know just enough about the gospel to be dangerous. It's about time you both got baptized."

Winnie smiled and rubbed her wrist against her forehead so the flour on her hands didn't spread. "Your family are good teachers, and most of what they say seems very familiar to me, but . . . there's time enough for all that. Old people have a lot more to change than young ones." She nodded at him. "So, are you going to get in touch with . . . what was her name, Ted?"

"Kiri . . . Kiri Karaitiana," he nodded. "Doesn't Karaitiana mean 'Christian' in Maori, Winnie?"

"It does." Winnie looked surprised, then she nodded knowingly at Dan. "Maybe it's an omen . . . a good Christian woman for you, Dan." She emphasized the word *good*.

"Meaning not a 'bad' one?" He shrugged as he caught her meaning. "Sarah's not bad—she just didn't want to marry me."

"She two-timed you!" Ted grunted. "Or that's what your mother said."

"Then I was better off finding out sooner than later, wasn't I?" Dan grinned ruefully. "I can't say being jilted didn't hurt, but in a way I feel . . . more free somehow."

"Free for a better relationship?" Ted winked at Winnie.

"Free to not have a relationship." Dan shook his head and raised his hands, palms upward, and looked meaningfully at the ceiling. "I only asked for help with building . . . and I get two resident match-makers. What did I do wrong?"

Ted chuckled again. "Nothing wrong . . . unless you don't go to see her. She's a tiny, wee lass, Dan." He touched his shoulder. "She'd come up to about here on you. Short, dark wavy hair, big brown eyes . . . and she's educated. She went to university in Dunedin, and she's been teaching over in Korea."

Winnie looked genuinely surprised. "Goodness me, Ted Morris. When did you ever talk that much . . . and to a complete stranger, as well?"

Her husband picked up his cup again. "It was easy, Winnie. I just felt like I was talking to a younger version of you . . . and I did most of the listening."

Chapter 2

Dan drove slowly down the short street, studying the numbers on the older letterboxes. Some were hard to distinguish, and he had to lean forward to tell whether there were letters added to the numbers.

"42A." He checked the house and the address on the docket, then pulled the four-wheel drive in against the curb outside a simple two-story weatherboard house. The downstairs had a large sliding glass door, and a small brass letter *A* hung crookedly on the doorjamb.

Dan hesitated briefly, then raised his hand and knocked firmly. He waited for a minute or so, but when there was no response, he knocked again more loudly. Even as he lowered his hand, the inside curtain on the door was pulled back slightly, and he saw a brief look of confusion pass across the girl's face. The curtain dropped down, and then the door and curtain were pulled back a few inches.

"Kiri?" Dan cleared his throat. "Kiri Karaitiana?"

"Yes." She too had to clear her throat as she coughed and tightened a dark blue robe across her body. "Can I help you?"

"Um . . . I'm Daniel Harvey. I believe you met a friend of mine the other night—Ted . . . on the bus?"

He watched her recognition lift a veil of concern and the door opened wider.

"Why, yes . . . he talked about you. You're a member of the Church." Kiri straightened her dressing gown and touched her hair. "I wasn't really expecting you . . . that is . . . ."

Dan noticed the dark shadows under her eyes and the way she suddenly coughed again. "Have you been sick?"

She waved her hand in front of her mouth. "Just a bit of flu from the change of climate. Really, I'm fine."

There was a brief silence, then Dan patted the sides of his legs. "Well, I just called in to welcome the newest member of our tiny Queenstown Branch and to see if I can help with anything or . . . Ted mentioned that you were on the bus, so to see if you could use a ride to church on Sunday."

Kiri hesitated. She was still holding the curtain and standing in the doorway, so she motioned him inside. "Um . . . I guess. Um, would you like to come in? It's a bit messy, I'm afraid."

Dan held up his hand. "No, no, I'm fine. Look, I know it's early. I'm just on my way to town to get some building supplies, but I wanted to see you and . . ." He shrugged. "Welcome you, I guess."

"Well, thank you. I appreciate that." She smiled shyly. "I must admit I was feeling a bit lonely, and being sick didn't help. When Ted started talking to me . . . well, he was so kind, I just opened up."

"He did say he surprised himself," Dan smiled. "He said you remind him of his wife, Winnie."

Kiri nodded and there was another brief silence, then Dan pointed to his truck. "So, would you like a ride to church on Sunday? I just live up the road, so it's not a problem."

He smiled again, and Kiri suddenly noticed how deep the dimples were on his left cheek and on his chin and how green his eyes were. She had to tilt her head back to look at him properly, and his wavy brown hair had a slight golden aura where the early morning sun shone behind him. She also noticed the width of his shoulders in the light blue denim shirt. The whole impression he conveyed was pleasant and . . . solid. She mentally chided herself for sizing him up, then stared at the top of his collar. He was, after all, just offering to help her out . . . like a good home teacher would.

"That would be lovely." She held out her hand. "I really appreciate the offer . . . and your coming to see me."

Dan reached forward. Her hand felt very small inside his large one, but she gripped his hand firmly and he responded in kind.

"It'll be nice to have another young person in the branch." He glanced at his watch. "I'd better go. So I'll see you Sunday morning about nine thirty."

"Nine thirty will be fine." Kiri frowned. "But will that be early enough? Ted said you help run things."

"That gives me plenty of time, although . . ." He hesitated, then asked, "Kiri . . . you don't happen to play the piano, do you?"

Kiri laughed self-consciously as she thought about the hours spent on the old piano at the University Hostel. "I do play, but I'm totally self-taught. Not exactly the concert pianist, but I'm okay on hymns."

"Then we'll go a little bit earlier so you can practice." Dan grinned. "That is . . . if you wouldn't mind being the pianist. I usually bluff my way as the chorister."

"Sounds like a great combination, Dan." Kiri smiled and felt a genuine surge of anticipation. "I'll look forward to it."

The rumbling sound of the truck's engine had died away before she closed the door thoughtfully and pulled the curtain back into place. She didn't even have to close her eyes to visualize his face and the way he'd smiled. Kiri looked sideways at the small, framed mirror on the wall by the door. She groaned slightly.

Her naturally curly hair had a tendency to do its own thing, and even the short style she'd chosen last year had to be kept under strict control. Right now several tufts stood on end where the quick brushing she'd given it hadn't helped, and one of her black eyebrows had decided to bush up in the middle. She put a hand across her mouth and rolled her eyes at her reflection, but for some reason, Dolly's prompting to enjoy life more came to mind.

She knew she avoided relationships, and it wasn't because she felt unattractive. But it seemed as though any time she let herself get close to a man, there was that same suffocating feeling that would almost physically overwhelm her and make her keep her distance, leaving her dates wondering what they had done when she declined any more commitment. Young adults at church had tried to include her, but she found that friendships with elderly people had filled the need for companionship without the complications of a romantic relationship.

She'd often justified her reluctance to develop a relationship as simply a way of putting her focus elsewhere—to keep working and studying hard to be independent. Her self-imposed solitude had paid off. So now she was starting again, trying to earn more money to further her education. She didn't need any commitments.

"But it would be nice just to have a friend," she sighed as she glanced at her reflection again and grimaced. "Oh well . . . Sunday's two days away. I can only improve."

* * *

"Shall I run up and get her?" Daniel glanced at Ted sitting beside him. "Or would you like to surprise her? She probably wouldn't be expecting to see you."

Ted grunted and looked down at the shirt and tie he was wearing underneath his favorite tweed jacket. "She probably wouldn't recognize me in this getup. I had to take a second look in the mirror myself."

Winnie leaned over from the backseat and touched her husband on the shoulder. "You look just grand, Ted. As handsome as I've ever seen you."

"Now don't you start getting mushy on me, Winnie. If I get out of the truck to get Kiri, I may not get back in."

"Then you go, Daniel. I'll make sure Ted doesn't get away," Winnie laughed. "But you'd better be quick."

They were all laughing as Dan pulled up outside Kiri's house, and Winnie peered out of the side window.

"Is that her place downstairs . . . the glass door with the curtain drawn?"

Daniel opened the door and looked up the driveway. "Yes, it is. It doesn't look like much is happening, does it? I did tell her the time I was coming to pick her up."

He tried to look nonchalant as he walked up the driveway, but his heart was beating faster than normal as he tapped lightly on the glass door. When there was no response, he knocked more loudly, but there was still no sign of movement. He turned toward the truck and gave an exaggerated shrug, to which Winnie and Ted responded by pointing toward the upstairs portion of the house.

Daniel tried knocking one more time, then made his way up the front stairs to a paneled wood door. On his first knock the door opened, and a small woman with purplish-gray hair greeted him abruptly.

"Are you here for the young lady?" She twisted her face and squinted up at Dan as if trying to make out his features more clearly.

"Yes. I arranged to pick Kiri up for church this morning, but there doesn't seem to be anybody there." He paused. "Have you spoken to her or seen her at all?"

The woman shook her head vehemently. "Not a sign, but I've been getting phone calls from the man at her work. Very surly man. Kept calling and telling me off for her not turning up at work—as if it's my fault." She pointed downstairs. "I only keep one phone, and I just buzz her to pick up the extension. I can only think she's gone out."

Daniel turned, then he hesitated. "Excuse me for asking, but when did you see her last?"

The lady peered upwards and squinted again. "Must have been . . . Friday . . . Friday morning." She nodded toward the truck. "After you were here."

"I see." Daniel smiled, getting a sudden picture of the woman watching out of her window behind a lace curtain, unseen, but missing nothing in her neighborhood. "So you didn't see Kiri go out at all?"

"It's none of my business what she does." The woman looked momentarily offended, then natural curiosity seemed to get the better of her. "Would you like me to call downstairs?"

"Would you mind?" Daniel glanced at his wristwatch. "That would be really helpful."

The woman seemed to take forever to return, and when she did she held out a small brass key. "There's no answer, but maybe we should take a look . . . just in case."

Daniel followed her down the stairs and waited while she fiddled with the lock. "I don't usually do this sort of thing," the woman mumbled. "But she seems like a nice girl. I'm sure she wouldn't mind . . . after all, you're a friend."

She stood back and gestured to Daniel to open the door. He hesitated slightly before sliding the glass door and heavy curtain back just enough to put his head in the opening.

"Kiri!" he called out in the loud whisper that the circumstances seemed to dictate. There was no answer, and he began to feel a sense of urgency. "Kiri . . . are you there?"

There was still no response, but he could smell the mustiness of a room that hadn't had any fresh air for a while. With a mounting sense of trepidation, he ducked his head under the curtain and stepped inside. The room was dark with only the shaded orange light filtering through the heavy curtains. He blinked to see more clearly and made out a small round table and two chairs, a set of drawers with some clothes on top, and a bed with more clothes lying across the end. There was a definite mound beneath the bedspread, but there was no movement.

"Kiri?" He turned back to the woman. "Can you come and see with me, please?"

They both walked across to the bed, and Dan heard a sharp intake of the woman's breath as she leaned over the still form in the bed.

"Oh, my goodness . . . is she dead?"

Daniel had the same thoughts as he reached over and gently touched Kiri's shoulder. There wasn't any movement, but he could feel the heat of her body radiating through the thin bed sheet, and her hair was damp and disheveled across the pillow.

"She's not dead . . . but she's very sick." He turned. "Can you go and get my friends out of the car? And do you know a doctor or emergency service we could call?"

The woman nodded and gripped her hands together as she went quickly to the door. "I'll call the emergency . . . but you know this isn't my fault. This hasn't ever happened before."

In the few seconds it took for Winnie and Ted to come inside, Daniel quickly tried Kiri's pulse. It was weak but steady.

"What's happened?" Winnie laid her hand on the bedspread as she leaned forward for a better look. "Oh, the poor child. How long has she been alone like this?"

She was whispering, but she stopped as Kiri suddenly moved slightly and groaned. The movement seemed to trigger another spasm of pathetic, hoarse coughing that made her body lurch as she moaned again.

"She's completely out of it." Daniel frowned. "She's probably dehydrated, so we'll need to get her to hospital as fast as we can. Ted, can you check with the lady upstairs to see if an ambulance is coming?"

As Ted left quickly, Winnie glanced at Daniel. "I hate to imagine what might have happened to her if we hadn't come to pick her up. She looks dreadful." She instinctively stroked Kiri's damp forehead. "The poor girl."

Daniel stood helplessly for a second, then he turned and checked the doorway, nodding as if making a decision.

"Winnie, I'm going to give her a blessing. Do you know what I mean by that?"

There was a brief silence, then Winnie nodded. "I think so. Our Mackenzie said something about it once, after she was baptized. She said that her fiancé Wade gave her a blessing when she was sick up in the States." She hesitated. "I know it's something to do with you men being able to heal people, and if it's going to help this child get better, then just do it."

* * *

It was always faces.

The same faces in the same sequence.

A woman's face, kind and calm, then suddenly contorting and fading away to be replaced by the old man's face. He stares, then his eyes close, and she can only see the back of his head as he turns away. Then two young men fill her vision. They are the same, but different, and then the feeling of being crushed, suffocated, and unable to move her arms or legs. Then the faces become one . . .

"No! No!" Kiri struggled to open her eyes as she turned her head restlessly from side to side. Her arms seemed to be pinned to her sides. As her eyes began to focus, she looked questioningly at the strange woman sitting beside her bed.

"Where am I? What . . . happened?" Her voice broke as the dryness of her mouth and throat caused her to cough hoarsely. She tried to lift her hand to her head but immediately felt the pull of intravenous lines inserted into her arms and dropped it back onto the bed.

Winnie leaned forward and gently patted Kiri's hand. "It's all right now, love. You've been very ill, but you're in hospital and you're improving very quickly."

Kiri felt the warmth on her hand and the comforting squeeze, but she still frowned in confusion. "Was I sick? How long . . . ?" She looked suddenly mortified as she took a deep, quivering breath. "My work. Oh, my goodness . . ."

"Don't worry, dear, that's all been taken care of. Dan called around to the restaurant and explained what had happened."

"Dan?" Kiri looked anxious again.

"Daniel Harvey. Dan came to pick you up for church. My name's Winnie, and you met my husband Ted on the bus and he told Dan you needed a ride to church," Winnie explained gently, then waited as the expression on Kiri's face changed, recognition dawning.

"Of course . . . I remember now." Kiri's voice was barely a whisper, and she tentatively reached up with her other hand to touch her hair. "Oh, this is awful."

"Tch, my girl. You're looking much, much better than when we found you." Winnie shook her head.

"Found me?"

"We came to pick you up for church and you weren't ready, so Dan got concerned and asked your landlady to let us in and check your flat. When we found you, you were quite delirious. The doctor said it was some sort of virus and that you'd developed pneumonia."

"Pneumonia." Kiri looked startled. "How long have I been here?"

"Two days."

There was a long silence as Kiri stared at the wall, trying to comprehend the lost time.

"I'm so sorry."

"Now what have you to be sorry about?" Winnie smiled and her eyes glistened slightly as she stood up and gently rearranged the pillows behind Kiri's head. "I'm just so glad we found you in time. Dan gave you a blessing."

Something in the quiet confidential tone of her voice made Kiri turn her head slowly. "He gave me a blessing?"

"Yes, love." Winnie nodded as she sat down again. "I've never seen the like of it before. He spoke so calmly, and soon after that you started breathing so much better . . . like you were listening to him even though you couldn't hear him."

Kiri lay back against her pillows as she tried to comprehend Dan laying his hands on her head. She closed her eyes again. No one had done that for her since she'd been baptized as a little girl.

"Now then, dear. You just relax. It's all a bit much to take in at once. Dan said he'd come up later with Ted." Her voice dropped a tone. "Do you want me to bring you anything from home . . . like a nightgown or pajamas? I didn't want to get anything without asking you first, but these hospital gowns aren't very pretty, are they?"

Kiri glanced down at the shapeless green tunic that she was wearing and smiled weakly. "That would be nice, thank you . . ." She hesitated, staring at Winnie with a questioning frown.

"It's Winnie, dear. Winnie Morris." She stood up. "Now, I'll just go and tell the nurse you're awake, then I'll call Daniel and Ted." She paused at the end of the bed. "I hope you don't mind me helping you . . . it's just, when I saw you looking so ill, I just . . . well, I just wanted to help and so did young Daniel."

"I'm glad you did." Kiri coughed sharply and lifted her hand off the bed. "I don't seem to be very good at looking after myself at the moment. Thank you, Winnie."

The women looked at each other for a second, and then Winnie quickly walked up to her side and dropped a quick kiss on Kiri's forehead, patting her hand.

"You take care, dear, and we'll see you later."

As the door closed behind her, Kiri raised her hand slowly and gently rubbed her forehead. It still felt warm as if the gentle kiss had lingered; it was as if her mother's lips were pressing a warm comfort against her head as sleep claimed her again.

She slept until the nurse woke her for the doctor's examination. She nodded her head as he told her what was happening, but her body and mind seemed to want to avoid reality. It was as if, in closing her eyes, she could finally shut out the pressure and demands she'd imposed on herself for so long, floating away with the sensation of Winnie's kiss and Dan's image, vague and pleasant, keeping her company.

When Kiri woke up again, the first pink shades of sunset were lighting up the sky. She looked around, noting the usual austerity of a hospital room—the plain walls and the stainless-steel bedside tray, a padded vinyl chair sitting at the end of the bed, and a single shelf holding only an empty vase.

She breathed deeply, then stopped as a sharp cough threatened to hurt her once more. She pressed her hand to her chest. The doctor had said the pain would ease within the next few days and that she would be able to go home in two days.

"Two days . . . then what?" She plucked at the bed covers, absently noting how the tubes in her arm moved. "I'm not allowed to work for at least two weeks, and by then Ben won't need me anymore at the restaurant."

It had seemed a great solution to work in Queenstown for her old employer when she first arrived back from Korea. Her loan was repaid, and she was independent with the option of finding work immediately in some field of occupational therapy. But recently the idea of returning to university to do post-graduate work had been lingering in her mind. Working in Queenstown for a few weeks had offered a familiar respite so she could make some final decisions.

"And now I'm stuck in hospital . . . unable to make money or a decision," she muttered to herself. "So now what am I going to do?"

* * *

The automatic glass door closed with a sigh as Dan entered the hospital behind a cluster of young people. They were laughingly assisting one of the girls in their group to hobble up to the reception desk. A girl of about eighteen years paused to brush a long strand of blond hair off her face as she used a tall young man as a crutch while resting a crudely bandaged foot. She obviously wasn't in a lot of pain as she laughed out loud at something he said and the rest of the group hooted in response. Dan felt his eyebrows rise in time with those of the nurse at the desk, but on his part it wasn't so much at the noise of the group as at the sultry good looks of the girl.

"A junior Sarah," he muttered under his breath and tightened his grip on the bouquet of flowers in his hand. "Always the center of attention."

With a decisive move, he turned his back on the girl and her friends and headed deliberately for the stairwell rather than wait for the elevator in the lobby. It still didn't take long before he was standing outside the room Winnie had told him to go to, but he hesitated before knocking. Winnie had described Kiri's shocked reaction to finding herself in hospital and the story of how they had found her. How would she respond to his visit when he'd only met her briefly? A vivid image of Kiri lying on the ambulance stretcher—frail, ill, and vulnerable—caused him to take a deep breath as he glanced down at the flowers.

"Mum says flowers are right for any woman at any time," he mused as he knocked lightly on the door. "She'd better be right."

"Hello . . . are visitors allowed?" A hand holding a colorful bouquet of yellow lilies and purple irises surrounded by bright terracotta–orange paper appeared around the doorway, and Kiri felt a smile light up her face as Dan's head made an appearance followed by the rest of his body.

"I wasn't sure if you were up to having visitors, but the nurse said you were doing fine." He nodded back toward the corridor almost apologetically. "And Winnie said you were looking forward to seeing me again."

She looked surprised, and he shrugged. "Actually . . . I made that up, but I thought it was a good excuse." He held out the flowers, then looked at all the tubes in her arm. "How about I put these in a vase? It looks like you're allowed one bouquet per room. That's thoughtful of them."

She watched as he took the vase off the shelf and filled it with water at the basin. Then he put the vase onto the bedside table and eased the bouquet in.

"The florist said to put an aspirin in the water so they'll keep longer, although I've never heard of drugging flowers before." He realized he was nervous, speaking quickly and not giving her space to respond, but the sight of her looking so small and helpless in the large hospital bed somehow made his heart beat faster.

"Thank you . . . for rescuing me," Kiri finally spoke quietly, but her voice broke before she could finish. She raised her free hand to wipe her eyes, unable to look straight at him.

Daniel pulled the chair up to the bed beside her and sat down, waiting until she seemed to get control.

"I'm just glad we made contact when we did." He shook his head. "I think there must have been a bit of divine intervention there—your meeting Ted and my coming to see you. And then after you said you played the piano, there was no way I wasn't coming to pick you up on Sunday."

His tone was almost laughing, but as she lifted her head she could see genuine concern in his gaze.

"Maybe I can play next week," she said, trying to match his light tone.

"And maybe you'll just take it easy for a while. We'll make it the week after." Daniel grinned and she noticed the deep groove in his cheek with happy familiarity.

"Is Ted coming up?" She tried to clear her throat and reached for the glass of water on the table. Before she could get it, he quickly reached up and passed it to her, turning the straw around so that it was near her lips. She leaned forward slightly to drink, feeling a flush of warmth run through her at the unexpected attention.

As she lay back against the pillows, Daniel leaned forward, resting his elbows on his knees and clasping his hands. "Actually, Ted and Winnie have been with you most of the time since we found you. I think they've practically adopted you."

Kiri frowned. "I can't quite understand how this has all happened. I meet this man on the bus and you all end up helping me . . ." She stopped again, unable to speak.

"It's just the way things work, Kiri," Daniel interrupted quietly. "We're just glad we were there at the right time." He shook his head. "In fact . . . you may be a blessing in disguise."

"Me? How?" Her voice was still croaky, and he offered her another drink.

"When I said that I was picking you up for church, Ted suggested that they come too, which would be the first time for them."

Kiri took the straw from her mouth. "You mean . . . ?"

Daniel shook his head. "Winnie and Ted aren't members of the Church, so when they said they'd come with you it was amazing. So, thank you, Kiri."

* * *

Winnie leaned over and picked up a fairly worn magazine, glanced at the date, which happened to be from the previous year, grunted, and leafed through it quickly without really looking at anything. Ted found himself an auto magazine and thumbed through it slowly, studying each vehicle and article carefully. Rather than wait in the car, they had decided to stay put in the waiting room inside the hospital while Dan was in the room with Kiri.

"Do you think she'll like the flowers?" Winnie folded her hands in her lap and glanced at her husband. "Ted . . . do you think she'll like the flowers?" she repeated.

"Mmm? 'Course she will," Ted answered absently as he raised his bushy, silver eyebrows over the top of the magazine. "Every woman likes getting flowers."

"If you know that, how come I don't get them?" Winnie asked primly but with a hint of a smile.

"Because I spend hours in the garden growing them for you," Ted grunted and nodded toward Kiri's hospital room. "If we'd been at home I could have brought some of my own."

"True." Winnie stretched her back against the plastic seat. "How long do you think we should wait?"

"Dan said to give him a few minutes . . . which was about five minutes ago if you count the walk from the car park."

Winnie sat quietly while he continued reading, then she tapped his arm. "She really seems like a lovely girl—not that we talked a whole lot, and she was very tired—but I just get that feeling."

"The same feeling you got when young Wade Fenton came to stay at Glencameron? Your woman's intuition?" Ted chuckled. "Our Mackenzie never had a chance once you decided Wade was the right person for her."

"Oh, and I'm sure she's complaining." Winnie nodded sagely. "Mackenzie's engaged to Wade now, holidaying in America. They're as happy as larks, and with a wedding and a home to look forward to here in New Zealand, I feel quite sure it was the right thing to . . . help them along."

"Well, I hope Dan knows what he's in for if you've got 'that feeling.' Should I warn him now?"

"Don't be silly," Winnie scolded him affectionately and looked meaningfully at the door. "I think it must be time for us to go in now."

She stood and picked up a plastic bag full of items, then headed for Kiri's room with Ted slightly behind as he finished reading the article. After a tentative knock, she poked her head around the door and quickly appraised the situation before stepping in.

"Hello, dear, you're looking so much better than before." Winnie held up a bag. "I picked up a few things for you. I hope they're all right."

Dan stood up and offered her his chair, and she sat down. Ted stood at the end of the bed, self-consciously rotating his hat in his hands.

"Good to see you looking well, lass," he finally croaked. "You had us all worried, especially Dan here."

Dan had the grace to color fairly rapidly, and Kiri felt her own cheeks heating up until a sudden spasm of coughing racked her body and the moment passed.

"So how long do all those tubes stay in?" Ted pointed to them with a disturbed frown. "And what are they all for?"

Kiri smiled and lifted her hand. "They tell me it's antibiotics and they'll be in for a couple of days. Then I get to go to physiotherapy to teach my lungs how to work properly again." She shook her head. "I had no idea this could happen. It was just a bit of flu."

Winnie rolled her eyes meaningfully. "You young ones don't take good enough care of yourselves. Tiny meals and rushing around—you need a lot more TLC."

"Well, I have to stay here till at least the end of the week, and then I'm not allowed to work for another two weeks after that." Kiri coughed hard again. "I promise I'll give myself TLC, Winnie, because I have to earn a living after that."

"What are you going to do?" Dan leaned up against the windowsill and folded his arms. The sight and sound of Kiri coughing was disturbing, and when Winnie suddenly stood up and began to rub Kiri's shoulders, he almost felt envious that she was doing something constructive. He breathed deeply and stared at the floor as he experienced a profound feeling of uselessness. It didn't seem normal to feel so protective of someone that he'd barely met.

"Aye, lass . . . what are you going to do?" Ted patted his own chest, then pointed at her. "Until you get better, I mean . . . there's time enough to worry about afterwards."

Kiri felt her eyes closing as Winnie methodically massaged her shoulders and neck as if it were the most natural thing in the world. The first touch had made her instinctively stiffen, but Winnie had seemed oblivious to her reaction and maintained a steady pressure. Then, as if her body sensed the nonthreatening kindness in Winnie's touch, Kiri began to relax, letting her neck drop forward. As the muscles in her neck responded, she realized it was the first time in nearly eighteen years that someone had actually cared for her like this. For the first time she welcomed the physical contact. Slowly opening her eyes, she forced herself to focus on Ted's question and she shrugged slightly.

"Um, sorry . . . I'm really not sure, Ted. I . . . I have a bit of money saved from my teaching in Korea, which I was keeping in case I went back to university, but I can always use that to tide me over."

"What are you planning to do at university?" Dan spoke quietly.

"I've trained in occupational therapy in Dunedin, and I was planning to do some post-graduate work so I could do more in management—run my own clinic sometime in the future." She paused to get her breath and began to cough again.

"That's enough talking for you." Winnie patted her gently on the shoulder to silence her, then stood to unpack the plastic bag. She stored the few items of clothing in the bedside locker. "You need to get as much rest as you can, my dear. We'll pop up again tomorrow, and don't you even worry about what happens after you get out of hospital. We'll be able to organize something, I'm sure. Won't we, Dan?"

Dan stood up and quickly nodded. "Absolutely . . . I've talked with the branch president, and although there's only a few of us here in Queenstown, everybody is more than willing to help out." He moved forward and held out his hand as if to shake hers, then hesitated and gently rubbed her fingers, avoiding the tubes. It was the briefest connection, but the contact seemed to create a current straight to her heart, and her lips trembled as Winnie leaned down to give Kiri a warm hug.

"See . . . there's nothing to worry about except getting better."

As the door closed behind them, Kiri lay back against the pillows and let the tears begin to flow unchecked down her cheeks.

She could still feel the pressure of Winnie's soft hands on her shoulders and the faint smell of lavender from when she'd hugged her. She drew a deep shuddering sigh and lifted one hand to touch the other where Dan had rubbed her fingers. It seemed almost impossible to think that she'd only met them a few days before and yet could feel so comfortable with them. She smiled through the tears. She felt so . . . loved.

Chapter 3

"Oh no . . . I couldn't possibly do that." Kiri shook her head emphatically as she eased herself off the hospital bed. "You've already been so good to me."

"We're enjoying it." Winnie was equally determined. "And it makes perfect sense. The house we're in is huge, and we'd be able to look after you much better if you're right there with us. You can stay downstairs in the little apartment until you decide what to do about university or working."

Kiri put her hand up to her cheek. "It just seems so . . . presumptuous. I've only just met you all."

"Don't be silly." Winnie held out Kiri's dressing gown. "We've been friends for six days now . . . eight, if you count the bus ride with Ted. That's plenty long enough to get to know somebody, and I trust that you won't run away with the family silver."

Kiri bent over slightly as a fresh spasm of coughing shook her body.

"Not that you'd be running anywhere with a cough like that," Winnie muttered as she turned Kiri's slippers around to slip on her feet. "As of now, I'm not taking no for an answer. You may be well enough to leave hospital, but you still need looking after."

"I think I'm beginning to see how you kept control of all those shepherds and shearers all those years." Kiri managed a weak smile. "You bullied them."

"Only when they needed it." Winnie smiled back. Over the last week of hospital visits the two women had developed a comfortable relationship, and despite the difference in their ages, they had found that they could talk easily. Winnie had enjoyed listening to the girl's stories about Korea and her occupational therapy experiences, while Kiri seemed to respond to the many stories about life on the isolated sheep farm. "So, it's settled then. You can come home with us now."

"I . . . I guess so." Kiri frowned slightly. "But what about Mrs. Adams? I'm meant to give her two weeks notice."

Winnie flapped her hand as if to wave away the protest. "Tch! With the state of that room you were staying in, it's a wonder you didn't get sicker much sooner. The damp and mold were terrible, so Dan suggested to her that the tenancy tribunal might be interested. She agreed very quickly that it would be nice for you to come and stay with us and said there was no need to worry about giving notice."

Kiri stared at the metal bed rail. "I didn't realize it was as bad as it was until there was a storm one day and it leaked."

"Well, it was shocking, and the sooner you're out of it the better." Winnie walked over to the window and checked to see if Dan's truck was parked below. "There's the truck, right on time. They just went to get a few supplies for the cabin."

Kiri fiddled self-consciously with the collar of her dressing gown. "Winnie, are you sure I have to stay in this? I can easily get into some track pants or something."

"And risk catching cold again?" The older woman shook her head. "It's straight home and straight back to bed for you, my girl. You'll only be outside for a minute or so."

"Hello . . . is everybody respectable in there?" Dan's voice came through the doorway.

"Come in." Kiri pulled the gown tighter around her thin body as Dan walked in with Ted close behind. She noticed that her heart beat a little faster as he gave her a swift glance from head to foot.

"You're looking a lot better already." He nodded approvingly and turned to Winnie. "Were there any objections to the plan?"

Winnie pursed her lips and tilted her hand from side to side. "Mmm . . . a little bit. I think I've convinced her, though."

Kiri folded her arms shyly and leaned back against the bed. "If you mean about my coming to stay at your house . . . she didn't actually give me much choice." She turned and smiled at Ted. "You have a very persuasive wife."

"You're telling me?" Ted chuckled. "Who do you think she's practiced on all these years?"

Loading up took about two minutes, and then they made their way out to the truck, which Dan had brought right up to the door.

"You know, most people come to Queenstown for a holiday," Dan commented as he swung the truck into the road. "Have you ever done any of the touristy things down here?"

Kiri shook her head. "No, I've always come down to work. Being a waitress doesn't pay too well, so I'd earn just enough for my next year's fees. There wasn't much left to spend on activities."

"Then maybe it's time you had a holiday." He turned off the engine at her place and jumped out of the truck before she could respond.

Less than five minutes later, Dan and Winnie walked back up Kiri's driveway with a suitcase and some small bags and put them in the back of the truck. It then took only another few minutes to drive down the road before they turned into the driveway of a large, rectangular brick house with a white block base. The whole house was well maintained, and a neat pebble garden with tidy, succulent plants contained in rubber tires ran up the side of the concrete driveway.

"I told you we were just around the corner." Dan helped her out of the truck and kept hold of her elbow as Ted led the way to a varnished wooden door on the bottom level. He unlocked it and stood back for the others to walk in.

"This'll be a lot nicer for you, love." He winked. "This gets sun most of the day, so you'll be a lot better off here."

"Oh, my goodness . . . this is so lovely!" Kiri glanced around the tiny apartment with its cheerful maize-colored walls and cornflower-blue and white couch. "This is like a motel . . . are you sure it's . . ."

"It's absolutely all right," Dan finished for her as he walked past carrying her suitcase and opened a door to a small bedroom. "And this is your prison until Winnie says otherwise."

Winnie turned from putting some groceries on the kitchen bench. "Daniel, you make me sound like such a tyrant," she complained good-naturedly as she followed him into the bedroom. "I don't know that I deserve it."

Kiri walked in slowly behind them. The bedroom walls were the same pale gold color, but the single bed had a plain white bedspread with a thick, hand-pieced quilt folded on the end. She immediately put her hand out and stroked the tiny pattern pieces which formed an intricate textile rainbow. The pure cotton fabric felt soft and responsive to her touch.

"This is wonderful." She concentrated on the quilt so they couldn't see the tears welling in her eyes. "Everything is wonderful. I really don't know how to thank you all enough."

"You thank us by getting better." Winnie instinctively gave her a tight hug, then picked up the quilt and efficiently fanned it out over the bed before turning back the sheets. "Now, you've been up long enough. The doctor said just an hour or so at a time for the first couple of days."

"And the sooner there's more hours to stay up, the sooner we can go exploring." Dan turned toward the door. "Meantime, I'll get back to work."

He paused in the doorway. "I'll see you this evening. And Kiri . . ." He looked directly at her, his smile slightly crooked and boyish. "I'm really glad you got so sick."

"Now that was a backhanded compliment, if ever I heard one," Winnie stood with her hands on her hips as the front door closed behind him. "I think he's pleased you're here."

Kiri was still staring at the doorway, and she faked a cough as she felt her cheeks burn. "I think he's glad he doesn't have to run around so much now," she responded quietly as she slipped her robe off.

Winnie chuckled as she waited for Kiri to get into bed. "And that too. Seems like everyone wins by your being here, my dear."

Kiri climbed in between the crisp, white sheets and felt her whole body relax as she stretched out and Winnie fluffed the top covers over her. It was an oddly comforting sensation, even familiar, and she frowned slightly.

"Something wrong, love?" Winnie noticed her expression immediately.

"No . . . not at all." Kiri laid her arms down at her sides and smoothed the cover. "I just felt like I'd had that happen before . . . when you did that with the cover."

"Your mum probably did it when you were little." Winnie patted her hand. "My Mackenzie is about the same age as you, and she used to love it when I did it for her when she was young. She said it used to help her sleep better . . . like she was floating on a cloud."

Kiri smiled sleepily. "It does feel like that . . . like I could happily float away in a dream right now."

* * *

Dan opened up the back of the truck and began to pull some lengths of timber out as Ted walked around the side. The older man glanced up at the sky before reaching in for a wooden box.

"We're going to have to get a move on with that roof. The weather forecast isn't too promising for the next few days."

Dan wrapped both hands firmly around the timber and began to carry it up the slight hill behind the truck. "We're all ready to go, and Jens said he would come down and give us a hand tomorrow. We should have it done by Tuesday."

"If there aren't any distractions." Ted grinned behind him. "Funny how we've been side-tracked lately."

"And it was your fault, if I remember rightly," Dan puffed slightly as he adjusted the bundle of wood. "You were the one who wanted to take the bus into town that day."

Ted shrugged as he moved ahead to clear a space on the veranda of a partially completed cabin.

"Strange thing, that. I never take buses and I don't usually talk to strangers . . . especially young women . . . and I did both."

"And now she's staying with us as a guest in our house." Dan eased the pile of wood onto the ground, then flexed his arms. "What do you think of Kiri, Ted?"

"I think she's a lovely lass." Ted nodded approvingly. "Winnie's gotten to know her better and feels right at home with her—like she's another daughter."

"Taken Mackenzie's place?"

"No, lad. No one could do that. But I think she has filled a gap there for Winnie." He hesitated. "She did mention something the other night, though."

Dan turned slightly. "About Kiri?"

"Aye. Winnie said that they've talked a lot about Kiri's time at university and this past year in Korea, but . . ." He frowned.

"But?"

"Well, it's probably nothing, but she . . . Winnie . . . says that Kiri never talks about her home or family. She says that she mentioned she was from up north, but that's about it—even with prompting from Winnie. Rather tight-lipped about it."

Dan was silent for a moment, then he shrugged. "It does seem unusual for a Latter-day Saint but, then again, not everybody gets on with their family . . . and she has been away from home for a while."

Ted nodded as he began to set up two sawhorses. "Fair enough . . . meantime it gives Winnie something to do."

"What? Looking after Kiri or trying to get more information from her?" Dan grinned as he swung a length of timber across the sawhorses. "Let's get these bracing pieces finished. I want to bring Kiri up to have a look as soon as the roof is on."

"Aah . . . nothing like a bit of incentive to get a man working." Ted picked up a circular saw. "You planning some activities with Kiri, are you?"

"Mmm . . . a few." Dan laid another piece of timber alongside the other. "Ted, did you notice that Kiri only ever talks about working and trying to save money? She's obviously put herself through university, and now she's planning to go back. I don't think she knows how to relax."

Ted frowned. "You might be right. Winnie said something similar the other night—that it was time the girl had some fun. It felt a bit like Mackenzie all over again."

"There are a few similarities, aren't there?" Dan nodded, remembering what his parents had told him about Mackenzie Cameron, the young woman that Ted and Winnie had virtually raised after her mother died and her father became engrossed in running his high-country sheep station. "Maybe you and Winnie are just the right sort of people for these situations. You certainly worked for Wade and Mackenzie . . . which reminds me. When do they get home?"

"In about two weeks," Ted grunted. "Then it's all go for their wedding two weeks later."

"So they are going to stay on at Glencameron?" Dan rested his hands on the timber.

"Yep . . . for a while, anyway." Ted buzzed the circular saw. "I wonder if Kiri will still be around by then."

* * *

The early morning sun was making the worn outlines of the flowers seem even more transparent as it pushed its way through the thin cotton fibers of the printed sheet curtain. Finding a crack in the torn fabric, the light rested on her cheek and played there until she felt its warmth and tried to brush it away with grubby fingers.

She rolled over to snuggle closer to her mother, and waited for the arm to reach out and draw her close. When nothing happened she opened one eye and patted the empty space beside her.

"Mama?" She barely whimpered as the realization hit as swiftly as the coldness of the sheet under her hand. "Mama." It wasn't a question anymore, and she pulled the sheet up closely under her chin.

She lay still, listening for the early morning sounds, but there was only the sea noise—comforting in its hushed monotony. The immediate silence around her in the house was like a trigger to move as she slid down off the narrow bunk bed and padded through the curtain in her bare feet.

"Mama." It was the only word that she'd uttered for nearly a month, and it was the word that repeated itself with the motion of her little legs as she let herself out the kitchen door and began the climb up the hill behind the house. The dew-damp grass came nearly to her waist and tangled with her long, black hair. It tickled her legs as it swept under the thin cotton of her dress, but she didn't pay it any attention as she struggled on, intent on reaching the top of the hill.

She didn't even cry as she sat beside the headstone. She didn't know how to cry anymore. She only knew how to wait until her mother came back. Her uncles said Mama was here, under the headstone and the rounded pile of solid dirt—with new strands of grass pushing through—that resisted her fingers as she began to claw at it.

"Mama . . ."

Chapter 4

"These are really beautiful, Winnie. I can't believe you've only been quilting for a year." Kiri held up a lap quilt made up of squares with deep red centers and opposing sides of light and dark fabrics making a distinctive step pattern. "What's this one called?"

"That's a Log Cabin quilt." Winnie smiled proudly. "That was my first attempt. Dan's mother, Sheryl, said it was a good one to start with, but after I'd done four squares I honestly thought it might be the one I ended with."

Kiri held the quilt closer to inspect the tiny stitches. "Are you sure I could make one? It looks so detailed, and I've never really sewn much." She pulled a face. "Only at intermediate school, and that was a really bad apron and some ugly shorts."

"Then now is as good a time as any to start." Winnie pointed to the smaller quilt. "I like the story behind this as well as the pattern. I read something about how the Log Cabin quilts were used in America to show the runaway slaves which were safe houses to go to. See the red squares in the center? Well, that's meant to signify the fire on the hearth. The story goes that if a quilt was hanging up on the porch or clothesline and it had black squares in the center, then it was a safe house for the slaves to go to for refuge."

Kiri was thoughtful for a long moment, then she touched a central red square with her forefinger. "I can just imagine some poor person being really afraid and running for their life. It must have been such a relief to see a quilt and know that they were somewhere safe."

Winnie nodded. "Something we can't begin to comprehend."

"No," Kiri murmured, then she gripped the edge of the quilt decisively. "Winnie . . . I'd like to do the Log Cabin quilt . . . but I'd like to make it with black squares in the middle."

* * *

Three days had passed since Kiri had been installed in the downstairs flat and she hadn't even been allowed out of doors. Winnie had become the self-appointed guard and caregiver, and under her watchful eye, Kiri had regained her health and spirits very quickly. This morning Kiri had changed into jeans and a sweater for the first time in over a week, and then Winnie had introduced the idea of teaching her how to make a small quilt as a way of passing time.

"Well in that case, we'd better get Dan to run us into town later to get some more material." Winnie rummaged through a basket of brightly colored fabric pieces. "In the meantime, you can sort out some designs that you like here, then we can coordinate them with bigger pieces at the shop."

"Will we need to get much fabric?" Kiri held up the small blanket. "It's funny, but I look at this and I just want to do one exactly like it so I don't get it wrong."

"You'll be surprised once you see all the colors. I loved Sheryl's quilt, but it was in yellow tones. I ended up going for more blues and deep pinks with little floral patterns. I've always loved my flowers and ferns."

"Ted said you both spend a lot of time in the garden." Kiri laid the quilt across her lap and sank back onto the bed. "Do you enjoy doing things together?"

Winnie chuckled. "Probably more than we should. I tend to get a bit bossy, but Ted just does what he feels like anyway." She nodded. "We've spent a lot more time together this last year . . . especially since the house is being renovated and Mackenzie's been away. The idea was that this stay in Queenstown was a holiday with Ted helping Dan if he needed it . . . but Ted's been the one getting up early and telling Dan to hurry up. That old man just can't stop working. I'm surprised he didn't bring his dogs with him."

"Dogs?"

"Sheepdogs." Winnie tut-tutted in her throat. "His children . . . and he spoils them rotten. He's dead scared they aren't going to recognize him when he gets back."

Kiri smiled. "Ted is such a lovely person . . . he's just so comfortable to be around. I wish I had a grandfather like that."

Winnie hesitated as she recognized the wistful tone in Kiri's voice and the first subtle reference to a family life.

"Don't you have a grandfather, child?" she asked quietly.

"Not really." Kiri studied the finely worked stitches on the quilt. "I never knew one of them, and the other . . . I haven't seen for a long time."

The way she finished seemed to end the conversation, so Winnie spread the fabric pieces out. "Well, I won't tell Ted that you said anything nice about him or he might get shy on us. Now . . . let's choose so you can get started."

* * *

The television was still playing even though Kiri had dozed off to sleep again. She woke up suddenly as Dan switched the children's program off.

"What . . . oh, Dan . . . did I go to sleep?" She looked around the lounge room blearily and unconsciously pulled the quilt farther up under her chin.

"Again." He grinned and folded his arms as she stretched. "I think you must have caught up on your yearly quota by now."

"Oh, I know." Kiri put her hand to her mouth to stifle another yawn. "It's embarrassing. The doctor says it's the antibiotics but I'm really feeling . . . anti-social."

"Yes, you are a bit, but you can make up for it later." He nodded. "I've got a stack of jobs lined up for you on-site. Not too much heavy lifting, but you should earn your keep."

She knew he was joking by the way his eyes teased, but she still felt an instant feeling of remorse.

"You know I'm more than happy to do anything I can," she began earnestly, her brows drawn together tightly. "I need to pay—"

She stopped as Dan suddenly leaned forward and pressed his finger gently against one furrowed eyebrow. As she felt the pressure of his hand against her skin, her head flicked sideways and the frown deepened across her forehead. She felt her pulse quicken but confused it with the instant churning in her stomach.

The swiftness of her reaction took Dan by surprise as his hand hung in the air and he watched the color drain from her cheeks. There was a brief silence as Kiri bit at her lip and stared at the floor, then she slowly shook her head.

"I need to pay my way," she repeated quietly but firmly.

"Will you please stop talking about repaying," his tone was equally firm. "At the moment we can help you and we're enjoying it. One day you'll be able to help somebody else . . . it may be one of us or it may be a complete stranger." He put his hand down. "Don't you remember your seminary scripture mastery about when you're in the service . . ."

"Of your fellow beings, ye are only in the service of your God," Kiri finished quietly, suddenly remembering long hours spent memorizing the scriptures off small cards that she'd begged from some older cousins. They had been more than happy to hand them over to her.

"So stop worrying about repaying and concentrate on dinner." Dan pointed toward the kitchen. "Winnie's whipped up some lamb chops and vegetables, probably enough to feed a whole shearing gang, so I hope you're hungry."

"Starving." Kiri stood up and noticed again how she only came to beneath his shoulder. "Um . . . did Winnie mention going into town?"

"She did." He stood back to let her go through the door before him. "She said it's absolutely essential that you go tonight or the sky may well cave in, or at least my life will be in danger."

"Oh . . . it's not really that important," she responded immediately, then held up both hands as she realized he was teasing again. "But it would be really nice if we could."

"Great. We'll go straight after dinner." Dan nodded as he led her into the dining room.

Chapter 5

Kiri glanced up at the clock on the wall and then over at a small free-standing calendar on the breakfast bar. It was her fifth day out of hospital, and she had woken up feeling unreasonably healthy and happy. A few deep breaths had started no spasms of coughing, and she'd even tried a few subdued lunges and stretches as the early morning sun had streamed in through her bedroom window.

Even her shower had felt more invigorating, and drying her hair and shaking out the short curls had seemed as if she was shaking off a heavy burden. With a truly overwhelming sense of gratitude, she had spent a long time on her knees praying and had finally risen with a renewed feeling of anticipation and determination. The evening before, Dan had arranged for her to go out to the cabin in the morning, and as he had jokingly outlined a long list of tasks for her, she had felt a mounting sense of happiness at the thought of being involved with anything he and Ted were doing.

She glanced again at the clock and then at her wristwatch. The clock was slightly faster, and she quickly walked into the tiny bathroom and began to apply makeup from the few pieces she owned. A touch of pale peach lipstick and a thin smear of apricot eye shadow were all that she usually bothered with as her black eyelashes were thick and long and didn't need any mascara on them. She licked her finger and tried to smooth her eyebrows into a neater shape, but they didn't respond. Neither did her hair when she tried to turn it under into a neater style.

"Stupid curls," she muttered, then jumped at several sharp taps on the front door. "I'm coming!"

She took another critical look in the mirror at the blue jeans, white T-shirt, and apricot hooded sweater she'd decided to wear. Her first choice had been a gray marl sweatshirt, but the freshness of the apricot jacket had suddenly been more appealing as she'd contemplated the day ahead.

"All ready?" Dan turned as she opened the door. "Wow . . . I think I just woke up springtime. You look . . ." He stopped and shrugged admiringly.

"Springy?" Kiri tried not to sound pleased at his open admiration. "I woke up feeling so much better—like the sun was pouring right through me."

"I think it stayed inside. You look *sunny!*"

They both began to laugh, then Dan held out his arm.

"Allow me, ma'am. I believe the carriage awaits to take you to the workplace."

She hesitated briefly, then with new confidence she placed her hand in the crook of his arm and stepped through the doorway.

The back of the truck was loaded with a wooden bathroom vanity unit and various boxes that were marked with pictures of tap and shower fittings.

"Today you have to make sure that we get the vanity in exactly the right place." Dan gestured toward the load. "And then you have to watch for the shower to be delivered."

Kiri stopped as she got into the truck. "I hope I get to do a bit more than that."

"We'll see." Dan pushed her gently into her seat. "You'll have to do extremely well on those jobs before I'll trust you to do any more. It's hard to get good help these days, and I have to be sure about my employees."

Kiri laughed as she swung into the seat then tried not to watch as Dan walked around to the driver's side, but he smiled broadly as he caught her eye. As he swung himself up into the truck, she shook her head and closed her eyes briefly, almost unwilling to respond to him, but enjoying it at the same time.

"So, have you ever been out Glenorchy way, Kiri?" Ted asked as he strode to the truck and settled himself onto the narrow backseat behind her. She turned to him, excited.

"No." She buckled up her seat belt and kept her attention on Ted as Dan got in beside her. "I've only visited Arrowtown and done the gold-mining thing out there."

"Ah . . . you're in for a treat then. Even the drive out is pretty spectacular." He frowned. "Didn't you say you'd worked down here a few times?"

"I think that's all she did," Dan joined in the conversation. "I think she's a chronic workaholic . . . which is why I'm employing her."

"So you're going to get your pound of flesh after all?" Kiri responded to his teasing. "And I thought you were just being kind to a sick person."

"I can do both," Dan replied easily. "Get you better quickly and then put you to work. I certainly wouldn't have gotten much labor out of you last week."

He glanced sideways as Kiri tilted her head back against the seat and laughed out loud, in a totally uninhibited way that he hadn't seen before. He glanced in the rearview mirror and caught Ted's eye as the older man smiled and winked.

"We'll see if she's still laughing at the end of the day," Dan spoke over his shoulder. "Eh, Ted?"

"Aye, lad." Ted tapped Kiri on the shoulder. "I warn you, girl. This man may look harmless, but he's a hard taskmaster . . . a real perfectionist. Makes me do the smallest thing over and over until I get it just the way he wants," he chuckled. "He's also a right pain in the neck at times."

Dan stared straight ahead as he drove onto the main route out of town. "I just know what I want it to look like," he shrugged nonchalantly. "Why settle for anything less than the best?"

Kiri felt a swift intake of breath at his words and sat quietly as the truck moved easily along the road with the gray-green waters of Lake Wakatipu glimmering out to the left. She gradually exhaled as the beauty of the scenery forced her to concentrate on her surroundings.

"The road gets pretty close to the cliff edge in some places," Dan pointed ahead. "Just up there," he pointed, "the original road surveyors had to use ropes to stop from falling into the lake."

"Really?" Kiri forced herself to concentrate in the direction he was pointing. "Wouldn't it have been easier to just go farther inland?"

Dan chuckled. "They were pretty rugged in those days. They probably thought they were taking the easy option going around the top of the bluffs because it was too swampy down along the old bridle track."

The road climbed around high bluffs, with striking views out across the lake and toward the mountains which still held the glistening remnants of winter snow on the very top peaks. At other times, the road dropped down to pass secluded bays right at the level of the lake where tall pine trees, tinkling streams, and the first spring flowers beckoned hikers and picnickers.

"I had no idea this was so beautiful." Kiri strained her neck to catch a last glimpse of a small pine-clad peninsula. "It's so . . . untouched."

"And hopefully it can stay that way," Dan indicated back toward the peninsula. "There's so much potential here, but if we plan it right, good property development can still keep the feeling of the place."

"I hope so." Kiri looked back across the lake. "It would be such a shame to lose this atmosphere."

Dan nodded. "My brother-in-law works for an adventure travel firm. He's always talking about the potential for bringing in tourists, and he's shown me a few places they're focusing on. Queenstown is already inundated, but I think Glenorchy is far enough away to keep uncluttered."

"Aye . . . most tourists go the other way toward the big lakes." Ted nodded. "I didn't even know about this place, and now I really love it."

Kiri folded her arms and squinted at the sun reflecting off the lake. "I can't believe I've missed all this even though I've been in the area."

"Well, if you work hard I might even take you to some of the places Carl showed me." Dan nodded indulgently and she smiled at the dimple in his cheek. "I'll whisk you away to the really beautiful and exciting places."

"And if I don't work hard?" Kiri tried to sound offhand as the goose bumps intensified at the thought of doing any activities with him.

"I guess you'll just have to speculate about what might have been," Dan dropped his voice dramatically and gave her a huge wink.

"You'll put the girl off working completely," Ted grunted behind them. "She'll need a lot better incentive than that."

Kiri coughed, suddenly embarrassed at the attention, and quickly pointed ahead. "What do they do on those islands out there?" She pretended sudden interest in the landscape.

"I don't know," Dan answered easily, although he noticed how she'd abruptly changed the subject. "They have really original names, though. The tiny one is Tree Island, the big one is Pigeon Island, and the front one is Pig Island. They used to graze about three hundred sheep there until some wild pigs were put there. They ate all but three lambs from all the sheep."

"Oh, no!" Kiri put her hand to her stomach and wrinkled her nose in genuine disgust. "That's just awful. I hate to think what happened on Pigeon Island."

"Probably nothing, seeing as pigs can't fly," Dan commented, then grinned as Kiri rolled her eyes at the joke.

They drove on in comfortable silence as the vista of lake and mountains unfolded. After a few moments, Dan pulled to the side of the road and pointed toward a small settlement spread out on the river flats with a spectacular mountain backdrop.

"That's Glenorchy township down there, but we go up this way a bit," he indicated toward some pine-clad slopes on their right. "The property developer I work for wanted his log cabins nestled in amongst pines instead of on the river flats. He's doing a development of about eight cabins over a few acres."

"Are you building them all?" Kiri ducked her head to look up at the hill slope.

"I'm working with a guy called Jens." Dan headed the truck toward a well-concealed entrance and up a long, bulldozed driveway. "He's the expert on log-cabin construction. He works for a friend of my cousin who's doing the development . . . which is how I came to get this job in the first place."

"So how did you get roped in, Ted?" Kiri put her hand out to steady herself as the truck lurched over a particularly deep pothole.

"Winnie and I were staying with Dan's parents when he got this job, and he needed extra man power. We were planning a holiday in Queenstown because we've never had a real holiday away from Glencameron . . . so Dan's dad suggested we stay a little longer, help with the building, and stay in their house with Dan."

"Their house?" Kiri looked puzzled. "I thought they lived in Christchurch."

"Mum and Dad bought the house we're staying in as an investment property." Dan glanced sideways. "They plan to rent it out to tourists."

"Oh, I see." Kiri thought about the last few days that she'd been staying with them. It had never occurred to her to ask whose house she was staying in. In fact, it had been easier to just be looked after and not ask any questions. She swallowed hard as she suddenly realized that she hadn't wanted to ask questions—or change anything.

"So what do you think?" Dan tried to stifle the pride in his voice as they drew up into a clearing. "Have you ever seen a genuine log cabin before?"

Directly ahead, the morning sun filtered through a canopy of pine needles and birch leaves to cast a speckled silhouette over a two-story cabin. The exterior was constructed of carefully layered logs whose pale golden hue shone warmly in the sunlight. A long wooden veranda ran along the front and side of the building. Dried pine needles lay in random orange and yellow piles on the gray sheet-metal roof, and an occasional twin needle drifted down the shafts of sunlight to lie with the others.

Kiri leaned forward, resting both hands against the dashboard of the truck as she let her gaze move slowly over the clearing and the cabin. She finally drew a deep breath and instinctively reached her hand out to Dan, but she didn't speak.

"You like it," he stated rather than asked, and she stared and nodded silently, inexplicably at a loss for words. "I'm glad," he added simply, and reached out to squeeze her hand. It was the gentlest touch, but she felt the warmth from his fingers suffuse immediately through her body, and her heart pounded so hard that she began to cough again.

"I'm sorry." She pulled her hand away and covered her mouth as the cough wracked her body. After a few seconds she patted her chest and smiled weakly. "I don't usually get so overcome by the sight of a house."

"Ah . . . but that's because this isn't just any house," Dan joked as he swung his door open, but he could still feel the exact imprint of her fingers on his hand and see the instant tears that had shone in her eyes as she'd studied the cabin. He gripped the rim of the door tightly then abruptly swung it shut as if the slamming of the door would keep his feelings in check.

He went around to open her door, but Kiri had already jumped out and was standing facing the cabin, her hands tucked into the front pocket of her sweatshirt.

"Come on . . . let me impress you with Ted's and my amazing construction skills." He bowed at the waist beside her and swept one hand out in an arc toward the building. "Then you'll know how high a standard you have to maintain."

Kiri pretended to look at him disdainfully, then she smiled.

"I'm already very impressed." She looked toward the cabin. "It looks so . . . cozy and . . . safe."

Her voice softened as she stared straight ahead for a long moment, then she turned to Dan.

"Winnie told me a story about the quilt I'm making . . . that in America in the old days, when there were runaway slaves, if a Log Cabin quilt was hung up and it had black squares instead of red, then the slaves knew that that house was a safe house for them to go to." She swallowed. "When I saw the cabin it was strange . . . I just had a really strong sense that this was . . . a safe house."

There was a long silence, then Dan slowly rubbed the back of his head. "I like that . . . a safe house, solid and reliable. I'd like to think I was building something like that." He paused. "Like how the gospel makes a home feel."

Kiri nodded thoughtfully, then she clasped her arms around her body. "Some people don't have that sort of place to go to . . . even if the gospel's there."

Dan frowned and shook his head. "I think it's part and parcel. If people are living the gospel then there's got to be that sense of security that goes along with it. I can't imagine it any other way."

"Maybe that's the point . . . it may be too hard to imagine any other way." She dropped her hands to her sides and began to walk across the clearing. "Anyway . . . let me have a better look and see if it's as good inside as it looks from here."

Dan stood still as she walked ahead, and Ted joined him with his arms laden with boxes. They both watched Kiri as she walked up to the veranda of the cabin and ran her hand along a newly milled post.

"I think she likes it." Ted tightened his grip on the boxes. "Did you see the look on her face when we drove up? I think she fell in love with it on the spot."

"Mm . . . she said it felt like a safe house." Dan kicked at a sinewy tree root that rose slightly above the ground by his foot. "Ted . . . do you get the feeling Kiri hasn't had much of a life . . . a family life, I mean?"

Ted grunted. "Funny . . . Winnie asked me the same thing the other night. She said that when she was teaching Kiri how to do the quilting it was like she couldn't learn quickly enough . . . but it was more like she wanted to please Winnie than learn how to sew."

"Mmm." Dan nodded thoughtfully. "It's almost like everything is new . . . even smiling and laughing."

Ted chuckled. "I noticed you were entertaining a bit more."

Dan glanced at him quickly, then smiled. "Mum and Dad always said I responded to a good audience. She has such a great laugh."

"When she lets herself," Ted commented dryly. "I think she holds back a lot."

"Oh well, I guess she'll talk about things when she feels comfortable." Dan turned to the back of the truck, then hesitated. "I'll get the rest of the stuff after I've shown Kiri the cabin. It does look much better with the roof on, doesn't it?"

He left the question unanswered as he walked to where Kiri waited at the top of the four wooden steps leading onto the veranda. As he reached her side she inhaled deeply.

"I love the smell of the pines and flowers and the native bush." She sniffed appreciatively. "And to know it's the real thing and not sprayed out of a can."

Dan laughed. "I never thought of it like that." He looked around. "I just know I love coming to work out here. It's so peaceful, and it's got all the things I've ever wanted."

"You mean the trees?"

"Not just the trees. There's the mountains and the lake close by, and just the fact that I'm building something to last. I just love the construction side of things and working with timber." He hit the post beside her firmly with the palm of his hand and then left his hand resting there. "It's something tangible that you can take pride in doing, and you know that someone will benefit from your doing a good job."

Kiri studied his hand on the post. It was so much larger than hers, and even though it was well manicured, the skin was tanned and hardened and there were several small scars of varying shapes and shades of pink to white. She immediately remembered the warmth she had felt from them earlier, and then for some reason, the thought came of his hands laid on her head when she was unconscious, asking the Lord to make her better. Strong hands . . . physically and spiritually. She resisted the sudden impulse to reach out and touch his resting hand; instead, she turned abruptly away toward the front door opening.

"Then show me more. I want to know everything about it." She clasped her hands together and took a deep breath. "I want to visualize it from start to finish . . . how it's built and what it will look like when it's all ready to live in."

Dan turned as he sunk his hands deep into the pockets of his jeans.

"Start to finish, eh? Well, right where you're standing, I visualize a big, old rocking chair . . . maybe two side by side where you can look out over the lake and watch the sun set over the mountains."

"Where?" Kiri turned quickly, then she gasped as she looked out beyond the canopy of trees. "I hadn't even looked that way . . . oh, that makes it even more beautiful."

They both stood quietly as she studied the northern part of the lake and the snowcapped mountains visible through a gap in the trees, framed by the boughs of pine needles.

"Why would you want to live anywhere else?" she finally whispered, then turned to Dan with a frown. "I'm beginning to wish you'd never brought me here."

The genuine frustration in her voice made him give a short laugh as he took her by the elbow and guided her toward the doorway.

"Come on . . . I'll show you around and then put you to work. That'll make some of the attraction wear off."

"Has it worn off for you?" she retaliated smartly, mainly in response to the feeling of his hand on her arm.

"Nope," Dan grinned. "Never."

It took a few seconds for Kiri's eyes to become accustomed to the darkness of the cabin's interior, and then, as they adjusted, she began to make out the skeletal shapes of the ceiling beams and a sturdy interior stairway leading up to a balcony. All of the walls were formed of robust layers of interlocking logs, with the exception of one at the end of the building which featured a half-completed stone fireplace. Even without furnishings, the structure felt solid and secure and comfortable.

Kiri took another deep, appreciative breath and ran her hand over the nearest wall.

"I've never seen this sort of construction before. I mean, I've heard of log cabins but I never realized how they actually looked." She turned to Dan. "When did you learn how to build like this?"

"Ooh . . . when I was about seven." He folded his arms and laughed at her expression of disbelief. "Honest . . . at least that's when I learned about how they were built. Our family have always stayed in touch with an American missionary they knew, and one time they mentioned to him how I was crazy about building things but that they were getting tired of finding nails hammered into furniture and walls. To cut a long story short, that Christmas I received a big box of Lincoln Logs from him that I could construct all these little cabins from . . . over and over again."

"No hammers and nails?" Kiri smiled at the thought of a young Daniel stretched out on the floor, absorbed with building the miniature cabins.

"No nails." Dan nodded. "I think it was one of the best presents my parents ever got . . . even though it was for me."

"So you've always been interested in building?" Kiri leaned against the log wall. "Even when you were little?"

"Always." He shrugged. "Even when we did scripture study. I was always pretty low key until they mentioned how Nephi built the boat, then I really got into it." He made an exaggerated hammering action. "I could just visualize myself up there building the boat with him, and later on when he built the temple."

"Temple?" Kiri frowned. "I don't remember that."

"That's because you're not a builder." Dan shook his head. "It says that he built a temple like Solomon's, and if you go to the Bible there are pretty exact descriptions of the measurements and everything that he would have used—right down to the colors and trimmings."

Kiri folded her arms and nodded slowly. "I never realized that. Now I'm going to have to go home tonight and look it up. I'll read it with new eyes."

They were laughing together as Ted walked into the big room securing a leather carpenter's apron around his waist. He adjusted it, then pulled a hammer out of a side loop.

"Have you two finished the guided tour yet, or shall I go on with the kitchen fittings?"

Kiri glanced quickly up at Dan as he pointed behind another wall.

"If you can finish those shelves, it would be great. We'll be with you in a few minutes. I'll just show Kiri the view up top."

Ted nodded his head upwards. "It's a grand view up there, lass. Makes you feel like you're really part of the big picture."

Dan held out his hand toward the staircase, and Kiri began to climb up ahead of him. At the top of the stairs, an open balcony looked out over the downstairs lounge, while three doorways opened off the other side.

"Wait . . . you have to do this dramatically." Dan stopped her and reached for the brass handle on the middle door, stepped past, and swung the door wide. Across the other side of the large, gabled room, a sheet-glass bay window surrounded a chunky window seat on three sides; it created the effect of the spectator being suspended in the air. The view of mountains and lake that Kiri had admired downstairs was even more breathtaking.

"It's amazing! It's like you're in the actual scene!" Her voice dropped to a whisper as she walked almost reverently across to the window seat. "Oh, you must love this."

Dan stood still in the middle of the room, feeling an almost childlike pride in her delight as he watched her gently touch the pane with a fingertip.

"I almost feel like I could become a wonderful painter with scenes like this to paint," she said, painting the air with an imaginary brush. "But you could never do it justice."

Kiri was unaware of the wistful tone in her voice, or the way the copper of her skin contrasted so strikingly with the blue-black sheen of her hair, or how her breath created a frosty backdrop as she leaned close to the morning-chilled glass. She paused, her finger on the glass.

"Your boss must have a very good architect just to think of putting a window like this here. It's wonderful."

"Thank you."

She looked puzzled. "Excuse me?"

"I said 'thank you.'" Dan bowed slightly and gestured toward the window. "The original plans just had small dormer windows, but once we'd built up to this level and I saw the view, I just felt it had to be more . . . breathtaking. So I put the window in."

"Well, you certainly achieved breathtaking." Kiri looked back at the view. "I hope your boss was impressed."

"Actually, he hasn't seen it yet, but he's due to come down in a few weeks and I'll find out if I really am clever or not." Dan smiled. "When I suggested changing the window he was quite excited about the idea. I've only met Mitch a couple of times, but he seems like a really good guy."

"So how and when did you meet him?" Kiri sat forward on the edge of the window seat, then quickly moved over as Dan came and sat beside her. He rested both hands at his sides and leaned slightly forward, lifting his head to survey the wooden beams.

"I came back off my mission a few months ago and wasn't certain about what to do. I'd finished my carpentry apprenticeship before I went away, so it was really a case of deciding who to work for."

"In Christchurch?"

"Yes. I wanted to stay reasonably close to home for a while, seeing I'd just got back." He shrugged. "I was prayerful about it, and next thing my cousin Meredith called from Auckland to say that a friend of hers who had joined the Church in Canada was looking for a builder in the South Island. He needed someone to work on a log cabin project near Queenstown and did I know anybody that might be interested."

Kiri couldn't suppress the laugh that bubbled in her throat. "Aah . . . and you were just a wee bit interested."

Dan grinned at the way she'd anticipated his response.

"Exactly. I told her straight off that I'd love to do it and spent the rest of the evening playing with the Lincoln Logs." He glanced at her sideways. "They were far more sophisticated constructions than when I was seven."

"Oh, I'm sure they were." Kiri smiled. "And they were obviously good enough for you to get the job."

"Yep . . . Mitch came down to visit and we got on really well. I showed him some houses I'd worked on before my mission, then we drove over here and met his supervisor, Jens. We had a look at the site and . . . that was it."

"So how did Ted and Winnie get involved?"

"That's another long story," Dan said, taking a breath in preparation. "Basically, my sister Charise helped her brother-in-law Wade convert his fiancée, Mackenzie, who is like Ted and Winnie's adopted daughter, and they were staying with my parents and . . ." He took a deep breath but Kiri held up her hand, laughing.

"I think I get it now . . . although there seems to be a lot of conversions and friends mixed in with your family. It's like listening to Maori *whakapapa* . . . everybody's connected in some way."

"Pretty much." He jokingly reached a brotherly arm around her shoulders. "If the truth be known . . . with the size of the Church in New Zealand, and considering my Maori great-grandmother . . . we could even be cousins."

There was a sudden silence as both sensed the heightened awareness of their touching. Dan heard Kiri's quick intake of breath and felt her back stiffen under his arm even as he felt his own skin tingle. Making a conscious effort to be casual, he relaxed his grip on her shoulder and pointed toward the door and stood up.

"Well, cuz," he coughed as his forced laugh caught in his throat. "We'd better go downstairs and get the bathroom organized before Ted goes on strike. Besides . . . it always gets more exciting when we start installing all the fittings. It's like making the house a reality."

"Turning a house into a home?" Kiri stood up quickly and moved toward the door.

"Nearly." Dan followed her, keeping a careful distance away. "I think it's the people who make the house a home. This'll be a home when there's a bunch of kids running around and a family sitting in front of the fire on a cold evening."

"That's very cliché." Kiri paused at the top of the stairs. "There aren't many people or families like that these days."

Dan hesitated briefly, then he nodded. "Perhaps . . . and maybe there are a lot of people who don't have a happy family life, but . . .

that doesn't mean it isn't possible." He shrugged. "I mean . . . that's what I plan to have . . . someday."

If he expected a response from Kiri, he was disappointed, as she merely stared at the stairway and tightened her grip on the banister before walking quietly downstairs. Dan frowned slightly as he noted the squaring of her shoulders and the determined lift of her head as she walked ahead of him. He gave the banister a thoughtful tap and followed her down.

An hour later, Kiri sat on the bottom stair, her chin resting in her hands as Dan and Ted maneuvered a wooden vanity unit through the front door. Although the waxed Rimu wood looked solid and heavy, both men seemed to handle the task with ease as they carried it through to the bathroom, bantering with each other about their respective capabilities.

"Slow down, lad." Ted quickly checked over his shoulder to check where the doorjamb was. "You're not in a race."

"Slow down? I'd be crawling if I went any slower," Dan retorted with a grin as he eased the end around the corner while ensuring that Ted's end was clear. "You're just too used to moving sheep . . . or counting them. Send you to sleep, either way."

"I'd like to see you mustering a few thousand sheep and getting them all through a gap no bigger than this doorway," Ted chuckled. "Yep . . . I'd really like to see that happen."

Kiri smiled as she listened. Although the two men had only known each other a short while, they seemed to have established a very easygoing relationship. Their conversation was largely bantering interspersed with specific instructions from Dan or Ted's subtle Irish brogue asking questions. She stretched her arms out in front of her as Dan's deep voice suddenly broke into the chorus of a hymn. His mellow voice echoed in the unfurnished lodge. It sent a warm shiver down her spine.

"Hey, Kiri . . ." Dan called from the bathroom. "Come and give us your valued opinion."

She started at the sound of her name.

"Kiri!"

"Coming!" She jumped up as Dan appeared around the corner. "I'm sorry. I was just daydreaming about safe houses and quilts."

"Winnie'll be pleased to hear that." He grinned. "We can tell her you were dreaming about them while you're supposed to be on the job, and she'll probably call my mother to tell her she's found a quilting protégée."

"Hardly a protégée," Kiri protested as she followed him down the short hallway and into the bathroom where they'd pushed the Rimu vanity up against the darker tones of the redwood walls. "Oh, my goodness! That looks so much better than in the back of the truck!"

"And a lot more useful here, as well," Dan countered.

She pulled a face. "You know what I mean," she said as she touched the ice-gray marble countertop. "Did you choose the fittings as well?"

"Pretty much." Dan picked up a box of tap fittings. "Mitch gave us a general idea and budget, and we just e-mailed pictures of the ones we'd chosen for his okay." He nodded. "I've always just followed instructions on the job, so I'm really enjoying being involved in the whole creative process."

"And it's great to spend someone else's money." Ted held out a fitting to see how it looked. "Just go in and order what you want. I'm enjoying it too. I've never done decorating or the like . . . just patched up whatever was wrong at the farm. I can't wait to get back and try some new stuff on the old house."

"When do you go back to Glencameron, Ted?" Kiri leaned back against the wall.

"Just after Mackenzie's wedding." Ted shook his head. "I can't believe our little girl's getting married."

"But . . . I didn't think . . ." Kiri's voice trailed off, and she instinctively glanced at Dan for clarification.

Ted saw her look. "Mackenzie's not actually our daughter, but she's as close to us as if she was blood. We lost our only son when he was a baby, so Mack has been a real blessing to us. We love her as if she was ours."

"So she's not your adopted daughter?" Kiri looked puzzled.

"No, lass," Ted shook his head.

"And you're not related at all?"

"It's a love connection, eh, Ted?" Dan nodded thoughtfully as he pulled another fitting from a box. "Friends of ours have adopted two children, and they all look so alike. It's like they are their actual children, but just came to them by a different path. It's pretty wonderful, really."

"Do the children know who their birth parents are?" Kiri asked quietly.

"Um, I think so." Dan glanced up briefly at the flat tone of her voice. "Their children have always been told they were chosen specially . . . luckily for them. From what I heard, both children came from pretty awful backgrounds."

"Aye, it's amazing what some of these poor wee bodies go through." Ted grimaced. "Do you remember that program on TV the other night, Dan? The one about abuse—just shocking what some people do to their own children. I couldn't believe it!"

"Some of them are no better than animals." Dan nodded in agreement and turned to face Kiri as he spoke. He watched in amazement as the blood literally drained from her face. Her dark eyes suddenly looked enormous against the instant pallor of her skin, and she swayed slightly.

"Kiri . . . are you okay?" He quickly put the faucet down and reached for her arm as her eyes closed and her legs bent. "Ted, bring the box over!"

He eased Kiri to a sitting position on the box and gently pushed her head down until the blood began to return to her face. She slowly rested both elbows on her knees and covered her face with her hands.

"I . . . I'm sorry," she whispered. "That was silly of me."

"Silly of you to apologize," Dan responded with a quick look at Ted. "We must have been working you too hard, eh, Ted?"

"Aye, lass." Ted touched her briefly on the shoulder to show his concern. "You just sit tight now . . . no need to do anything at all."

Kiri raised her head slowly and ran her hand behind her neck. "I don't know what came over me."

"Just a bit of postpneumonic stuff," Dan joked, but the concern showed in his eyes. "But I think we'd better have you rest in the sunshine or Winnie will be hauling us over the coals for treating you badly."

The sun was shining directly in through the window as Kiri sat quietly on the window seat of the upstairs bedroom. Her knees were drawn up to her chin as she listened to the sounds of hammering occasionally interrupted by the strident shriek of the circular saw. The noise slowly became muffled to her ears as she stared fixedly at the majestic mountain peaks, their cobalt-shadowed outlines blurring against the bright aqua sky.

Dan had ordered her to stay there until lunchtime and she hadn't objected. Her initial delight in the cabin and the surrounding scenic beauty had suddenly diminished as her mind began to replay parts of their conversations over and over again.

Kiri drew a deep breath and leaned her head back against the wall.

"Not everyone has a happy family, Dan," she barely whispered to the mountains. "Some do come from pretty awful backgrounds . . . and it does matter . . . to everybody, eventually."

* * *

"You can't stay . . . stay at the beach all day . . . girl. Your grandfather will get . . . really angry if you haven't . . . done your jobs."

"I've done my jobs." Her voice was muffled as she scrunched a thin shoulder to her ear and squinted at the unwelcome intrusion.

"Wha'? Sp . . . speak up, girl!" Her aunt's slurred voice lurched with a loud hiccup, and she sat down heavily on the sand beside her, clutching a nearly empty bottle.

"I said I've done my jobs." She turned her head away from the odor of alcohol and breathed deeply into the sea-laden wind. The faint ocean spray felt good against her cheeks. Good and clean.

"Your uncles'll be very . . . very upset . . . too."

"I don't care." She hunched her shoulders and stared hard at the large rock that sat permanently in the small cove, deeply embedded in the sand and resisting all that the relentless waves could hurl at it. From lots of practice, she knew that if she stared at it hard enough she could stop other images from coming into her mind.

"Well . . . I have to . . . care," her aunt's voice faltered as she pointed to herself repeatedly with buckled fingers. "I . . . I shouldn't have to care . . . not at all. Your mother . . . she didn't care . . . stupid . . ." The slurred curse was whipped away by the wind.

"My mother wasn't stupid! She was good . . . way better than you
. . . or anybody . . . and she did care! She cared about me!"

* * *

Kiri shifted uncomfortably on the window seat as the memories
left a cold-fingered impression on the back of her neck. She instinctively rubbed her shoulder where Dan had placed his arm so casually
a few hours before, and shivered again.

It had been the kindness and warmth of Winnie's embrace that
had started her thoughts turning back to the past, to dim recollec-
tions of her mother's warmth and of knowing how the woman cared
for her only child.

But then Dan's comments about families had caused carefully
buried memories to surface over the last few days. Memories that she
thought the years had successfully laid to rest.

"I'm sure my mother cared." She frowned slightly and rested her chin
back on her knees. "And the Jensons cared . . . but nobody else did." She
swallowed hard. "Until now . . . but soon they'll be gone as well."

"Hey, Kiri!" Dan's deep voice echoed up the stairs and interrupted
her thoughts. "You okay up there? We're nearly finished down here."

"I'm fine!" She raised her head. "I'll be right down!"

"Do you need a hand?"

"No!" She stood up quickly as if to stop him coming up for her.
"No, I'm just fine on my own!"

* * *

Lake Wakatipu was a darkening palette of gold, beige, brown and
gray, the sun casting a tanned haze over the entire scene as they drove
home from the cabin in the early evening. They quietly discussed the
plans for the next day until, closer to Queenstown, Kiri leaned
forward and peered through the front window of the truck, squinting
into the sun at the sharp slopes of the hills directly across the lake.

"Those sheep look like tiny miniatures from here." She put her
hand up to shade her eyes. "It looks like they haven't moved since we
came by this morning."

"They'll have moved all right," Ted motioned with his head in the direction she was looking. "They're just like lawn mowers—they'll eat about eight or nine pounds of grass each day when the growth is good."

"Eight pounds!" Kiri looked astonished. "And it all just turns into wool and meat."

"All the better for us to eat," Dan rhymed, then grinned at her expression of disgust. "Well, aren't they?"

"I prefer to think of them as cute and woolly." She wrinkled her nose.

"There's nothing cute about some of those older ewes," Ted commented knowingly. "The older they get, the more ornery they become, but they seem to make the best mothers."

"Sounds like a lot of females." Dan glanced sideways to watch Kiri's reaction, but she just raised her eyebrows and shook her head.

"How chauvinist . . . any astute person would realize that it's the protective instinct coming out in them." She folded her arms, enjoying being a part of the bantering that she had listened to all day.

"So you're saying I'm not astute?" Dan immediately retorted with a grin.

"I . . ." She hesitated. "I'm not sure." She was suddenly uncomfortably aware of him sitting so close beside her. "I really don't know what you are." She tried to sound offhand as she pointed to the sheep again. "But I do have another sheep question. When I was looking around the cabin today, I noticed that you had sheep's wool tucked in above the doors. What was that for?" She felt pleased at how steady her voice sounded even though her pulse raced again when Dan answered.

"It's to keep the house warm."

"You mean insulation?" She looked genuinely puzzled. "But that little bit wouldn't help much. I didn't see it anywhere else."

He smiled at the serious tone of her voice and noted the way her forehead creased into a frown, re-forming a deep v-shape between her eyes.

"That's very observant, ma'am." He nodded. "Actually, it's not really to keep the house warm, although it does seal up any draughts. The reason we put it in is that the timber actually shrinks quite a bit during the first few years, so we leave a gap around the doors when we build and then when it shrinks, it compresses the wool rather than the timber twisting or cracking."

"How clever," Kiri nodded thoughtfully. "I wonder whoever thought of doing that."

"Probably some pioneer innovation." Dan tapped his forehead. "Somebody uses his logic and the only available materials and . . . hey presto! Like all those great stories of the Mormon pioneers and all the things they used to create when they had nothing. I used to tell my mother that I could see the Lord's hand in their inventions." He chuckled at Kiri's surprised look. "I was very insightful as a youngster."

"Meaning you aren't now?"

Dan took a moment to answer as he stared straight ahead. "Not so much less insightful . . . but I probably doubt myself more."

"Really?" Kiri was genuinely surprised. "I don't see you as the sort of person who doubts himself."

"Aah . . . that's because I can fool some of the people some of the time . . ." He nodded meaningfully. "I'm actually a very insecure person."

Kiri didn't know how to respond, and she sat quietly until she heard Ted's wry chuckle behind her.

"And if you believe that, then he really can fool some people."

Both men laughed and Kiri joined in quietly, but she noted Dan's laugh didn't last very long and his hands tightened on the steering wheel.

Winnie was waiting at the door of the house when they arrived back home and climbed down out of the truck.

"So did they work you hard, Kiri?" She gave Kiri a firm hug as she reached the front door.

"Until I dropped, Winnie." Kiri felt an absurd feeling of warmth rise through her whole body as she responded to the older woman's embrace. It felt so good to be welcomed home.

"Literally," Dan commented right behind her. "We showed her what to do, and she just dropped in her tracks—couldn't handle it at all."

Winnie glanced quickly between them. "Did you?"

"No." Kiri elbowed Dan in the stomach, and he promptly doubled up as if he'd been hit hard. "He just likes making up stories. I was fine, but they talked so much while they were working that I fell asleep where I stood."

"Don't listen to either of them, love." Ted edged his way past them with his hands full of gear. "I was the only one to put in a decent day's work. These two were too busy looking at the view."

They all laughed at the bemused expression on Winnie's face as they walked past her, but she began to look thoughtful as she closed the door slowly.

"So things are happening, after all," she commented quietly to the door as she pressed it shut.

Chapter 6

"I'm glad you're going to be at church today." Dan warmed the engine as they waited for Ted to help Winnie down the driveway. He lowered his voice. "Can you look after Winnie and Ted? They're acting very casual about coming, but it's the first time they've been . . . and I have to keep things running in the branch."

"I understand," Kiri answered quickly as Ted opened the truck door for his wife. "It's been awhile for me too."

A few minutes later Dan looked around the car park at the small funeral home as they drove in. "We're never quite sure how many will be at church each week. Sometimes we'll have about twenty, and other days there'll just be a handful of us. It depends on how many tourists are in town."

"Looks like a few visitors today, then." Ted pointed to a group of people standing uncertainly beside the front door. "I hope that they speak English or that you can speak . . . something else."

Dan grinned as he stopped the car and jumped out quickly, giving Kiri a quick wink. "Here's where I pray for the gift of tongues."

She smiled at his comment, then pointed past him toward the group. "Can I help? I'm sure they're Korean."

Dan looked behind him, then bowed toward her. "That would be very, very much appreciated . . . and then if we can just get you to play the organ for sacrament meeting and then run Relief Society and nursery . . ." He laughed at the look on her face. "Just kidding. President has it all organized."

The father of the family acknowledged Dan warmly as they met them at the door, but the whole family smiled even more happily as

Kiri greeted them in their own language.

"Blow me down if that girl isn't a surprise package," Ted whispered to Winnie as Kiri knelt down to talk confidently to a tiny girl dressed in a pale pink dress, her silky black hair tied up into two thin pigtails on the top of her head. "I can't believe she can talk the lingo like that."

Winnie nodded, keeping an interested eye on Dan as he too watched Kiri talking with the little girl, a slight smile playing at the corner of his mouth.

"I think Dan thinks she's quite the package as well."

Ted looked up at Dan, then back to Kiri, then to his wife.

"Winnie . . ." His voice held a tone of reprimand, but she playfully patted his arm before he could say any more.

"I'm just a spectator, Ted . . . nothing more."

"Mmm," Ted grunted as he followed his wife inside the building. "That's what you said about Mackenzie. You better do some confessing when you get inside."

* * *

Kiri hummed quietly along with the hymns that were playing as she worked the tiny hand stitches that joined the quilt pieces lying in her lap. Winnie was working on a similar piece of handwork in another armchair across the lounge. Dan's and Ted's voices floated through the kitchen door as they cleaned and stacked dishes. She felt a complete sense of peace that occasionally brought a contented sigh as a hymn finished or she completed a row of stitching.

"That's a lot of sighing going on." Winnie didn't raise her head from her work. "Are you bored?"

Kiri stopped sewing and rested her elbows on the arms of her chair, taking her time to respond. She let the sounds filter around her awhile longer, then she leaned her head against the back of the chair. "You know, Winnie . . . I don't think I've ever felt so . . . content or peaceful. I just can't get used to it. It almost seems . . . wrong."

"There's nothing wrong with being happy, my dear." Winnie still didn't look up. "Especially when you're making other people feel the same way."

Kiri opened her eyes. "What do you mean, Winnie?"

"Oh . . . just that sitting here sewing with you makes me feel happy . . . and Dan is always singing or humming after he's been talking to you, and Ted . . . well, he's still gob-smacked about your being able to talk to that Korean family today. He thinks you're wonderful." She finally looked up, and Kiri was surprised to see her eyes were glistening. "Don't underestimate what you do for people, Kiri. You've got to stop feeling like you're a burden."

"But I . . ." Kiri began to protest, then stopped as Winnie raised her eyebrows at her. "Okay . . . maybe a little bit . . . but . . . I've never really had any reason to think otherwise."

"Well, child," Winnie frowned at her handiwork, "I don't know what happened to you to make you feel like that . . . but the way I see it . . . you're not back there anymore. Now it's time to just enjoy being Kiri, and not play any other role—no worrying about anything or anyone else."

Kiri sat silently. Enjoy being Kiri? She'd only ever been called "girl," or even worse, "goat." That uncomplimentary nickname came when one of her cousins had discovered that her star sign was Capricorn. So, finding the accompanying goat symbol amusing, he'd called her *koati,* Maori for "goat." The name had stuck. Then university people had regarded her as "the workaholic" or "the Mormon," and in Korea it had been easy to just keep her own company and be referred to as "Missee Teachee" because the students couldn't say her name properly.

Even the few times she had attended church with her grandfather throughout her life she'd been able to remain relatively anonymous.

She swallowed hard. A brief period where a missionary couple, the Jensons, had picked her up and taken her to church had been the most wonderful experience of her life . . . but then they'd left, leaving her with a Book of Mormon with her name written inside. It had become her secret treasure to be diligently hidden from her boisterous male cousins.

So how was Kiri Karaitiana meant to embrace her true name without recalling her past? Could she put it behind her and simply have a good time? She closed her eyes again, letting her mind wander over the events of the last few days. Maybe this restful feeling was a part of that.

"Hey, sleepy," she heard Dan's voice speak softly and opened her eyes to find him kneeling beside her chair. "Do you want to play a game?"

"A game?" She sat up straighter. "What sort of a game?"

"It's a matching game . . . pairs." He rolled back to sit beside her chair and pulled a small pile of colored cards from his pocket. Very deliberately, as if showing a child, he began to create three rows of cards, placing them facedown on the ground in front of them. "We take turns picking two cards each time. If you pick two of the same, you keep the pair. First to get three pairs . . . wins."

"O . . . kay." Kiri hesitated, then, sensing his deliberately childlike explanation, she grinned and began to play along. She carefully placed her quilt pieces on a side table and slid off the chair onto the floor beside him. "Is this a favorite game, Dan? Do you play it often?"

"Only when someone will play with me." Dan spread his hands out. "Winnie and Ted won't play because I always win. So you pick first."

Kiri carefully picked one card and turned it over.

"And it's number three!" Dan did a mini drumroll on the table with his fingers. "Can she make it a double?" He watched as she turned over a four. "No!"

She was sure he deliberately missed the next couple of pairs, but when she had three pairs and he only had two, he declared her the winner and pulled a sheet of paper out of his other pocket.

"And we have . . ." He checked the numbers she had beside her. "Threes . . . which are . . ." He looked back at his list. "Fishing! Yes!"

Kiri frowned. "Fishing?"

He ignored her and went back to the list. "Nines . . . and we have . . . jet boating! Yes!" He clenched his fist and raised his arm as if victorious.

"Jet boating?" She looked inquiringly at Winnie who just shrugged and smiled.

"And finally . . . we have . . . twos," his voice dropped dramatically. "Ah, well . . . I guess you can't win them all. It's horse riding." He screwed up his nose. "Are you sure we can't go for a six? I quite like the idea of tandem bungee jumping."

Kiri laughed at the expression on his face, then she pointed at the cards. "I think horse riding has more appeal, but what on earth are you talking about?"

"It's simple." Dan held up his list. "You have just chosen three activities for us to do over the next two weeks before you have to head back to university. Oh . . . and the rules are that you have to attend every activity and that enjoying yourself is compulsory."

"But I don't . . ." She stopped as he held up his other hand.

"I forgot . . . the other rule is 'no buts.'" Dan folded up the list. "Besides, we have to do it for my brother-in-law Carl. Because Charise is having trouble with her pregnancy, he can't do his assessment on these activities for his company . . . so it's all up to us, and it's paid for."

Kiri stared at him from under slightly furrowed brows. Three activities with Dan? Three major activities with only the two of them? She opened her mouth to protest, then caught sight of the expression on Winnie's face. The older woman nodded her head briefly and mouthed the words, "Have fun." Kiri shook her head slowly, then smiled weakly. "Then I'd be silly to object, wouldn't I?"

"Absolutely." Dan leaned back against the chair and clasped his hands behind his head. "So we'll have to get started soon, and I'd say we make fishing the first priority. I can arrange a day off on Wednesday."

"And that means me too." Ted settled himself on the couch beside his wife's chair. "How about a date, Winnie?"

Kiri had to suppress a smile at the expression on Winnie's face as she slowly raised her head from the quilting, stared at the blank television screen, then said, "I think I must have water in my ears. I'm not hearing right," and joked by patting imaginary water from her ears.

"Of course you are, girl." Ted chuckled at his wife's expression and folded his arms across his chest. "I got to thinking about what that fellow said in church today, about having a weekly date with your wife. Sounds like a good idea. It's been awhile."

"About thirty years." Winnie actually blushed as she laid her work in her lap. "And where are you thinking of taking me?"

"Oh . . . maybe up the gondola and to have dinner in the restaurant and maybe a movie afterward." Ted nodded at his own suggestion as Winnie's mouth fell open.

"But . . . that's so exp . . ." She stopped as Ted wagged his finger at her.

"I'm organizing it, Winnie, and it's a date. You can't tell me what to do because I asked first."

There was a long silence as the color in Winnie's cheeks deepened and she stared at her husband, then she mischievously glanced at Dan.

"Can we come to church next week? I can't wait to see what they'll say next."

After a few laughs and pleasant banter, they sat talking and quietly listening to music for another hour until Kiri smothered a second yawn. Dan noticed and stood up beside her.

"Time to get some shut-eye." He pointed to the clock on the mantel. "Are you coming to the cabin tomorrow, Kiri?"

"Actually, I'm going to stay with Winnie and learn the next stage of this quilting." She held up her handiwork shyly. "I'm gathering momentum and I can't wait to see all the pieces together."

He stood aside as Kiri placed her sewing in a plastic bag, then he followed her to the door after she'd said good night to Ted and Winnie. As they made their way through the kitchen, he held the door open and again followed her to the top of the outside stairs leading down to her apartment. The air was cool and crisp after the warmth of the lounge, and she shivered slightly.

"The lake breeze always feels so fresh," she murmured as the goose bumps raised up on her forearms and she paused to rub them. "Well . . . good night."

Dan leaned against the railing behind her and made no comment as she hesitated then turned down the stairs. He sank his hands into the pockets of his trousers, then took a deep breath as she reached the third stair.

"Kiri?" His voice held a tentative question.

"Yes?" She stopped and looked up. He seemed to tower over her in the half-light of late evening, and she swallowed with difficulty as she studied the now-familiar contours of his face.

"Um . . . I just wanted to . . ." Dan coughed, and she saw him frown uncertainly for the first time. "It's just that . . . going on these activities . . ."

"You've had second thoughts?" She felt her stomach constrict and she breathed deeply. "That's okay . . . I never meant to keep you from working, anyway. It was a lovely idea but I know that you need to be practical, and I need to keep working on this quilt or I'll never get it done before I leave . . ."

"Shh," he spoke quietly but firmly. "It's not that . . . I just." He hesitated again, then he folded his arms. "It's just that . . . I know that you were a bit uncertain about going . . . out and I'm not sure why, but . . . I just wanted to . . . oh, man . . . this is going to sound really conceited . . ."

"No . . . it sounds confusing," Kiri interrupted quietly, her heart beating faster.

Dan breathed deeply and ran his hand along the metal railing before he looked at her.

"The thing is, Kiri . . . I really enjoy your company. I think you're a great girl and I want to have a good time while you're here, but . . . I'm not really looking for a . . . relationship." He rolled his eyes. "I told you it would sound conceited."

There was a moment's silence, then Kiri smiled. "Then I guess I must be conceited as well . . . because I'm not looking for a relationship either." She grasped the railing with one hand. "Do you think it's possible that we can have a really good time as just friends?"

"A good time between good mates. That sounds fine." Dan nodded, then bit at his lip as he folded his arms. "Maybe I can explain a bit. The thing is, Kiri . . . when I came back off my mission I thought that I was going to marry a girl that I'd dated before I left. I was totally convinced that the Spirit had confirmed it all to me, but when I asked her, she turned me down flat and told me that she was going to the States and thanks but no thanks." He screwed up his face. "So apart from recovering from a severely wounded ego, I'm really not ready to test the waters again . . . especially the spiritual waters."

Kiri stood silently as she absorbed his words, then she gripped the rail more tightly and smiled brightly.

"Dan . . . you have no idea how much better that makes me feel. I really don't want to be involved with anyone at the moment either. I have too many plans with university and . . . everything." She hesitated, then dropped her hand to her side and tapped her fingers against her thigh. "But I'd like to be your mate . . . and have some fun together. It has been awhile."

She watched his face light up with the wonderful broad grin that she'd come to anticipate, and she breathed more easily.

"Then let's go for it." He nodded happily. "We'll just enjoy what we have here for now." He grinned. "Just friends?"

"Just good friends." Kiri gave him a thumbs-up, then quickly turned downstairs. "See you tomorrow!"

A few minutes later she lay down on her bed and clasped her hands behind her head on the pillow. "Just friends. That's good. That's a lot better than nothing at all." She closed her eyes, but the image of Dan laughing came so quickly into her mind that she opened them again, frowned slightly, then rolled over onto her stomach.

"It's exactly like I wanted. No ties . . . no commitment." She breathed the words into the pillow, then rubbed her face hard against the cool cotton. "And I will enjoy myself because I may never have this opportunity again!"

Chapter 7

"Can I ask a pretty dumb question?" Kiri whispered as she crawled along a small stony ridge topped with long grass and overlooking a shallow stretch of clear water. "What are we doing?"

Dan took awhile to answer as he leaned forward, carefully raising his head above the yellowed stalks of grass to study the barely moving water. "Can't you guess?" He motioned her forward with one hand, then just as quickly held it up to stop her.

Kiri lowered herself back onto her belly and rested her chin on her hands.

"I thought we were going fishing," she whispered again.

"We are," Dan barely murmured and pointed to their left. "We're stalking a very large brown trout that's resting in under that high bank near the bend."

"We're stalking a fish?" she tried not to sound too incredulous. "I thought you must have seen a deer or something . . . do you really mean we're hiding from a fish?"

"We're not hiding . . . we're stalking." He eased up onto his knees and pulled a large canvas bag up in front of him. "And now I'm going to teach you how to catch your first trout."

Kiri wrinkled up her nose. "I really don't mind just watching you do it."

"Then you won't experience the adrenaline rush of reeling in your catch." Dan picked up a long, fiberglass rod and undid the nylon line.

"How old were you when you learned to fish?" She kept her voice low as he held a finger up to his lips.

"I'd just turned eight. It was sort of like my coming-of-age experience after my baptism." Dan's voice was deep and soft as he undid a small plastic container and took out a folded cloth with small bugs attached to it. "Which fly do you think Mr. Trout might like the look of?"

Kiri leaned closer to study the delicate pieces of fur and filament wound tightly together to resemble an insect. She poked one gently, and it glistened in the sunlight.

"I think this one looks very edible." She tried to be serious but couldn't quite keep the smile out of her voice.

"You know the trout will be able to tell them apart?" Dan pointed to the next fly. "This one here is actually more like the insects around here . . . the ones he'll be used to eating."

"So you think they can really tell the difference?"

"Absolutely." Dan fastened the silver-and-brown fly to the line. "When we cast this out onto the water and flick it a bit, he'll think its dinner and—wham!"

"Wham?" Kiri repeated faintly. "That's the bit I don't like . . . the killing part."

"But we're not going to kill it." Dan looked up. "We almost always put the fish back. In fact, Dad spent as much time teaching me how to carefully handle the fish we caught as he did teaching me how to catch them."

"Oh." She frowned slightly. "I thought you always eat what you catch."

"Not necessarily. I mean, if we needed food then we'd take them home, but angling is just a really relaxing sport for us. It used to be 'talk time' for Dad and me."

"Did you . . . did you spend a lot of time with your father when you were young?" Kiri watched the gently flowing river as she asked the question hesitantly. Somehow it seemed all right to ask a more personal question when the river water and insect calls were the only other sounds around them and the sun was warming them gently.

"Dad was always busy at work or with his Church callings, but he always made time to take me fishing." Dan didn't look up. "Sometimes I knew he was preoccupied when we were driving out to the river or lake, but once he got his waders and jacket on . . . it was like he left all the hassles behind. Then I knew it was just him and me . . . and the fish." He gave a short laugh. "Quite often we didn't catch anything, but Dad would say it didn't matter . . . that we'd still been fishing."

"Did you enjoy being with him?"

The wistful tone in Kiri's voice made him look up, but she was staring at the river, her chin still resting on her fists.

"I loved it." He smiled. "Sometimes we didn't talk for ages . . . either because we might scare the fish or just because the scenery was so beautiful and relaxing you didn't need to . . . but afterwards I'd be amazed at how much we had talked . . . especially about things you don't discuss much when everybody's busy at home."

He leaned forward and reeled up the line.

"One time I wanted to tell him that I didn't want to go to university . . . that I wanted to be a builder. I just couldn't find the right time at home . . . so I asked if we could go fishing. He knew right away that I needed to talk."

"And did you tell him?" Kiri finally turned to face him.

Dan nodded. "On the shores of the Rakaia River. I started my apprenticeship the next week—and he arranged it for me."

There was a long silence as Kiri sat up and began to play with the tufted end of a long piece of grass. A slight frown pulled at her eyebrows, and she opened her mouth to speak, then shut it again.

"Have you done much fishing?" Dan asked the question innocently, but she looked surprised.

"I was just going to say that I have done some fishing." She frowned again. "But it was nothing like this."

"Was it sea fishing?" Dan watched the lines form on her forehead and felt his own brow furrowing in response.

Kiri nodded slowly. "We'd put out nets off the beach and just haul in lots of fish. I'd have to hit them on the head to kill them." She shivered. "I hated doing it, but if I didn't, *Koro* would tell me off . . . because it was our dinner."

"Koro?" Dan asked quietly, sensing the importance of her finally confiding something about her personal life.

"My grandfather." She ran the grass through her fingers. "He raised me . . . after my mother died."

She didn't offer any more information, and Dan somehow knew not to ask for any more. He knew that in the quiet solitude of the river there would be time to talk.

"Well, I think we've given Mr. Trout time to get used to our being here." He stood up slowly and held out a hand to help her up. "You're now going to have your first lesson in fly casting."

Just the touch of his hand on hers made the hairs on her arm stand up and she shivered. With a quick look to see if Dan had noticed, she pulled her hand free and rubbed her arms briskly as if to get the circulation going.

"I hope the river's warm." She put both hands into the side pockets of her fishing vest. "Or do I need to be intrepid and brave the icy waters?"

"Reasonably intrepid, but with your waders you won't feel too cold." Dan placed the fishing rod down carefully, then pulled a pair of long rubber leggings out of a bag. He held them out by the braces only to be met by a look of mild horror on Kiri's face. Then she giggled.

"This really isn't a beauty pageant is it?"

"Of course not . . . fishing is serious business." Dan kept a straight face, but as she climbed into the waders, he stood back and folded his arms. "Then again, if anyone was going to make a pair of rubber leggings look good, it would be you."

"Oh sure." Kiri almost surprised herself by laughing happily as she held the large leggings out by her sides. "I'll be this year's winner of the Miss Fish Award. How glamorous is that?"

The sun was already beginning to settle on its noonday pedestal as Dan showed her how to cast the fishing line temptingly in front of the trout that she could now see languishing in the crook of the river. Occasionally the light would reflect off its brown, spotted scales as it moved almost imperceptibly.

"You're bringing the rod too far back." Dan stood behind and braced his hand around her wrist. "Keep your wrist stiff. Don't bend it . . . and imagine that your arm is like the hand of a clock. Don't bring it back past twelve o'clock."

"So . . . keep it at about eleven o'clock?"

"That's it, and then keep your thumb pointing at twelve o'clock and roll back . . . and a quick, sharp snap of the wrist . . . and away it goes!" he whispered loudly, then gave a chuckle as she didn't snap her wrist and the line dribbled miserably in front of them. "Well . . . nearly."

"I think you'd better demonstrate some more." Kiri handed him the rod and stepped back onto the drier stones. "I'm very much a visual learner."

She sat happily in the sunshine as Dan took the rod and began casting again, tempting the fish with fluttering movements of the fly on the water. The sound of the nylon line humming was soothing, and she leaned her head on her arms, letting the sun massage her shoulders with its increasing heat.

"Quick . . . the net!" She jumped as Dan gestured toward the net on the ground behind. "He's taken it!"

There was a brief struggle as the trout tugged on the line, swimming out into the stream then darting back into its hideout. Dan played the line patiently until he finally wound in a large, brown-spotted fish and dropped it into the net that Kiri held out cautiously. "Great . . . it's at least six pounds! Not bad for the first catch. Look at the markings on him."

Kiri moved closer to look, then she jumped as the trout gave a final convulsive flip then lay still.

"Is it . . . dead?"

"Nope . . . just taking a breather." Dan grinned as he took the fish carefully out of the net and gently removed the hook from its lip. It wriggled slightly as he laid it back in the water, smoothing the scales with his wet hands. Then with a quick flap of its tail, the fish moved back into the current and away into the shadows of the far bank.

"Now it's your turn again." Dan reeled in the line. "But we'll try a little farther up the stream. It's a bit flatter and you can just practice the rhythm of casting."

They moved their gear, wading through some parts of shallow water and continually searching for the occasional flurry of fins under the water. When they finally found another spot, Dan set up the rod for Kiri and then left her practicing while he lay down under a large willow that draped its bright green tentacles into the stream. He settled his cotton fishing hat over his face, but from under the brim he kept a constant eye on Kiri as she waded out into the water.

Within minutes she was totally focused on flicking the line back and forth, her brow furrowing occasionally if the line settled limply in front of her, or clearing as the nylon hummed sweetly over her head and landed exactly where she was aiming.

Dan folded his hands on his chest, adjusted the hat over his forehead, and breathed deeply. Unbidden, thoughts of his last relationship passed through his mind. He'd never been able to convince Sarah to come fishing with him. She'd always found an excuse to do something else, and he'd usually agreed to her persuasive cajoling to stay with her and do what she wanted. In fact, the first thing he'd done when Sarah had announced she didn't want to marry him was to go fishing.

He sat up quickly at a short shriek from Kiri as she sat down heavily in the water, her hands out to her sides as she tried to keep her balance. Dan's first reaction was concern as his heart thumped with the echo of her scream. As he saw she was all right, he cupped his hands round his mouth and called out, "Don't let the rod go! It's expensive!"

Her face was a picture as she struggled to her feet, the waders bulging with the sudden intake of water and her hat hanging over one eye. With a shriveling glance in his direction, she waddled out to retrieve the rod, then back to the bank, the water slurping around her body and soaking the fishing vest that clung to her slight frame.

She stood helplessly for a minute with both arms outstretched, then dropped the rod to the ground and bent over to let some of the water flow out. Even when Dan started laughing she kept her head down . . . until he was laughing so hard that he was lying down holding his stomach. It was only a few feet up the bank, and she covered it quickly so that when he opened his eyes it was just in time to see a fountain of water pouring down toward his face.

"Aah!" he spluttered as he wiped his eyes, the laughter continuing. "I'm sorry . . . you just looked so . . ."

"Wet?" She shook herself and covered him with another spray of water. "I might have drowned and you wouldn't have noticed!"

He could see the beginnings of a smile at the corner of her mouth, but she pressed her lips tightly together.

"I don't think so." His voice dropped a tone and he nodded thoughtfully. "You just don't look like a trout . . . so I would have noticed . . . definitely . . . eventually."

Kiri put her hands on her hips as yet another laugh spilled from him, then she was laughing as well and kicking him playfully at the same time.

"So what do you expect me to do now?" She slowly peeled off the waders and jacket and stood holding the sodden items. "Do I just dry out in the sun?"

"You could, but I don't think we want to risk another bout of pneumonia." Dan leaned forward and rummaged through the large canvas bag, producing a pair of light tan corduroy trousers and a large green sweatshirt. "I always carry spares . . ." He hesitated. "Just not really the appropriate . . . um . . . underclothing for you."

She reached out and took the dry clothes, pretending a nonchalance she wasn't really feeling.

"These will be fine." She turned and scanned the trees round about for suitable shelter. "A tiny bit wet is better than staying soaked."

Dan took his time reorganizing the fishing gear while Kiri changed, and then he sat back down on the bank, staring into the smooth running water. It moved flawlessly over the spot she'd fallen, as if Kiri had never been there. Dan closed his eyes and a smile came back at the image of Kiri standing above him, vigorously shaking to get him wet.

"You're becoming way too noticeable, Kiri Karaitiana," he murmured as he leaned forward and picked up a small, smooth gray pebble. He rolled it thoughtfully between his fingers before pulling his arm up and back and throwing the pebble in a high arc out over the stream. It landed with a single sound and sunk into silent circles. "Way too noticeable."

"Shall I just put these clothes out to dry?" Kiri spoke behind him. He turned and the smile came again at the sight she made. "What are you smiling at?" she prodded.

She had rolled up the trouser legs several times, but they still hung down over her feet, and the sweatshirt reached below her knees like a large green blanket. She'd rolled the sleeves up as well, but they ballooned over her tiny wrists.

"Nothing." He stood up slowly. "I just never thought my clothes could look so . . . huge."

Kiri grinned and held out the wet clothes in one hand while she carefully held the waistline of the trousers with the other.

"Huge is not the word. They're enormous." She pulled at the waistline. "And if I could have a spare bit of fishing line or something to use as a belt, it would be most appreciated." She laughed a natural, unrestrained chuckle. "I tried tucking the sweatshirt in to hold the trousers up, but I looked like a lumpy green ball."

Dan laughed as well as he reached out to take the wet clothes, but as his hand touched hers, he suddenly took hold of it and pulled her toward him. The unexpected movement took Kiri by surprise, and she clutched at the trousers as his arm came round her shoulders in a tight hug.

"You're a great girl, Kiri. A lot of girls would have been complaining about this. You just make me laugh." He released her just as quickly and turned away to spread the clothes out on the larger rocks behind them. "It feels good."

Kiri nodded as she took a deep breath and bent to look through the bag, her mind trying to cope with the sensations that were racing through her. She could still feel the strength of his arm around her and the warmth of his chest against her shoulder and . . . it did feel good. She swallowed hard.

"So . . . can we eat now and feel even better?" She pulled a plastic box out of the bag. "All that swimming has made me hungry."

* * *

"So did you catch anything?" Winnie turned from stirring some gravy on the stove as Kiri and Dan walked into the kitchen. One eyebrow moved upwards as she looked at the way Kiri was dressed.

"Only a cold," Kiri grinned as she spoke with a heavy nasal intonation. "Dan wants me to stay, so he tried to give me pneumonia again. I nearly drowned."

"Guilty." He didn't even look up from the cupboard as he bent to put some food away. "But she's a hardy type, Winnie . . . couldn't even get a sneeze out of her."

"That's because I'm so warm in these blankets." Kiri held out the trousers and pirouetted in front of Dan and Winnie, the sleeves drooping down over her wrists.

"You look like a little lost orphan." Winnie's smile turned to a frown as a darkness briefly shadowed Kiri's eyes.

"And the cutest one around." Dan saw the look too as he stood up. "Actually, I think it's more of a fashion statement. Very appealing."

Kiri glanced quickly between them, realizing that they had seen her reaction. She hesitated for a second, then she looked at Winnie, her shoulders straightening as if making a decision.

"When I first met all of you, I did feel a bit like an orphan, but you've all made me feel so welcome and . . ." Her voice caught and she glanced quickly in Dan's direction without looking at him. "I'll just go and get changed."

Neither Winnie nor Dan spoke for a while after she left the kitchen, and then Winnie took the pot off the stove and thoughtfully wiped her hands on her apron.

"Seems to me it took a bit of courage for her to say that." She bent her head slightly toward Dan. "You must have had a good day."

Dan folded his arms and leaned back against the bench. "It was a great day, Winnie. The sun shone, we caught fish, we laughed and joked." He nodded his head. "In fact, I can't remember when I had such a good time with a girl . . . even Sarah."

"Even Sarah . . . or especially Sarah?" Winnie pulled some place mats from a drawer. "From the little I saw of that lass when we were in Christchurch . . . I think you were lucky she decided to go to America."

Dan looked surprised, then he grunted. "I think you and my mother must be tuned into the same wavelength. That's almost exactly what she said when I told her I wasn't marrying Sarah."

"Your mother's a good woman." Winnie smiled knowingly. "I wonder what she'd think of Kiri."

"I think she'd like her." He raised his head and looked out the window. "Not that it matters . . . they'll probably never meet. Kiri goes back to university in ten days."

"Are you sure?"

"Pretty much." He nodded. "We were talking about it today, and she's determined to get the extra qualification so she can run her own practice and be independent."

"Very independent." Winnie straightened a place mat carefully on the table. "Almost too independent . . . like she doesn't want to let anybody into her life."

There was another long pause, then Dan stood up and turned to get some plates out of the cupboard. "It's good to see a woman that knows her own mind. She's got her career all mapped out, and she's determined to be debt free when she finishes school. I really admire her."

"Is that all?" Winnie took the plates he handed her.

"Yes, Winnie . . . that's definitely all." Dan deliberately bent to make eye contact with her. "Kiri needed help. We could give her that . . . and now she and I have the opportunity to have some fun together. She has her plans all worked out, and I don't want any commitment for a long time. It works well to just be friends."

Winnie smiled submissively as she patted his hand on the plates. "All right, dear . . . if you say so."

Her tone and smile couldn't hide the knowing sparkle in her eye, and Dan groaned.

"Did my mother send you here as her agent? She seems to think I need help in choosing a wife."

"Not at all." She pretended to look offended. "I don't need your mother's instructions at all . . . I'm quite capable of meddling on my own. You ask Ted."

She smiled as Dan leaned his head back and laughed loudly.

"Oh, Winnie . . . to think that I didn't even know you existed a few months ago." He was suddenly serious. "In fact, it feels like you've always been a part of our family."

"Then I'll take that as a total compliment because I think you have the nicest family I've ever met." Winnie stopped as her eyes became moist. "Maybe we knew each other before."

"Before when, Winnie?" Dan watched for her reaction.

"Before this life," she answered naturally.

"So . . . you think we lived somewhere before now?"

"Yes . . . don't you?" she countered. "I've heard your father and Wade talk about it."

"The premortal life?" Dan felt a warm shiver run the length of his spine.

"That's it." She nodded. "I never said anything but I recognized a lot of what they were saying."

"Winnie . . . how long have you known about the Church now?" Dan leaned forward and rested both hands on the table.

"Oh, mostly since Wade came to stay . . . about a year. Why?" She narrowed her eyes slightly. "Are you going to start preaching at me, boy?"

"Nope." He smiled and turned toward the door. "I don't think I need to."

The door swung shut behind him, and then his head reappeared as he cracked the door open.

"But if you have any questions—and I know you have—don't hesitate to ask. I'm sure Kiri can answer them for you. I'll go get Ted for dinner."

Winnie drummed her fingers on the bench as he disappeared again, and then she gave a low chuckle. "Cheeky young rascal . . . now I'll really get on his case about Kiri." She walked over to the stove and opened the door to pull out a large casserole dish. She placed it on the table and looked back to the closed door. "Then again . . . he might just be right."

Chapter 8

"There's such an amazing combination of colors in this stone." Kiri ran her hand over the variegated layers of schist rock that made up the large fireplace in the log cabin. Each piece of rock looked as if it had been split apart to reveal a different tone or color. "It's so different from the big, round boulders and pebbles you see in most rock fireplaces."

"It's made from the local quarry stone." Dan paused behind her as he lowered a small kitchen cabinet to the ground. "Otago schist rock. When the gold miners set up here in the 1840s, they found that they could split it really easily and layer it to make their chimneys and houses. Some didn't even bother with mortar."

Kiri rubbed the thick gray concrete mortar that barely showed between some small slivers of terra-cotta and beige stone. "It's like a big jigsaw puzzle . . . there's the great big obvious slabs, but the little pieces fill in the gaps to make the big picture."

"Mm . . . a bit like some people." Dan picked up the cabinet again and walked into the kitchen, leaving Kiri staring after him.

She looked back at the chimney, and the layers of stone suddenly blended together as she pressed her finger hard against one of the small pieces of rock. "But if you did know about all the pieces . . . you probably wouldn't want to know the big picture."

She reached down and picked up the broom that she'd laid against the fireplace and began to sweep, making a pile of the sawdust and shavings that had been lying on the floor. It had become her job to sweep and tidy up each day, and she found it suited her perfectly as she allowed herself to dream as she swept—to dream that this log cabin was her own home . . . that she was sweeping her own floors and caring for her own family . . . in her own safe house. She'd tried to laugh at herself and even called it her "Cinderella" time, but the fact remained that she loved the log cabin and the thought of leaving was becoming more painful each day.

There were eight more days until the date that she had originally planned to be back in Dunedin to enroll for school. Dan didn't know that she'd fabricated the deadline to ensure some closure on her time with him . . . and with Winnie and Ted.

"Eight days to reality and no more Cinderella dreams." She gripped the broom harder and swept briskly for several minutes as if hard work would whisk away the thought.

From the darker recess of the unlit kitchen area, Dan watched thoughtfully as she swept vigorously. One minute she would be laughing, then making some thoughtful observation, then asking pretty technical questions about construction—and actually listening intently to his explanations— then suddenly she would back off into her own silent place and her face would mirror some confusion of emotions that left her shy and quiet.

His lips pursed as he took off his leather carpenter's apron and walked toward her.

"We've already sanded the floors . . . you don't need to take another layer off them." Dan gently took the broom from her hand and leaned it up against the wall. "Besides which . . . you'll need some energy for this afternoon. If we leave now, we can have some lunch before we go jet boating."

"Okay, then." Kiri relinquished the broom and brushed her hands together briskly. "Although I can't believe I'm actually going in the jet boats. It feels so . . . touristy."

* * *

"Still feeling touristy?" Dan yelled in her ear some time later as they settled themselves three abreast in the bright red jet boat and the driver revved the Chevrolet engine loudly. Kiri turned her head until her cheek rested against the orange life jacket.

"Absolutely." She grinned. "My heart is pumping already and we haven't even left the jetty." She glanced over the side, then back at the other people filing into the seats behind them. "The boat just seems too little to take all of us."

Dan settled himself into the seat beside her. "That's because the engine is all underneath and it works on propelling the water out the back. That's why it can go in really shallow water."

"As shallow as four inches of water," shouted their driver Pete, who was leaning against the metal bar in front of their seat. "And we'll do a three-sixty spin especially for you, young lady."

He laughed and showed a row of white teeth that gleamed against his tanned skin. Kiri looked up, but she could only see her reflection in the lenses of the sunglasses that curved fashionably around his face. He wore a tight black T-shirt under his yellow life jacket, which seemed to accentuate the lightness of the bleached tips of his brown hair.

"I take it this is your first time on the jet?" His voice held the trace of an accent. "First time in Queenstown?"

"Umm . . . no," Kiri answered hesitantly.

"You mean you've been here before and never visited me?" He pretended mock horror, and the charming smile lit up again. "I'd better make this a trip you never forget, then."

Dan sat quietly as the driver continued to ask Kiri questions about where she was from and what she'd already done in Queenstown. Shy at first, she was laughing as Pete finally directed the boat out onto the fast-flowing waters of the Shotover River.

Despite the exhilaration of the ride, Dan found it difficult to concentrate as Pete skillfully took the boat within inches of the sheer granite walls of the canyon. And when he sent the boat skimming through a narrow channel made dark by the height of the canyon walls, Kiri squealed along with the rest of the female passengers. Dan found himself frowning at the driver's blatant exhibitionism.

He finally focused on the ride as Pete swung the boat into a hair-raising, full-circle spin which sent Kiri forcefully against him as one of her hands lost its grip on the metal bar. A shrill scream was forced out of her lungs by the speed of the turn, and Dan instinctively reached his arm around her to steady her. The pressure of his hold on her increased as the spin continued, then they were lurched upright and the boat continued, skimming along the shallow braided estuaries.

"Oh, wow." Kiri reached up and brushed the watery drops off her face. "That was better than a roller coaster. I couldn't even stop that scream." She glanced up at Pete grinning at her, and blushed as he gave her the thumbs-up sign. "I don't know if he's a reckless driver or just very good."

Dan grimaced as Pete held up his hand and rotated it in a circle to indicate another spin. *He's just very good.* Then Dan held onto Kiri tightly as the boat executed another spin.

"That was so much fun!" Kiri undid the buckles on her life jacket and slid it off her shoulders as they climbed onto the jetty at the end of the ride. "Thank you so much, Dan."

"It was a pleasure." He took the jacket from her and placed it on a rack on the jetty. "I think we were given an extra special performance . . . just for your benefit."

He nodded his head toward Pete as the driver leapt up onto the jetty and made his way toward them.

"So . . . did you enjoy that?" He addressed the question to Kiri.

"Wonderful . . . thank you." She glanced deliberately at Dan. "We had a great time."

"So . . . would the two of you like to join me in town this evening? We have a group that gets together at one of the hotels most nights." He tucked his thumbs into the side buckles of his jacket. "Plenty of action happening."

"Actually . . . we're pretty busy." Kiri pointed to Dan. "Dan has a lot of work on. He's a builder," she finished quietly and clasped her hands in front of her, uncertain what to say next.

"Thanks for the offer, anyway . . . and thanks for the ride." Dan gave him a brief salute. "You're a great addition to the Queenstown tourist industry."

They had to cross a gravelly ridge, then walk up a steep grade to the car park, and neither spoke until Kiri was standing by the truck door waiting for Dan to unlock it for her.

"He was very charming, wasn't he?" She suppressed a grin as Dan paused with the key in the lock.

"If you like that sort of in-your-face personality." He twisted the key and swung the door open. "I prefer the guy that was here last time I came with Carl. A bit older . . . more mature."

"It was very kind of him to invite us out." Kiri knew she was needling him, but she felt an absurd impulse to get a reaction. Perhaps the attention she had received from Pete had had an effect after all . . . on both of them.

"You could always go on your own." Dan barely suppressed his sarcasm as he waited for her to get into the truck. "I'm sure Pete would be delighted."

"Daniel Harvey." She looked straight at the top button of his shirt—her heart pounding hard. "Were you jealous?"

"Ha!" His response was instant and vigorous as he ran a hand through his dark hair. "Jealous . . . I don't think so . . . more like disgusted!"

"Disgusted?" Kiri felt her heart jump at the impact of his response, and her voice came in a small gasp. "He wasn't that bad."

"Well, heck . . . it was fairly obvious that we were together." Dan rested his arm along the top of the door. "And he was still trying to hit on you."

"Maybe he didn't realize that we were . . . together," Kiri allowed a note of cynicism into her reply. "We aren't . . . technically."

"Then why don't you take up his invitation?"

"Because I don't want to go. You should know that. Why would I want to go to a hotel with a bunch of drinkers?"

"You might enjoy yourself . . . something different."

"You're just being silly!" Kiri planted both hands firmly on her hips, and her dark eyebrows almost joined together as she scowled. "And there's absolutely no need for it."

For a moment they both stood still, the only sounds coming from the rest of the tourists as they made their way to their cars.

"Are we arguing?" Dan stared at the billboard behind Kiri's head.

"I think so." She kept her gaze on his shirt button.

"I'm sorry." He frowned at the sign. "He was just such a . . ."

He stopped as Kiri held up her hand and touched his lip lightly to stop the coming words.

"Such a friendly person," she finished for him as she quickly put her hand down again.

"Just what I was thinking." Dan looked down at the top of her head. "A bit too friendly."

"Dan!"

"Just kidding!" He grabbed her hand as she brought it up again but he didn't let it go. Instead, he shook it gently. "You're my mate, Kiri. I just . . ." He hesitated again.

"You were just protecting my interests." She didn't want to move her hand and it made her slightly breathless to feel him so close. "And I appreciate that, Dan. I couldn't ask for a better friend."

"So . . . we're okay?" He finally looked at her.

"Definitely." She grinned. "Because if we're not, then I'd miss out on seeing you horse riding and I've been waiting for that all week."

"Sadist." He let go of her hand and gave her a quick squeeze around the shoulders. "I thought you were my friend."

"Only sometimes." She nudged him in the stomach and quickly pulled herself up into the truck. Then she laid her head back against the headrest and closed her eyes.

* * *

Kiri rested both hands on her knees and rolled her shoulders several times to ease the muscles that were tightening up. She had been working on the quilt pieces since early in the morning, and the radio had just announced the midday news. With just a hint of pride, she smoothed out the multicolored fabrics over her lap, delighting once more in the neatly worked Log Cabin design.

"Only four squares to go and you're all done," she murmured to herself as she folded them tidily and laid them in the lidded cane basket that Dan had bought her the day after their jet boat excursion. She had protested when he'd given it to her, but he'd just ignored her objections and told her it would be better than the plastic bag she'd been using. She thought about his parting words and absently rubbed the handle of the basket. "A memento of my Queenstown experience. Well, at least I'll have a basket and a quilt."

"Kiri?" Winnie opened the door into the lounge. "Oh good, you're still here. I have some friends here that I'm sure you'd like to meet."

She came into the room followed by two women—one middle-aged and the other a younger, very pregnant version of the older one.

"This is Dan's mother and his sister . . . Sheryl Harvey and Charise Fenton. Ladies, I'd like you to meet Kiri Karaitiana."

There wasn't a moment's hesitation before Sheryl Harvey crossed the room and gave Kiri an enthusiastic hug and a kiss on the cheek.

"Kiri, I'm so pleased you're feeling better. Winnie has been keeping us informed about your progress since you were so ill. Isn't it wonderful that they were here just when you needed them?"

"Mum, slow down or you'll frighten the lady." Charise moved more slowly to her mother's side and held her hand out to Kiri. Even holding her hand forward threatened to tip her off balance, and she leaned slightly back with one hand on her hip. "Excuse my teapot pose." She smiled happily. "Five hours sitting in the car makes the baby settle right in the middle. It's good to meet you, Kiri . . . and now I must make a comfort stop."

Her tone was warm and friendly, and having introduced herself, Charise immediately left the room.

"Poor girl." Sheryl shook her head as she watched her daughter leave the room. "I told her I was fine to drive myself over, but she insisted on coming with me. Now, where were we?"

"Um . . ." Kiri glanced at Winnie then back to Dan's mother. "It's good to meet you too, Sister Harvey. Your family have been wonderful to me . . . I don't know how I can ever repay you all."

"Oh, my dear, don't be silly. There's no question of repaying. We're all here to help each other, aren't we?" She moved to Winnie's side and gave her a hug as well. "Actually, I just really enjoyed the drive over. I forget how beautiful the countryside is between Christchurch and Queenstown, and then once I see the lake . . . well . . . I'm just so glad Rob convinced me that we should buy this house. He sees it as an investment, but I think I could easily retire here."

"It is lovely." Kiri nodded. "And out where Dan and Ted are building the cabin is really amazing as well."

"And how is my son?" Sheryl looked around the lounge. "You ladies must be doing the housework because I'm sure it would be a lot messier if he were caring for it himself."

Her words sounded abrupt, but Kiri could tell from her tone that she was speaking endearingly about Dan. Sheryl Harvey was simply an enthusiastically affectionate woman, and Kiri felt herself warm to her just as she had to Winnie.

"Dan and Ted are still out at the cabin." Winnie gestured toward the couch. "I didn't tell them you were coming because I thought it would be a nice surprise."

"Thank you, Winnie." Sheryl grinned. "It will definitely be a surprise for Dan to see Charise looking like this. When he left she wasn't anywhere near this big. She seems to have exploded the last few weeks."

"Thanks, Mum." Charise walked carefully past her mother and maneuvered down onto a firm chair. "The couch looks cozy, but I don't know if I could get back up right now."

"So how long have you got to go?" Kiri tried not to stare at the roundness of Charise's stomach.

"Technically . . . about four weeks." Charise rubbed her stomach lovingly. "Mentally . . . I was ready days ago. I seriously think I'm producing an elephant. How on earth do those animals put up with a two-year gestation? That is really horrible to even imagine."

"Well, you can guarantee your brother's going to have something to say to that effect." Sheryl patted her daughter's hand. "When do you expect them home, Winnie?"

"They'll probably be a couple of hours. It'll take them a bit longer today because Kiri is usually out helping with the cleanup, but she decided to have a quilt day today."

"Oh yes. Winnie said she'd been teaching you how to quilt." Sheryl immediately looked interested. "How is it going, Kiri?"

"Very well . . . at least . . . I feel like I'm making progress." She spread her hands almost apologetically. "I'm sure it's very amateurish compared to your work . . . but I'm really enjoying it."

"And that's the whole point of it," Sheryl laughed. "When I started quilting Rob would watch me cutting out these little shapes, and for the life of him, he couldn't figure out why I would take so much time to cut up pieces of material only to sew them back together again in the same shape I started with."

They all laughed, then Kiri self-consciously bent over and picked up her basket. "Would you like to see what I've done so far?"

"Absolutely!" Sheryl patted her lap. "Bring it here, dear. Oh, that's a lovely basket. I have one very similar and it's perfect for holding quilt things. Did you get it here?"

"Uh, yes." Kiri glanced at Winnie. "Actually, Dan bought it for me the other day. He said the plastic bag that I was using didn't do my work justice."

"Well . . . good on my son!" Sheryl chuckled and nodded at Charise. "I think there is hope for your brother, after all."

Kiri felt herself relax as she pulled the folded quilt blocks from the basket. Dan's mother and sister obviously felt completely at ease with her being here, and as she listened to their joking about Dan, she felt increasingly comfortable in their presence. She felt even better as Sheryl studied her work carefully and pronounced it "quite beautiful."

"I really like the strong colors you've used." Charise held one block up. "The way you've used the black centers, and then those deep autumn tones on the dark side look great."

Winnie pointed to the black squares. "Kiri liked the idea of using the black squares like they made the quilts in the slave days . . . to show the safe houses."

"I've never heard of that." Sheryl looked up. "But I like the idea, and besides, I think homes with quilts tend to be that sort of house anyway. Like a modern-day equivalent."

The minutes slipped into hours as Winnie brought out juice and homemade cheese scones and they sat around laughing at the stories that Sheryl and Charise had woven together. Suddenly the lounge door opened, and Dan walked straight to his mother and gathered her up in a huge hug.

"I thought I recognized the car." He squeezed her hard until she hit him on the shoulders, gasping for breath. "How dare you sneak in on us?"

"Daniel!" She patted her chest to emphasize her shortness of breath. "And we didn't sneak, either. Winnie knew we were coming," she said, as she kissed Daniel's cheek.

"And I'm not quite up to sneaking anymore." Charise grinned as she beckoned to her brother and held her cheek up for his kiss.

"You're not joking." Dan gave her a look of genuine concern as he pecked her on the cheek then stared at her stomach. "You're huge."

"Thank you for telling me, brother dear." She thumped his arm. "I wouldn't have known if you hadn't told me."

"Mum, were you ever like this?" He frowned as he pointed at Charise.

"Mmm . . . close." Sheryl smiled. "Only for you, though. Charise was a respectable size. It was you that ruined my youthful figure forever."

Kiri sat back watching the familiar interaction between Dan and his family. Even Winnie seemed completely at home with them all, and Ted's face was a picture when he walked in a few minutes later.

"I'll be . . . it's a reunion." He greeted Sheryl warmly. "Did Rob come over?"

"Not this time." Sheryl shook her head. "Someone had to stay with Grandma and Grandpa. We can't trust Dad to watch Grandma like he needs to. He just doesn't realize how dangerous it is to leave her alone."

"Is Grandma getting worse?" Dan sat down on the arm of the couch beside his mother and rested his arm behind her. She leaned back against him, and suddenly the happy expression on her face faded a little and Kiri saw the lines on her forehead deepen.

"Physically, she's fine." Sheryl toyed with the television remote control. "But she's beginning to wander a lot more, and the other night she actually went out onto the street . . . in the middle of the night." She ran her fingers over her brow. "I just happened to get up and I saw the door open. I hate to think where she might have ended up if I hadn't found her."

"Mum's hardly been able to sleep since." Charise's face had a slight frown as well. "Everyone is feeling quite exhausted . . ."

"And the only really happy one is Grandma." Sheryl tried to laugh. "She has no idea that anything is any different. And now I'm getting worried about Grandpa because he tries to get her to do things they've always done. Sometimes she'll start talking about completely fictitious places and people or things from her past like she was there yesterday, but treats him like a total stranger."

"Wow." Dan squeezed his mother's shoulder. "That seems to have happened really quickly. I mean, it was a surprise when she didn't recognize me when I got home, but she didn't seem that . . ."

"Away with the fairies?" Charise nodded. "Even the social worker is surprised how quickly this stage has developed. Ever since she moved into our home it's like our real grandma has disappeared."

"It sometimes happens like that," Kiri suggested quietly and hesitated as they all turned to look at her. "Um . . . it's just that . . . I've seen quite a bit of dementia during my training . . . and it seems like when they're shifted out of their own surroundings, they seem to slip into a fantasy world quite quickly." She smiled. "I used to have wonderful conversations with one lady about her home and where she grew up, and then her family told me that it was all made up. It used to frustrate them, but she and I had some great times together."

There was a moment's silence, then Charise leaned forward. "Didn't it bother you that she was . . . lying about everything?"

"But she wasn't lying . . . not in her mind." Kiri shook her head. "And she felt confident talking to me because I didn't question everything like her family did."

"Youch . . . guilty." Sheryl raised her hand in her lap. "But Rob gets very frustrated with her as well. He can't stand that his mother is doing such weird things when she used to be so competent. She's been the president in all the Church auxiliaries and raised a large family, and suddenly she's putting shampoo on her toothbrush."

"Why does she do that?" Dan looked straight at Kiri, and she felt her heart tremble at the concerned look in his eyes.

"Well, I was taught that it's all about choices . . . rather than ability," she began carefully, reluctant to be too outspoken. "Your grandma remembers how to brush her teeth, but given the choice in a bathroom cabinet of shampoo or soap or toothpaste . . . she'll just take any one." Again, she smiled. "I had to take a group in a rest home for crafts when I first started training. I was very enthusiastic and I thought I was highly organized. I had painting and needlework and knitting—all things that the hospital had told me they could do. But when they sat down with all the choices . . . I ended up with one lady painting with knitting needles."

"That's funny, but it's sad," Charise laughed and then put her hand over her mouth. "And it's so like Grandma."

"Which leads me to the main reason we came." Sheryl leaned forward and looked straight at Kiri. "I wasn't going to mention it straight away, but seeing we're on the subject . . . Kiri?"

"Yes?" Kiri glanced at Winnie, who shrugged and smiled and nodded toward Dan's mother.

"When Dan called and said you were staying here, he told us a little about you . . . that you were an occupational therapist." Sheryl folded her hands in her lap. "And later, I was talking to Winnie and she said that you were looking at going back to university but you hadn't quite organized everything yet."

"Um . . . not quite." Kiri avoided Dan's questioning look. "But . . . I was planning on beginning my master's papers . . . next semester."

"I understand." Sheryl took a deep breath. "And I know this is a huge thing to ask but . . . I . . . we . . . were wondering if you would even consider helping us out with Grandma for a while. The thing is, the social worker says she's going to need a lot more supervision, especially at night. And we've just found out that my sister-in-law needs chemotherapy up in Taranaki and I need to go up there for her for a while, and Charise is due to have the baby, and frankly, I just don't trust Grandpa with the responsibility." She paused for breath. "The hospital recommended getting a therapist to come and help on a daily basis and someone else at church mentioned that they knew someone who had a live-in help . . . anyway, after I'd spoken to Winnie I just got to thinking that maybe . . . maybe I could ask you if you'd consider one or both of those options . . . for a few weeks. We'd pay you, of course, and you could live in the guest room beside Grandma's room . . ." Her voice trailed off. "And the more I talk the more absurd it seems to even think of asking."

No one spoke, and then Ted cleared his throat. "Seems to me like 'nothing ventured, nothing gained.' It never hurt to ask."

The simplicity of his words broke the silence, and of one accord they all seemed to look at Kiri.

"Of course, we wouldn't expect an answer right away." Sheryl tightened her fingers in a ball. "But if you could consider it . . . well . . ." She glanced around the room. "I think I'll just be quiet now."

"And I think my pork casserole should be just about ready." Winnie stood up and nudged Ted. "Why don't you give me a hand with the vegetables and we can eat sooner."

As they left the room, Sheryl stood up and ran her hand over her hair.

"And I think I'll go and freshen up before dinner." She paused by Kiri's chair. "I'm sorry if I've put you on the spot, dear. It just seemed like such a good idea."

"I understand, Sister Harvey." Kiri swallowed. "And I'm honored that you'd think of me. I . . . I'll just have to think about it for a bit."

"Well, we're here for a couple of days." Charise stretched her back as her mother left the room. "I told Mum I needed to blob out for a while before baby comes, but she's the one that really needs the break. Dad has taken a couple of days off work to look after Grandma and Grandpa."

"I had no idea things were so bad." Dan stood up and thrust both hands into his jeans pockets. "Isn't it funny how you can just go about doing your own thing and be completely oblivious to what's going on somewhere else?"

"I reckon." Charise laid her hand on her stomach, and Kiri watched as it suddenly rose as the baby moved. "Whooa . . . that was a cartwheel. I think I'm giving birth to a gymnast."

She grimaced as Dan leaned over, fascinated, and put his hand over hers.

"Hey . . . make it do it again, sis." He pressed his hand down, and his eyes widened in delighted surprise as the baby moved again.

"*It* happens to be your nephew, and this really isn't my idea of entertainment." Charise chuckled and moved Dan's hand. "Back to our topic . . . how long do you think it'll be before you finish the cabin?"

"Ooh . . . about a month if all goes well. We're ahead of schedule." Dan looked puzzled. "Why?"

"Well, I just thought that you could come back and give a hand at home for a while after you're finished. You won't be starting another house straightaway, will you?"

"Not starting one, but Mitch was talking about sending me up to Canada to work on a project up there . . . experience the 'real' thing in the wilderness."

"But you've got plenty of wilderness right here." Charise spoke Kiri's thoughts out loud. "I just think you should spend a bit of time with Grandma before . . . well, before she's not the grandma we remember. She may have to go into a home. And it would help Mum and Dad."

"I guess so." Dan looked thoughtful and he glanced at Kiri. "Do you think there's a chance you could work for a while . . . until I could take over?"

Kiri tried to look calm as her thoughts and feelings raced.

"Can I let you know tomorrow?" She chewed her bottom lip. "I'll need to make a few phone calls first."

"Of course." Dan pointed back toward the kitchen. "What say we eat and then just relax after dinner? No more talk about grandmas."

"I agree." Charise tried to get up unsuccessfully and held out a hand for Dan to help her up. "Let's talk about your impending responsibilities as Theodore's uncle."

"Theodore?" Dan stopped with his hand outstretched. "You're kidding . . . right?"

"You'll just have to wait and find out, won't you? No forgetting that we exist while you labor in paradise." She pushed herself to the edge of the chair. "Now come and help Theodore and his mum get to the dinner table."

Chapter 9

"I think he's trying to eat me." Dan's voice was low as he stepped back a respectful distance from the dapple-gray gelding that he'd been given to ride.

"He's not trying to eat you. He's just feeling the bit in his mouth," Kiri spoke quietly as well as she led her own smaller, bay-colored horse up beside him. Even as she spoke, Dan's horse suddenly extended its neck, pulled its top lip right back, and shook its head vigorously.

"Look at the size of its teeth!" Dan took another involuntary step back. "Those would take a fair-size chunk out of my rear."

"I think you're safe . . . he's already been fed. Just be nice to him." She stifled a grin as he walked toward the horse and gave it a tentative pat on the side of its neck. "I didn't realize you were serious about horses . . . about not liking them."

"Oh, I don't mind them . . . I just don't think they like me." He kept rubbing the horse's neck, but at the same time keeping a wary eye on its ears that kept flattening. "Charise went through a horsey phase when she was about eleven, and she'd make me go riding with her. I got dumped about three times."

"That's not bad."

"It is if you only went three times." He gave her a rueful grimace. "These beasts just think they're all powerful."

"Well, stop calling them 'beasts' for a start. They can hear you." Kiri reached up and scratched her horse behind his ears, and he dropped his head in against her chest with a satisfied whiffling noise. "You know, we needn't have come riding if you felt this bad about it."

"No, fair's fair." He shook his head and copied her in scratching his horse's ear. The horse flattened them again and Dan frowned. "Do you want to swap horses?"

"That might work." She compared the height of their mounts. "That way your feet would touch the ground and you could just brake when you wanted."

"Oh, you're so smart." Dan pulled a face. "Just because you're used to horses."

Kiri shook her head in protest. "I like horses but I haven't sat on one since I was about ten, and that didn't really qualify. It was about thirty years old, and my cousins and I used to ride her all at once . . . about five of us. She never went faster than a plod."

They were both quiet for a second, then both burst out laughing at once.

"So why did you include horse riding in the choices?" Kiri giggled.

"Because I thought you liked riding. You'd mentioned how you liked a certain horse when you were growing up." Dan rolled his eyes. "I didn't know you were describing the local taxi."

"I did like her . . . she was the one thing I could talk to that didn't mock me." Kiri stopped and lifted the reins over her horse's head. "Anyway . . . let's make the best of this. It's only for a few hours, and I really have been looking forward to it."

"A few hours." His voice was a low moan. "A bungee jump would have been all over and done with in a few seconds." He stood back. "So how do you get up on this thing, anyway?"

The guide arrived just as he spoke and gave them their instructions as he took the lead of the group. Within minutes they were ambling down through the town of Glenorchy and out onto a narrow trail that opened onto the reaches of the Rees River. Even Dan's face cleared of unwilling concentration as the raw beauty of the scenery settled on them. The crystal-like greens and blues of the river changed to shades of beige as it washed over rounded rocks. Underneath the outstretched arms of gnarled green-leafed trees, the water provided a soothing musical backdrop to the steady clomping of the horses' hooves as they moved automatically along the well-worn path.

"This really is wonderful." Kiri took a deep breath and exhaled slowly. "The air just feels so clean and fresh."

"Except for the horsey smell." Dan screwed up his nose.

"Oh, Dan." She shook her head at the expression on his face. "If only you could see your face . . . you're going to get a permanent wrinkle over your nose."

"No . . . it'll be fine as soon as my feet hit terra firma again." He exaggerated the rolling movement as dictated by the horse's gait. "I must admit this is really quite soothing."

Kiri nodded as she straightened her back. "Dan . . . I really do appreciate your including the riding in the choices . . . especially as you don't like it. That makes it even more special."

"The ultimate sacrifice?" He grinned. "Do I get extra points for that?"

They continued along the river walkway, then the guide led them back inland and into an amazing labyrinth of tall trees where the sunlight filtered through the leafy canopy that intertwined high above their heads. The pale light seemed to illuminate the greenness of the lush native undergrowth and the golden brown of the dry leaves that lay in piles against the crawling tree roots.

"Primeval Beech Forest," Dan quoted the tourist brochure they had read on the drive out to the stables.

"It feels very . . . ethereal." Kiri gave a slight shiver as she gazed around her. "You can almost imagine little forest people popping out of the trees."

"Mmm, very Tolkienish." Dan nodded in agreement and pointed out into the woods. "And the guide told me we don't even get to see the best surroundings on the short trek." He readjusted his seat in the saddle. "Four hours being the short trek."

They rode silently for a few minutes, letting the atmosphere soak in, then Kiri glanced at Dan.

"Do you read a lot? You mentioned Tolkien."

Dan nodded thoughtfully. "I read quite a bit now. My mother used to despair of me when I was young . . . I just couldn't see the point of sitting for so long just to read words. There were so many other . . . fun things to do." He turned his head toward her. "Did you . . . read?"

"Mmm . . . quite a bit." Her hands tightened on the reins. "Books weren't really available in our house . . . but I used to read as much as I could at school."

"Why only at school? Why didn't you take the books home to read?"

She smiled. "My cousins weren't exactly into books. They liked to tease me if I was reading, and the best way was to throw the book around so I couldn't catch it. I used to get told off by the teacher when the book got wrecked." She shrugged. "It was easier to read at school, and . . . I got to be a very fast reader, which really helped in my studies later."

"So it turned into a positive thing?"

"I guess it did." She stared ahead. "I never really thought of it like that."

"Most things can have a positive outcome . . . if you look hard enough." Dan moved past her as his horse suddenly decided it wanted to walk ahead. "I'm working on the positive side of this exercise."

"It's definitely the delightful company," Kiri called as he tried to pull on the reins and the horse only moved faster.

"Let me know if you mean me or the horse!" His voice was lost as the horse broke into a trot.

They stopped for lunch in a sheltered glade where the trees opened out to form a crescent around an area of soft green grass. The sun shone down directly onto them as they rested back against a straight tree trunk. Their horses grazed nearby, tearing at the long strands of grass in a steady rhythm.

"They're really loud, aren't they?" Dan lifted the brim of his cap to stare at the horses. "Sort of changes the atmosphere."

Kiri didn't bother opening her eyes as she held her face up to the sun. "No, it adds to the atmosphere . . . the sounds . . . the smells. It reminds me of when I was little and the horse was my quiet friend. I would lie down in the grass while she grazed . . . her bigness was comforting somehow." She paused. "Thanks again . . . for bringing me out."

"Hey . . . I've only been kidding most of the time." Dan pushed his cap farther back and rolled sideways to face her. "I really like horses. They're very noble."

He chuckled as her eyes flicked open and she let the deep mellow sound roll over her. Suddenly it was the perfect day . . . the perfect company in the perfect place . . . and she didn't want it to end.

"Wouldn't it be nice to just stay like this?" Dan gave voice to her thoughts, and she felt her cheeks flush as though he'd read her mind.

"Nice . . . but totally unrealistic," she murmured as she played with a long strand of grass that waved against her leg.

"But you don't have to be realistic all the time." He reached out and picked another long strand from the same patch. "It's good to let go and dream occasionally. That's when you allow yourself to imagine a future . . . then you just have to have the courage to go ahead and make it happen."

"What if you don't want to dream . . . for fear of it never happening?"

"Then I guess you'll never know," he persisted. "Seriously, though . . . what made you go to university? Wasn't it following a dream?"

Kiri took awhile to answer as she watched some small white clouds temporarily fill the space of sky overhead. They cast a fleeting shadow, and she shivered in the passing coolness as she thought about the fears she'd faced as she'd left home and then as she'd begun her first semester at university.

"I saw it as meeting a need . . . not following a dream." She finally looked down. "I was scared stiff and very alone."

"But you did it. You made it through, and now you're going even farther." Dan twisted the grass between his fingers so that the fluffy tip ran up and down the upturned cuff of Kiri's shirt. "What do you dream of doing now?"

Kiri watched the grass dancing on her sleeve. She didn't want to move her arm or speak. She wanted to keep watching the way his dark hair curled out around the edges of his cap and the way his shoulders strained the light cotton fabric of his shirt as he rested on his elbows. She quickly averted her eyes as he looked up.

"Seriously . . . what does Kiri Karaitiana want . . . in the future?" He spoke very softly which seemed to fit the mood in the glade. Even the horses had stopped chewing.

"Um . . . I want to finish my master's and get into some sort of clinical practice . . . or even health administration." She bit her lip. "I want to make a difference . . . for people who can't really help themselves."

"That sounds like a long-term commitment," he responded quietly, and she nodded.

"That's how I see it."

"And where does marriage and a family fit into the picture?" Dan twisted the grass again, and it tickled against her skin so that she leaned over to scratch it.

"Maybe it doesn't." She rubbed the skin longer than she needed to.

Dan looked up with a surprised expression on his face. "Not at all?"

"Well . . . possibly . . . but marriage doesn't have to be the only option."

"I guess . . ." He frowned. "It just seems like there's a classic Latter-day Saint image. You know . . . loving husband and five children . . ."

"What if you've never known that image?" Kiri pulled her legs up to clasp her arms around her knees. "And what if you don't want to repeat the only image you do know?"

"What's that?" He rested his chin on his hand and didn't look at her. At that moment he felt as close to finding out about her past as at any time throughout the last few weeks . . . a past that she seemed to adroitly avoid mentioning.

"Nothing you could relate to," she answered briefly. "No mother, no father . . . the only girl amongst a heap of boy cousins and uncles . . . one auntie who didn't really care about anybody, and a grandfather who ruled."

"So your grandfather brought you up?"

"He was in charge . . . I wouldn't really say he brought me up." Kiri briefly rested her forehead against her knees. "He's a member of the Church, but he's not your 'classic' LDS image."

"But you turned out really well."

She tried to detect any mockery, but there wasn't any and her eyes suddenly filled with tears at the genuine caring tone of his voice. If only things could stay as they were right now . . . nothing changing.

"Thank you for that." She still didn't look at him. "It actually means a lot to me."

"And actually . . . you mean a lot to me." The stem of grass sat still in his hand as he realized the depth of his words—the way he'd felt when he'd laid his hands on her hot, fevered brow when she was sick; the fun they'd had fishing at the river; the resentment he'd felt when Pete, the guide, had made overtures to her. "Really, Kiri. You're an awesome woman."

She had no idea how to respond, and though the words wouldn't come, warm tears began to slide silently down her cheeks until she could taste their saltiness on her lips.

"Kiri?" Dan sat up slowly and bent his head to see her face properly. When she tried to turn away, he took her chin firmly in his hand. Her immediate reaction of flinching and lifting her arm in defense took him by surprise. He lowered his hand as the tears fell and she bit at her bottom lip. The tears made him angry at himself and ache for her in the same instant. "I'm so sorry. I didn't mean to hurt you."

For just a moment she looked back without restraint, taking in every detail of his face and the concern showing in his eyes.

"Don't ever be sorry, Dan." She tried to smile through the tears. "You've given me the happiest time of my life in the last few weeks. You're the best friend I could ever ask for."

The familiar endearment seemed to create a large knot in Dan's stomach, and he lifted his hand tentatively to cup her cheek as he swallowed hard.

"Suddenly I hate that word." He leaned forward slowly and gently kissed the tears on each cheek and then paused somewhere between her nose and lips. He could sense her body stiffen and he immediately drew back slightly. But then, in quivering consent, Kiri lifted her face upward. There was the slightest hesitation, then both felt an overwhelming sense of completion as their lips met in the gentlest of kisses.

"Time to move on, folks!" Their guide spoke from behind a stand of bushes. "When you're ready, that is."

"Oh, boy," Dan muttered under his breath as he rested his forehead against Kiri's. "I never . . ."

"It's . . . it's okay." Kiri quickly began to stand up and brush off her jeans. "I never intended it to happen either. It must just be the setting."

Dan stood up and adjusted his cap. "Actually . . ." he began, but she turned away.

"Honestly, Dan . . . being friends is good and I'm fine with it." She walked over to her horse and began to undo the tether rope. "Let's just enjoy the day . . . no complications."

He thoughtfully tucked his shirt firmly into the back of his jeans as she led her horse toward the rest of the group.

"Actually . . ." He leaned forward and muttered to his horse as it eyed him warily. "I meant I never realized a kiss could feel that way."

Kiri was very talkative on the ride back to the stables. She commented on the scenery and asked him a lot about other books he'd read. If he was quiet, she talked to their guide and the two other trekkers, a couple from Germany. She was animated and there was a distinctive flush to her cheeks, but she couldn't look straight at him.

He watched as Kiri led her horse up to a tethering post and thanked the guide for the excursion, then waited as he brought his mount forward. He could see that she was thinking hard because there was a tiny frown line deepening over her left eye.

She took a breath as if she was going to speak, but the words didn't actually come until they had nearly reached the truck. Then she stopped walking and made a line in the dirt with the toe of her boot.

"We both stepped over the line, didn't we?" She retraced the line as she stared down at it.

"I think so." He folded his arms and waited for any indication that it was all right.

"And I'm sorry, too. I really don't want anything to change the friendship we have, Dan. I value it too much." She bit at her bottom lip. "I know how you feel about commitment and I really still want to be your friend . . . if that's okay?"

"It's completely okay." He held out his right hand. "Friends?"

"Friends." She smiled and he could see the relief in her face as they shook hands very briefly.

They traveled home with the car stereo playing louder than usual, and even sang along with the songs. It was a contrived lightheartedness, but it worked, and by the time they drove up the driveway to the house, she was feigning horror at Dan's rather strained version of a country singer. They unloaded their gear and then Dan assumed an exaggerated cowboy gait and groaned as he walked up the stairs.

"I'm sure glad we didn't do the two-day trek. I don't think parts of my body would have stood it."

They were both laughing as they entered the lounge and Charise looked up sleepily.

"Sounds like you two had a good day." She switched off the television with the remote control. "Horse riding must suit you."

"I . . . don't know about that." Dan shook his head. "But I'm sure it would have made things happen for you if you'd come along."

"Oh, there's a good idea." She pulled a face at her brother. "I'm dreading the drive back tomorrow. Baby's been giving me some definite warning signs that he thinks it's time to leave this little haven I've created for him."

"You're in labor?" Kiri and Dan spoke in unison.

Charise wagged her finger at them both. "You're even starting to think alike," she scolded innocently. "No, he's just practicing. We've got weeks to go." Charise waved her hand airily. "And we've got to get through the wedding first. We forgot to mention that Wade, Carl's brother, and Mackenzie are due in next week and we've got the wedding to organize for the week after. Winnie and Ted are going to come back next week just before they arrive."

"Is everyone going to be at the house?"

"No . . . that would really throw Grandma." Charise shook her head. "No . . . Carl's parents and sister are going to stay at a motel, and Mackenzie is coming to stay with us in the flat until they fly up to Hamilton, to the temple."

"Are you sure you'll be able to manage all that?" Dan looked down at her stomach.

"Of course." Charise patted her swollen stomach. "I'm pioneer stock . . . I can handle anything." She laughed, and then her face tightened into a grimace and she leaned forward uncomfortably. "If only the midwife hadn't told me he was going to be at least nine pounds . . . I could happily have him tomorrow."

Kiri stared at her for a long time, then turned toward Dan.

"Do you think your mother would mind if I went back to Christchurch with them tomorrow? It might help ease the load a little."

Chapter 10

It didn't take very long to pack up her few belongings the next morning. After she zipped up the suitcase, she set it on the floor with the quilt basket. On the spur of the moment, she picked up the basket and took out the large rectangle that she'd finally formed the other day when she joined most of the squares together. There was something about seeing the finished connection of light and dark blocks forming a ladderlike pattern that gave her a great feeling of accomplishment. She stroked the soft cotton pieces gently, running her finger around the perimeter of one of the black squares.

"This really has been a safe house," she murmured and traced the outline again, then began to fold the quilt up. Just as she placed it back in the basket, Sheryl Harvey knocked on the open door of her bedroom.

"Kiri?" She stood hesitantly in the doorway. "I just wanted to thank you again for agreeing to come back with us. I know it's a huge imposition . . . but I'm so grateful . . . so very grateful."

Kiri was startled to notice Sheryl's eyes begin to moisten, and she stood uncertainly near the bed as the older woman wiped at her tears.

"Now I'm just being a big crybaby." She smiled and fanned her face. "I . . . I've been trying to handle everything for the last few months, and I thought I was doing quite well but . . . my hormones seem to go amok when there's a family crisis . . . or two . . . or three." She leaned against the door. "What with Dan's engagement breaking up, and my sister-in-law getting sick, and then Mother and now Charise . . . well . . . I just really do appreciate you coming on board."

Kiri didn't really hear the rest of her explanation. Dan had actually been engaged?

The look on Kiri's face somehow communicated itself to Sheryl and she hesitated.

"Did Dan not mention he was engaged?"

"Um . . . not really." Kiri waved her hand dismissively. "He just said that he'd expected to marry a girl . . . Sarah . . . when he got off his mission . . . but it didn't happen."

"Well, that's definitely the *Reader's Digest* version." Sheryl rolled her eyes. "The poor boy went through a lot of drama. Sarah wrote to him the whole time he was on his mission, and she was there at the airport when he got home. They dated again for several weeks, then he asked her to marry him and she said yes. He gave her the ring and everything." She shook her head. "Then about a week later he got an envelope with the ring in it and a letter saying she'd been e-mailing a returned missionary in America for the last seven months and she'd decided to go to him."

"Oh my goodness." Kiri felt her heart fill with compassion for Dan. "That's just dreadful."

"It was dreadful." Sheryl clasped her hands in front of her. "I thought he handled it very well, and the next week my niece's friend offered him the job up here at the cabin. It didn't take him long to decide to do it."

She paused, then cleared her throat. "I've got to say, Kiri . . . that when I heard you were staying here . . . I did wonder a bit about you and Dan. I was worried he might be rushing into a . . . rebound relationship." She made a juggling motion with her hands. "You know . . . off with Sarah . . . on with Kiri—not that you're much alike."

"I assure you," Kiri held up one hand, "there's nothing—"

"I know that now." Sheryl nodded briefly as if dismissing any idea of a relationship. "Dan has assured me you're just friends and Winnie says that you have a really good sibling-type friendship."

"Dan has been wonderful." Kiri clasped her elbow with her other hand. "He's helped me a lot since I was sick, but . . . I'm keen to pursue my career."

"Well, I hope we haven't upset that." Sheryl took a step inside the room and enveloped Kiri in a warm hug. "Just thank you again before we face the business of the next few weeks."

Kiri didn't sleep well that night. The full moon seemed to create larger, stronger shadows than normal that played on the walls and ceiling of her room. Even the birds seemed to be having a midnight party, and at some point in the early morning hours, two cats decided to confront each other. Their intermittent wailing reached full crescendo right outside her bedroom window, making her sit bolt upright as they screeched and fought.

"Be quiet!" She finally leaned out of the window and banged the side of the house. The cats dispersed, slinking off down the driveway in opposite directions. "And stay away," she muttered with the tartness borne of sleep deprivation, then she slowly closed the window. With a sigh of resignation, she lay back down on the bed and stared up at the ceiling.

Dan had actually been engaged . . . had actually committed himself to a temple marriage just a few months ago. She felt a lump form in her throat and pulled the sheets up more tightly under her chin. "No wonder he doesn't want commitment." The shadows suddenly grew lighter above her head as she turned over and punched the softness of the pillow. "What a stupid woman that Sarah must be."

* * *

She could feel him approaching even before the long grass flattened under his heavy work boots.

Her mother's grave had become a sanctuary for a while. Out in the open, up on the hill. The stark headstones stood almost like vigilant sentinels protecting her. Her uncles left her alone here . . . but he wasn't her uncle. She didn't know where he'd come from. She didn't want to know his name.

"C'mon, don't be shy. Girls are meant to kiss . . . boys." The mustiness of his breath seemed to seep inside her ears and eyes and settle in her throat as she tried to turn her head away. The more she resisted, the more his fingers sunk into the flesh on her cheek, then she felt her hair locked into his hand.

"No . . ." She could barely manage a whisper as her neck strained back and his head obscured her vision.

"You know . . . you want to." His heavy breathing was interrupted with a throaty hiccup and she felt her stomach retch. With a desperate show of strength, she pushed him and rolled away. For his size he moved surprisingly quickly, and she felt the jarring pain as her head hit the headstone.

"Girls just pre . . . pretend. You're all the same. You know you want . . . kisses."

* * *

Kiri pressed both hands over her mouth as she kept her eyes tightly closed. She could feel the wet trails of tears fall down the sides of her face and into her hair.

How long had she been crying?

She lifted both hands and ran them over her face and breathed deeply. The softness of the pillow under her head suddenly seemed suffocating and she sat up suddenly.

"I do want kisses . . . but I can't. It's wrong . . . it's wrong!" She felt the sob in her chest as she pressed her hand to her mouth and felt her teeth dig into her lip. "It's wrong, Dan. I can't!"

* * *

They loaded the car up early so it wouldn't be too hot for traveling, and within a few minutes Charise was settled into the front seat with pillows around her for a more comfortable ride. She laughed at Dan as he made exaggerated efforts to get the pillows in exactly the right place for her.

"You are such an idiot." She thumped him on the shoulder as he bent in and put another pillow under her elbow.

"Hey . . . I'm just looking after my nephew. You just happen to be the vehicle he's traveling in." He pretended to wince as she hit him again, then he bent and kissed her on the forehead. "You take care, now, little sister. Call me when you get into town."

"I will." Charise's tone was suddenly soft. "And thank you for the blessing. He's definitely calmed down a lot since then." She placed a hand horizontally above the bulge of her stomach. "In fact, I think he might have dropped. It feels a lot easier."

"That'll make for a better trip, then." Sheryl walked around behind her son and lifted her face for a kiss as he straightened up from the car. "Thank you for everything, darling . . . and we'll see you." She looked thoughtful. "When will we see you?"

Dan kissed his mother lightly and ran his hand through his hair.

"I should be finished in time for the wedding. I'll try and be on deck to stay with Grandma while you all go up to Hamilton."

"You don't think you'll come?" Winnie spoke behind him.

"Well . . . I just don't know Wade and Mackenzie that well, and it seems like Grandma needs to have someone close." He shrugged. "Besides, I'd like some time with her . . . before . . . you know."

His mother nodded as she gave Winnie, then Ted, a hug. "Whatever suits you, dear. We'll keep in touch."

"And we'll be there in a few days." Winnie patted Sheryl's arm. "I'll try to be useful, but I must confess . . . I'm getting so excited to see our girl again."

"It's going to be wonderful." Sheryl smiled. "Mackenzie is going to be thrilled to see you too."

Kiri stood back slightly as they all said their farewells, then she moved toward the backseat behind the driver. Just before she slipped in, she felt a hand grip her elbow firmly and Dan pull her gently back to stand in front of him.

"Think you're just going to slip away?"

She tried to ignore his hand on her arm as he stared directly into her eyes.

"Uh . . . no." She forced a slight smile. "I did intend to wave."

"That's all . . . a wave?" He raised one eyebrow, and she felt his grip tighten slightly. "After teaching you all I know about fishing and building, and protecting you from predatory guides, and risking my life on giant horses . . . I only get a wave . . . from my mate?"

As soon as he said the word *mate*, Kiri relaxed and leaned forward to give him a brief, hesitant hug.

"I'm sorry," she murmured into his shoulder. "I'm just not big on good-byes."

"Me neither." He let go of her elbow and suddenly wrapped both arms around her. They were both silent, then Kiri pushed herself back without looking at him.

"Thanks for everything . . . mate," she whispered as a lump formed in her throat. "I'll do my very best for your grandmother."

"I know you will." He was equally serious as he stood back and folded his arms. "You're the best, Kiri."

His words played over and over in her mind as they drove away, traveling north through the town of Cromwell, past the man-made reaches of Lake Dunstan, and up through the arid reaches of the Mackenzie Basin.

As the car made its way past ruggedly barren hill country, Sheryl glanced out the window.

"Glencameron lies over that way." She pointed in a vague westerly direction. "That's the sheep station that Winnie and Ted live on usually, and Mackenzie Cameron, who owns the station, is going to be Charise's new sister-in-law soon."

Grateful for the distraction from her own thoughts, Kiri stared out the window. "So you met Winnie and Ted through your brother-in-law?" She turned to Charise who was lying back with her eyes closed, although she'd been humming quietly for some time.

"Mmm . . ." Charise nodded but didn't bother opening her eyes. "Wade flew out here to do some photography for his dad's wool mills and stayed at Glencameron. It turned out that his hostess was none other than Mackenzie, whom he'd seen during his mission a few years before when he served down here in Christchurch."

"But she wasn't a member?"

"No . . . but he decided to try and teach her . . . and that's when he called me to go and help with his photo shoot." She smiled, remembering. "Poor Mackenzie . . . she'd been a tough, independent high-country girl all her life, and Wade suddenly turns up and wants to dress her in all these beautiful clothes, have her wear makeup, and try to get her to understand the Book of Mormon all in a matter of days. It was insane when I think back on it."

"But it all worked out in the end. She was a beautiful model and she joined the Church." Sheryl smiled. "The Lord truly works in mysterious ways."

"So that's how you met Winnie?" Kiri found herself intrigued with the story.

Charise nodded, wide awake now.

"I flew out to do the makeup for the shoots . . . and to be Mackenzie's . . . confidante, I guess. Wade was hopeless. He was so smitten with her that he couldn't even get the right words out at the right time. I think I was more like his interpreter."

"But they got together?"

"Not initially." Charise shook her head. "Mackenzie was unofficially engaged to the farmer next door, who happened to be quite a hunk . . . so when Mackenzie got confused about everything, she turned back to him."

"You mean she got engaged to him?" Kiri couldn't keep the surprised tone out of her voice.

"Yes . . . and Wade didn't want to hurt her anymore and decided to ride off into the sunset." Charise grinned. "Except they didn't bargain on Winnie taking control of the situation."

"Winnie?"

"Winnie . . . our treasure," Sheryl joined in. "She called Charise and basically told her that Wade loved Mackenzie and she loved him, but they were both too considerate of each other to admit it."

"So . . . what happened?"

Charise sat up a little. "Well . . . Wade went back up to Auckland and meantime Mum and Dad had been in touch with his parents and they decided to come down."

"From America?" Kiri raised both eyebrows. "That's such a long way!"

"Charise!" Sheryl frowned at her daughter, which only made her giggle.

"Okay, Mum." She waved her hand. "Don't let the truth get in the way of a good story."

"And the truth is . . ." Sheryl waited.

"Wade's parents were already on their way down with Carl, my husband, for our wedding." Charise screwed up her nose. "It just doesn't sound as dramatic."

"It was dramatic enough." Her mother turned back to Kiri. "They all went out to Glencameron, and next thing they arrive back in Christchurch with Mackenzie in tow. So on top of all the wedding preparations, we're also teaching Mackenzie the discussions and preparing her for baptism."

"Oh, my goodness." Kiri's eyes were getting wider. "But Wade didn't know any of this?"

"No." Charise smiled proudly. "He didn't know a thing until he turned up at the temple . . . or at the chapel by the temple . . . and Mackenzie was waiting for him . . . all dressed in white ready for him to baptize her."

"Oh, my . . ." Kiri gasped. "That is amazing."

"It really was." Charise nodded. "It was a wonderful wedding present for us, as well. We went straight from the baptism up to our temple sealing. It was perfect."

There was a long silence as they became occupied with their own thoughts. Then Sheryl reached out and patted her daughter's hand. "And now we're having a baby, and Wade and Mackenzie are getting married next week."

Kiri swallowed hard and took a deep breath. It had been relatively easy to just keep aloof from other people over the last few years, and, in that way, she'd managed to keep a safe distance from family situations. The Church members in Dunedin had invited her into their homes as they often did with the many university students who lived there on a temporary basis, but she'd always managed to find an excuse for not going. Not that she wouldn't have enjoyed it, but it was just easier not to be involved. The gospel provided a wonderful framework for personal striving, and as long as Heavenly Father was there, she didn't really need the complications of involvement with others.

She suddenly thought of Dan and the strength of his hug, then she closed her eyes tightly, blocking out the memory of his kiss that threatened to sneak into her thoughts. In just a few weeks she'd allowed him to reach into her heart where she'd never let anyone go before . . . and now she was even committing herself to staying with his family!

"I'm pleased you're going to meet Mackenzie," Charise spoke again. "I think you'll really enjoy her company. I've noticed a lot of similarities between the two of you."

"Winnie said that as well." Kiri nodded thoughtfully. "Tell me, is Winnie really as perfect as she seems? I mean, she's raised Mackenzie and now she's looked after me. Sometimes I feel like she's the Church member."

Sheryl glanced over her shoulder. "It is quite uncanny isn't it? We felt like that when we first met her. It's like nothing phases her and she seems to be able to . . . love everybody . . . almost unconditionally."

Charise grinned. "She didn't have unconditional love for Brad Stanning when he got himself engaged to Mackenzie." She giggled. "What I love is how she's prepared to step up and help people if she thinks they're heading in the wrong direction . . . like a little Maori warrior."

"Do you think she and Ted will ever join the Church?" Kiri asked. "It doesn't seem like they'd have to change much at all."

"Maybe." Charise hesitated. "I think Winnie would accept it tomorrow, but Ted is a lot more reluctant to change . . . and even though she appears to boss him around, Winnie loves him to bits and she'd never do anything to upset him."

As they continued traveling, Charise resisted her mother's efforts to stop more often, reassuring Sheryl that they were better to keep moving while baby was lying quietly. They drove past the pristine turquoise waters of Lake Pukaki and gazed appreciatively at the stark grandeur of Mount Cook as it gleamed in snowcapped brilliance in the distance. Then, as they descended through Burke's Pass, the more level rural farmland opened up into rolling green pastures, and Charise breathed a sigh of relief and patted her stomach.

"Well, at least we're on the homeward stretch from here. Why don't we stop at Temuka and have lunch at that nice little café on the main street?"

"Sounds good to me." Her mother rolled her shoulders. "I'm needing a break." She looked in the rearview mirror. "I forgot to ask whether you drive, Kiri. Do you?"

"Yes, I have my full license." Kiri nodded. "I wasn't sure whether to ask if you wanted a break."

"Well, I think it's probably a good idea if you take the wheel for a while after we leave Temuka." Sheryl rubbed her neck. "I'll have a wee rest so that I can face home again."

Kiri drove cautiously at first, having not been behind the wheel for several months, but the car was a large sedan and it handled easily. Within a short time she relaxed and settled more comfortably into the seat. Sheryl had already laid her head against a pillow and fallen asleep.

"My mother has an amazing ability to fall asleep anywhere, anytime." Charise half turned to check her mother. "She used to be on the go all the time when we were younger—I think it's all caught up with her."

"She does seem to have a lot on her mind." Kiri glanced in the rearview mirror. "Maybe it's her way of escaping. I used to go to sleep if I wasn't comfortable or happy."

"I think I could too." Charise grimaced and readjusted her position. "But someone else has different ideas. I think we should have just kept driving."

"Not long now, and you can get to bed for a proper rest."

"The only time I get a proper rest is if I'm lying close to Carl." Charise smiled. "Then I let baby kick his back, and there's some sort of vengeance in doing so that lets me sleep."

Kiri laughed, then sobered. "It must be nice to look forward to this together." She stared at the road ahead.

"Nice doesn't even come close." Charise arched her back and pushed a pillow more firmly in place. "I thought it was wonderful just finding Carl as an eternal companion. I didn't think I could be happier . . . until we found out baby was coming. It takes your relationship to a whole new level." She actually blushed. "I love my husband even more now than I did when I married him."

The statement didn't seem to invite a reply, and Kiri drove on quietly as Charise hummed a random assortment of hymns. As they passed the signpost indicating the way to Geraldine, the humming suddenly stopped and Charise's face contorted in a momentary spasm.

"Kiri?"

"Mmm?"

"What do you think happens when your water breaks?"

"Are you serious?" Kiri felt her heart skip a beat and she glanced at Charise nervously. The spasm of pain that crossed the other girl's face made her grimace as well. "I mean . . . um . . . aren't you meant to have lots of contractions first?"

"Well, something's happening . . . and it's not something that I'm familiar with." Charise tried to smile. "I'm just trying to decide whether to panic or not."

"You don't need to panic." Kiri forced her voice to sound calm as she slowed the car and pulled onto the side of the road. "But why don't we wake up your mum and get her opinion."

The sensation of the car stopping had already wakened Sheryl, and she sat up with a small gasp. "Is everything all right?"

"Everything's fine." Kiri pulled on the hand brake. "But we think Charise's water may have broken, and we just wanted some motherly advice."

"Darling?" Sheryl leaned over into the front seat. "Are you sure?"

"As sure as someone who's never done this before." Her daughter flashed a bright smile. "We were just trying to decide if I'm going to panic or not."

"Oh no, dear." Sheryl patted her daughter's shoulder comfortingly. "You've got plenty of time yet. You came hours after my water broke, and Dan . . . well, he always takes his time. Now, where did I put those extra towels?" She began to search under the backseat and promptly produced a plastic bag with two towels in it.

"You brought towels?" Charise's voice was a little higher than normal. "Were you expecting a delivery, by any chance?"

"Not really." Sheryl's voice was muffled. "I always take towels on a long trip . . . in case you children make a mess."

Somehow her statement seemed to capture Charise's amusement, and she began to chuckle so heartily that Kiri was soon laughing as well.

"So I don't have to call for a police escort?" Kiri checked for oncoming traffic and pulled away from the side of the road.

"Not yet." Charise grinned as she reached into her bag for her mobile phone. "But I think I'll call Carl . . . just in case."

Chapter 11

"Well, I certainly never expected things to happen so quickly." Sheryl turned away from the window where she'd been watching for her husband to arrive. "I always took much longer. Imagine . . . four hours from start to finish. He really was in a hurry."

Kiri looked up from the water dispenser and passed Sheryl a drink. "I didn't think we were even going to make it to the hospital. Thank goodness you knew the shortcut past the town traffic."

"Thank goodness you were driving." Sheryl took a sip of water. "I don't think I could have handled driving and helping Charise."

They had barely passed through the town of Ashburton before Charise had begun experiencing cramps that had settled into a regular pattern of contractions which had increased in intensity on the outskirts of Christchurch City. A brief call to Carl had been enough to send them all straight to the hospital where Charise had delivered her baby just minutes after Carl had arrived. Kiri had caught a brief glimpse of a tall, blond man as he whisked past her with a completely preoccupied look on his face and only his wife's name on his lips.

"I'm so glad he's a healthy size as well . . . even being a few weeks early." Sheryl took a deep breath and rolled her eyes. "Imagine how big he'd have been if Charise had gone full term."

"Hey, Grandma!" A middle-aged man with thick, silvery hair came round the corner of the waiting room and enveloped Sheryl Harvey in a long embrace. She clung to him for a minute, then he held her back and the question was all in his look.

"Everything's fine." Sheryl nodded and leaned her head against his shoulder. "It was all a bit quick and he had the cord round his neck, but they checked him thoroughly and the nurse said he's good. The doctor thinks Charise's dates were wrong because he's not like a premature baby."

"You haven't seen him yet?" Rob Harvey looked surprised.

"No, of course not." Sheryl nudged him. "We do that together."

Kiri stood quietly watching their conversation . . . and feeling completely out of place. She turned to pour herself another drink and tried to be as unobtrusive as possible in this family scene. She hadn't even known these people three days ago, and now she was part of one of their most intimate family times.

"Kiri." She turned slowly as Sheryl spoke to her. "I'd like you to meet my husband, Rob. Rob, this is Kiri Karaitiana who has saved the day for us . . . again."

"Oh no . . ." She began to protest at Sheryl's description as she felt her hand disappear in an enthusiastic handshake.

"Very glad to meet you, Kiri." Rob Harvey's smile reached his eyes, and Kiri felt herself warm to him immediately. "Sheryl was so excited that you agreed to help us out. We can't thank you enough."

"Believe me, it's a pleasure." Kiri smiled shyly. "You have a wonderful family, Brother Harvey."

There was a brief silence as Rob Harvey looked at her, then at his wife. He nodded soberly. "You're absolutely right, Kiri. I do have a wonderful family, and it takes times like this to really appreciate it."

She declined when they asked her to go in with them to see the baby, but she watched as they held hands down the corridor and tiptoed into the delivery room. The room wasn't far, and before the door eased shut she heard Sheryl's voice, slightly higher as it trembled with emotion. "Oh, Charise . . . he's beautiful." Then Rob's deeper tone. "Boys aren't beautiful, love . . . he's downright handsome . . . like his grandfather."

Kiri took a long, cold drink of the water and deliberately let it work its icy trail before she shivered. A new generation . . . wanted and loved. Not some dysfunctional mess of children who didn't know who they belonged to.

She gripped the plastic cup tightly, and it caved in underneath her fingers before she realized it. With a resigned sigh, she tossed it neatly into the rubbish bin and settled into one of the waiting room chairs.

* * *

"Who's your mum, Herewini?" Kiri asked.

The stick made irregular furrows in the damp sand as Kiri tried to form the letters of her name.

"Not like that . . . it's a little line with a dot on top." The stick was taken gently from her hand as her cousin rubbed out her work with his foot and then wrote the letter correctly. "I'm not sure about my mum. Koro says she was a cousin from north somewhere."

"Is she still north?" She managed the next letter and looked up for approval, then wrinkled her nose in a puzzled frown. "Where's north?"

"North is back over the hill." Herewini nodded with his head. "I guess she's still there. She and Koro didn't get along, so I stayed with my dad . . . and now I'm with Koro."

"Will you always stay here?" She used one hand to push the unruly strands of hair tangled with salt spray off her face. "Will you stay with me?"

He looked out toward the sea for a long time, his older-boy features squinting into the morning sun as it hovered over the broad stretch of beach and ocean that was their safe place. Out here in the open, where the sky watched over them, he could protect her. Even the sea began to sound louder as the silence grew longer. She stubbornly dug the stick into the sand.

"If you ever go away, I'm coming with you." She pouted and frowned as he took the stick from her hand. "I don't want to stay with Koro or the uncles. I want to stay with you."

He looked down at the sand where their footprints mingled—his large and deeply sunken in the wet sand, hers small and barely making an impression. In several places her print was set into his where she'd tried to follow his steps, giggling as he'd deliberately lengthened his stride and she'd struggled to keep pace. He raised his face to the wind as it whipped away the moisture from his eyes, and he straightened his young shoulders.

"I'm not going anywhere, little one. I'll always be here for you . . . and Koro. I'm your family."

* * *

"Kiri . . . Charise would really like you to come in." Rob stood at the door of the room, and he smiled as she hesitated. "Please . . . you're an important part of this arrival."

The baby was round faced, and the thin growth of blond hair on his head had a distinctly auburn tinge to it. His eyes were tightly closed, but his slightly squashed features contorted often as he squirmed in his newly exposed skin. Occasionally he would stretch his arms and extend tiny fingers that opened and shut as if to work their way into the minute layers of wrinkles.

"Isn't he perfect?" Charise crooned over her new son as she lay on the bed cuddling him. "Here, Daddy . . ." She held the baby up to Carl. "You hold him so Kiri can see him better."

Carl leaned forward and held his arms out awkwardly, trying to negotiate the best way to hold his son while not taking his eyes off the little face. Even the blanket that the baby was wrapped in proved a challenge, and Kiri had to grab the end of it as she moved forward to take a look. As she reached up to tuck the blanket around the tiny body, the baby moved its arm and touched her hand. It was the smallest movement, but she jumped back as if she'd been shocked.

"I . . . oh, that startled me." She clasped her hands and looked at Charise. "He's beautiful, Charise."

"Handsome," Rob corrected playfully behind her as she took a step back.

"Very handsome." She nodded her agreement, then turned back just as the baby yawned and began to cry. "I think I have that sort of effect on babies—either bore them or make them cry." She gestured toward the door. "I'm so glad everything's okay . . . and ummm . . . I'll just wait outside so you can have more time together."

* * *

"Well, that's a totally different end to the day." Sheryl put her handbag down on the narrow hall table and waited as her husband carried in a small suitcase. "Let's leave the rest until we've seen Grandma. Sister Roberts has already left."

Rob left the suitcase on the floor and indicated for Kiri to go ahead of him behind his wife. She quickly took note of a homely looking lounge off to the right-hand side and the rows of family photos arranged along the wall of the hallway. Sheryl led the way through a narrower passageway beside a staircase and into a smaller lounge room where an elderly version of Rob Harvey sat watching television. Close by, a tiny, wiry woman with white, thinning hair was bent over a fold-out table with large jigsaw puzzle pieces spread over it.

"Dad . . . this is Kiri, the lass we told you about that's come to help us with Mum." Rob leaned forward and turned down the volume on the television as his father rose slowly to his feet and offered his hand.

"How do you do, Kiri?" His voice was soft with a faint rolling of the *r* as he said her name. "It's lovely to meet you, and I'm sure my wife will be delighted as well." He turned to the elderly woman who didn't seem to have noticed them enter the room. "Emily . . . you have a visitor." He spoke quite loudly, and the woman lifted her head with eyebrows raised.

"What's that?" She stared blankly at all of them for a second, then her gaze fixed on Kiri's face and she leaned forward with her arms outstretched. Tears began to flow down her cheeks.

"Oh . . . oh, my darling girl . . . you've come back to see your mama!"

Chapter 12

There was a moment of confused silence as Emily Harvey continued to hold her arms out to Kiri. Her tears seemed to contradict the radiant smile that lit up her face. As Kiri remained standing by the door, Emily began to stand up and walk toward her, oblivious of the tray that fell to the ground, scattering the jigsaw pieces.

Sheryl automatically bent to pick them up, still watching Emily in wonder, and Rob moved to his father's side as the old man began to cry silently, his thin shoulders shaking as he lifted his hand to shield his face.

"My baby . . . my girl." Emily reached Kiri and held her arms out wide. "You finally came to see me . . . . oh, how I've missed you."

Emily's voice began to tremble as she leaned forward, and Kiri caught her close, her arms instinctively wrapping around the woman's frail body to protect her. Emily, in turn, held onto Kiri with surprising strength and then began to rock quietly, her head resting against Kiri's chest while she kept repeating "my baby girl" in a soft, singsong voice.

As the rhythm of her movement persisted, Kiri felt her initial confusion disappear and she began to respond completely to the woman she held in her arms.

She bent her head and gently kissed Emily on the forehead, rocking gently with her until the tears had stopped, then she quietly led her back to her chair.

"Maybe we should put her straight back to bed?" Sheryl spoke in a whisper. "The bedroom is just through here."

Kiri nodded and walked Grandma through to the small room that contained two single beds and a simple bedstand with a framed family photo and a flashlight sitting on top. Sheryl moved ahead to turn down the sheets as Kiri guided Grandma to sit down on the edge. Within a few seconds they had her into a nightgown and tucked up in the bed. The whole time, she never took her eyes off Kiri and would gently touch her face or hands as they helped her dress.

"Good night, Emily," Kiri whispered as she leaned down and again kissed the warm, wrinkled brow. "Sleep well."

"Yes . . . and we'll play tomorrow, darling." Emily smiled happily and closed her eyes, her face and body completely relaxed. She seemed to be asleep in seconds.

"Wow," Sheryl whispered to Kiri across the bed. "That's Emily today . . . now we have to deal with Grandpa."

Rob and his father were both sitting on the small, two-seater couch when the women went out into the lounge. He motioned them to sit down on the two other chairs.

"Well . . . I'd say, 'Welcome to the family,' Kiri . . . but it seems you're already a part of it." He shook his head. "I really don't know where Mum got that idea from, but she's obviously happy to see you . . . again."

"Maybe Kiri reminds her of someone she knew once." Sheryl sat forward. "You know how much better her long-term memory is than the short-term."

"Possibly," her husband sat back and looked at his father. "Although she was calling her 'my baby' . . . and Kiri's an adult. That doesn't make sense."

James Harvey sat quietly with his elbows resting on his knees, but at his son's words he looked up to the ceiling.

"It does make sense, son." He pointed a shaking finger toward the bedroom. "There are a few things that your mother has always preferred to keep to herself . . . but maybe it's time you knew . . . so you can understand."

Once again his shoulders began to shake, and it took awhile for him to compose himself. As Sheryl took him a box of tissues, Kiri stood up and indicated toward the door.

"Maybe it's better if I leave," she began hesitantly. "I can wait in the other lounge."

She went to move but Rob held up his hand to stop her.

"No, Kiri . . . I think it's best that you stay." He smiled kindly. "You're obviously a fairly pivotal person here, and if you're going to be looking after Mum, it's better to know what you're dealing with. Is that all right, Dad?"

Grandpa blew his nose loudly and nodded while he shrugged his shoulders.

"I'm not sure about many things concerning your mother anymore," he answered in a tired voice. "But maybe it will help . . . to understand."

He took awhile to begin, the first words creating a spasm of coughing, then he finally stood up and walked over to a small circular table in the corner and picked up a sepia-toned photo in a burnished gold frame. He looked at it for a while, then walked over and handed it to Kiri.

"This was Emily when I married her." His voice broke again, and Kiri studied the photo until he regained his composure.

The couple in the picture were obviously James and Emily on their wedding day. He was standing tall . . . resplendent in the uniform of the armed forces while she wore a long, cream satin gown that flowed down over her slim figure and formed a long train behind her. She carried a small bouquet, and her hair was done in a classic bob that barely showed under a long, lace-edged veil. Both of them were smiling happily while they looked directly at the camera.

"She was a beautiful woman." Grandpa sat down again. "I fell in love with her at first sight, and she came round to my way of thinking fairly quickly."

"I'll say," his son chuckled. "Didn't you get married two months after you met?"

"Two months and three days." Grandpa smiled. "I'd gotten home from the war about two months before that."

They waited in silence again while he clasped his hands together in an attempt to steady them.

"Emily was a few years older than me, but that didn't really matter. The war upset a lot of relationships, and people were just happy to be together . . . and alive."

"It must have been terrible," Sheryl murmured as she moved her chair closer to her husband's side.

"The main thing was to forget the terrible things, and so we did . . . at least we tried." Grandpa hesitated. "We'd been married a few months when your mother got quite ill. She wasn't sleeping well, and one night she was a bit delirious with a fever . . . she began to talk in her sleep and . . . she was saying a man's name. Another man's name."

Sheryl reached out immediately and took her husband's hand, and Kiri felt her breath catch in her chest.

"You can imagine I was a bit . . . upset." Grandpa tried to smile. "I tried to forget about it, but one day I managed to slip it into the conversation . . . like a joke. I said, 'Just who was this *Hoani*, anyway?'"

"Hoani?" Sheryl and Rob spoke in unison.

"Mmm . . . a man's name, and a Maori name at that." He shook his head. "It took her awhile to talk about it, but I managed to convince her that if we were to make a success of our marriage . . . that there shouldn't be any secrets between us."

Again he took his time speaking, and Kiri began to feel a cold finger of anticipation creeping down her spine as the hairs on her arms begin to stand on end.

"Apparently, before the war started, Emily had gone to a dance in the town where she grew up. She was seventeen and it was the first time she'd really been allowed out with her friends. Her parents were very strict Catholics and she'd been raised in a convent setting." He waved his hands as if that explained all the background. "Anyway . . . on this night a young man asked her to dance and . . . they danced all night. He was Maori and twenty-two, and she knew her parents would disapprove of her even dancing with him. They parted at the end of the evening, and she swore her friends to secrecy."

"But they met again?" Rob squeezed his wife's hand as he already anticipated the response.

"Again . . . and again," his father nodded. "Hoani was at the dance the next week, and soon they were seeing each other regularly. It was all very secret . . . but aboveboard, of course. Walks in the park and the occasional movie."

"Did her parents find out?" Sheryl leaned forward, captivated by the story.

"Oh, yes . . . and that's when the problems began," Grandpa frowned. "Her father ran a hardware store, and one of his customers duly reported seeing his daughter with this Maori boy . . . more than once. Emily was immediately confined to the house and forbidden to see him again."

"But it was too late?" Rob asked gently.

"Too late in that they had already decided they wanted to marry . . . even though they knew how her parents would take it . . . or not take it. Emily tried to plead with them, but they came down even harder and her father actually beat her."

"Oh, my goodness," Sheryl gasped. "I've never thought of that sort of thing happening."

"It definitely did . . . but it was never talked about . . . just accepted as appropriate punishment." Grandpa shrugged. "But it was the last straw for Emily and she ran away . . . with Hoani. They went down to Wellington together . . . just a few months before the war broke out. He helped her find a job and a place to stay with one of his family until they could find someone to marry them."

"And then he went away to war," Rob anticipated again.

"And never came back." His father nodded. "He never even saw action . . . it was just a freak accident on board the ship he was on. Of course, Emily was devastated when she got the news . . . especially because she had just found out that she was pregnant."

"With a daughter?" Sheryl glanced at Kiri.

Grandpa coughed and looked at Kiri as well. "Yes . . . she gave birth to a little girl . . . very prematurely . . . and the baby only lived a couple of days."

There was another long silence, and Kiri felt as if her heart were breaking.

"So . . . in her mind . . . I'm the baby she lost?" she whispered.

"It would appear that's the case," Grandpa began formally, then he began to cry again as he reached out toward his son. "She was always afraid that you wouldn't think much of her if you knew the truth, so I promised I wouldn't say anything until she was gone . . ." His shoulders began to heave. "But she has gone . . . my Emily's gone now."

* * *

"Well . . . that was quite an introduction to the Harvey family, wasn't it?" Sheryl tucked a pillow under her chin and slipped a fresh pillowcase up over it as Kiri hung the last of her clothes up on coat hangers on a mobile wardrobe. She was going to use the sunroom next to James and Emily's room so she could be on hand if she was needed. "Dropped right into the middle of a family crisis and then hearing one of the dark secrets. I hope it hasn't been too over-whelming for you." She smiled apologetically. "We're really quite boring usually."

"I certainly feel like I've known your family a lot longer than a few weeks," Kiri nodded. "Or days . . ."

"Or hours," Sheryl plumped the pillow and set it down on the bed. "I've never seen Grandpa break down like that, and poor Rob is trying to figure it all out. It's best we leave them alone for a while." She put her head to one side as she studied Kiri. "Do you think Grandma will think you're the same person tomorrow . . . or was that just a one-of-a-kind occurrence?"

"It's hard to say." Kiri took hold of the other side of a pale green duvet and helped spread it over the bed. "She was quite convinced I was . . . her daughter." She hesitated. "She'll probably be happier thinking that way, but . . . it could be very painful for everyone else having to listen."

"I'm sure we'll get used to it." Sheryl glanced round the room to see if anything else was needed. "We've had to get used to a lot of different things since Grandma became ill."

"Um . . . if it would help . . . I could leave." Kiri toyed with the corner of the duvet. "It might solve the problem."

"I thought you might say that, dear, but it's really not necessary. That would just solve one problem and create another. I think that seeing as you're the main person that's going to be dealing with Mother, as long as you're fine with it, then we are too."

The way she finished seemed to discourage any further discussion and Kiri took a deep breath.

"Then I guess I'm here for a while. I'll do my very best for you." She swallowed hard. "Thank you . . . for trusting me."

Sheryl looked at her thoughtfully.

"It really is all about trust, isn't it? I confess I'm usually a lot more reluctant to have anything or anyone encroach on the family circle, but . . . thank goodness the gospel is common ground for both of us . . . it makes for a much better start." She smiled. "And I also trust Dan and Winnie, and they were totally confident in your abilities. And after the day's events . . . I have no doubts either." She smiled and put her hand to her cheek with a mildly shocked expression. "I'm a grandma and I've hardly thought about it since we got home. Grandpa doesn't even know he's a great-grandfather yet . . . and we haven't told Dan either!"

As if on cue, her husband walked in with the cordless phone in his hand.

"It's Dan wanting to know what's happening and how come he had to wait five hours to find out he's an uncle."

Sheryl gave a delighted laugh and took the phone, holding onto her husband's hand as she spoke to her son.

"Dan? . . . yes, a handsome wee boy . . . six pounds two ounces. He's got his dad's fair complexion, but he looks a lot like Charise when she was born . . . no, that doesn't mean he looks like a girl! Charise is fine . . . oh, she did?" She put her hand over the receiver. "Charise and Carl just called him from the hospital, and he's already heard him cry."

"Ask him if they said a name yet?" Rob folded his arms. "Like Robert or something?" He turned to Kiri with a look of mock horror on his face. "They were talking about calling the poor child Theodore or something."

Kiri laughed as she remembered the conversation between Dan and Charise.

"Maybe it's Robert Theodore." She tried not to stare at the telephone, knowing that Dan was at the other end of the line, then her heart leapt as Sheryl held the phone out to her.

"Dan wants to talk to you." She quickly turned to the phone again before handing it over. "Kiri was absolutely wonderful today . . . so calm with all the baby fuss and then when Grandma saw her." She looked up. "It was just like she was greeting a long-lost relative."

Kiri felt her hand beginning to tremble as she reached out, so she quickly pretended to wipe something on her jeans. But as she took the phone from Sheryl her fingers trembled again. For a split second she glanced at Sheryl, and her stomach sank as she saw an undeniable flash of understanding in Dan's mother's eyes.

"Hello," she cleared her throat. "Hello, Dan."

"Hi . . . how's the heroine?" His voice was deep, and just hearing it sent a shiver down Kiri's back, which she tried to disguise by sitting down hard on the edge of the bed. "Sounds like you've had a busy day."

"Yes . . . yes, we all have." She licked her lips. "You have a lovely new nephew and Charise was really great. She's the heroine . . . I was just a driver."

"But according to both her and Mum, you were the calm in the storm and they couldn't have done without you."

His words had a very sudden effect on Kiri as she realized how much it meant to hear that she had been of help—that Dan's family appreciated her. It took a moment to get control of her voice.

"It's good to be able to give at last instead of receiving all the time."

She couldn't tell whether he sensed the trouble she was having with her emotions, but he took his time responding.

"It's really quiet here without you." She could hear the smile in his voice. "And Winnie keeps telling me off for getting under her feet. She says it was much better with you here . . . it kept me occupied."

"Then you're obviously not working hard enough." She felt her confidence returning. "Besides . . . it's only been a day."

"Is that all?" he responded dramatically. "I feel like my mate's been gone for ages."

"It does feel a bit like that." She stared hard at the wall and tried not to read anything into his words. "So much has happened. It's going to be good establishing a routine with your grandmother."

"How is she?" He sounded genuinely concerned, and she thought about the love that she had seen all his family members demonstrate toward each other. It was a completely new experience for her, and she suddenly realized how precious the whole experience had been.

"She's fine. She's asleep right now, and we're all heading that way as well."

Suddenly she wanted to keep talking . . . about anything . . . as long as she could hear him speaking.

Once more she heard him chuckle.

"I can't believe this . . . I have absolutely no desire to hang up. Shall we just talk for a while?" He seemed to read her thoughts again, and she gripped the telephone hard.

"Don't be silly, Dan Harvey . . . we all need to get some sleep." She glanced around the room, but his parents had gone. "It's going to be another big day tomorrow . . . now, good night," she finished lamely.

"Okay . . . you're a hard woman." She heard an exaggerated sigh. "I'll keep in touch. Good night, Kiri . . . sweet dreams."

She heard the telephone click but she didn't put it down.

"You have sweet dreams too, Dan."

She took the phone back out to the lounge, and Sheryl Harvey glanced up from where she was reading on the couch. Instinctively, Kiri knew she had waited for her to come in.

"I think Dan is going to make an excellent uncle." Sheryl nodded as she took the phone and placed it in its cradle beside her. "He's always been very good to Charise, so I imagine he'll spoil his nephew."

Kiri stood uncertainly at the end of the couch.

"I noticed they get on really well." She folded her arms. "Your whole family seem very close."

Sheryl nodded thoughtfully. "It's something we've worked hard to achieve over the years. Some people say we're lucky, but there's a lot to do to keep a family together and loving each other. Heavenly Father supplies the tools of the trade, but you have to learn how to use them." She hesitated. "Dan said you lived with your grandfather growing up."

It was a statement rather than a question, but Kiri felt the inquiry behind it and she shook her head slowly.

"I did live with my grandfather . . . and uncles, but I wouldn't call it your usual family." She faltered, then added almost defensively, "Certainly nothing like yours."

"Families are all different . . . as we learned from Grandma tonight. Everyone comes from a different place." She shrugged. "My father was an alcoholic, and it was like living with Jekyl and Hyde. He was lovely when he was sober but . . ." She frowned. "I couldn't change him, but I thank Heavenly Father every day for a wonderful husband who doesn't drink or belittle his children."

There was a brief silence, then Sheryl stood up.

"Well, I think we've had enough excitement for one day. Tomorrow we'll get organized and I'll check with my sister-in-law in

Taranaki to see how she's doing. I may not go up there if Charise needs me now." She rested a hand briefly on Kiri's arm. "It was good to see Dan so cheerful. I think he misses your company."

Chapter 13

Over the next few days Kiri quickly established a routine of rising early and taking a brisk walk, exploring the tree-lined streets and the paths along beside the Avon River as it wound its way through the city. The chill of the morning air seemed to heighten her senses, and the thought of having a job and a place to stay where she felt appreciated was oddly comforting and uplifting. She felt a compulsion to work hard to justify their faith in her. Usually, by the time the rest of the family were waking she was already showered and ready to look after Grandma.

Despite a feeling of apprehension when she had looked in on Emily the first morning, Kiri soon found that she liked to be called "my girl" and that Grandma was very biddable as long as "my girl" was around. Sometimes she would get agitated if anybody else asked her to do something, but she would calm down when Kiri spoke to her.

"I'm not sure if I'm overwhelmingly grateful for her preference for you or just a tiny bit jealous," Sheryl confided on the third morning as Kiri settled Grandma onto the couch with a large, colorful magazine. "But it does mean I can spend more time with Charise, which is lovely. And Wendy—my niece—called yesterday to say she was coming over from Australia to stay with my sister-in-law for a couple of weeks." She nodded. "That'll be nice for Nan to have company. She hasn't seen Wendy for a while, and her other daughter, Meredith, is on a mission over in Sydney."

"And it takes some pressure off you for a little while." Kiri squinted at the small calendar on the wall. "When does Mackenzie arrive home?"

"They had to come a day later, so they'll be here on Tuesday now. Charise is so delighted that she'll have baby all ready to show them." She smiled indulgently and patted her handbag. "I've already got two lots of photos in my brag book. Isn't it amazing how a tiny baby can create so much fuss and love all at once?"

Sheryl didn't notice Kiri's faint smile as she turned to kiss her mother-in-law on the cheek, then stood back as Grandma kept slowly turning the pages of the magazine as if nothing had happened. "Sometimes I wonder if there's any point in saying good-bye or kissing her at all . . . there's just no reaction."

"Not outwardly . . . but she knows . . . and especially when it doesn't happen." Kiri folded her arms. "You know how it is when you have lots of hugs and then you don't for a while. You miss it."

"Yes . . ." Sheryl paused to think and nodded. "You're right . . . I'd hate it if I didn't have Rob and the children to give me hugs." She bent down and gave Emily a tight hug and was rewarded with such a sweet smile that tears sprang to her eyes. She wiped them quickly and then reached over and gave Kiri a quick squeeze as well.

"Thank you, Kiri. You're making Grandma seem real again. I must tell Rob."

* * *

Charise dropped by two days later, without notice, staggering dramatically as she carried in the baby bundled up tightly in a plastic car seat and with a bulging nappy bag slung over the other shoulder.

"I cannot believe that such a tiny person can create so much . . . stuff!" she moaned as the bag slid off her shoulder and bumped the car seat, causing the baby to whimper. "And please, please don't be hungry again," she crooned at him until he settled again. She pulled a doleful face at Kiri. "I thought I'd be up and about in a few days. This is my first time out on my own and I'm feeling shattered. I even forgot Mum wasn't going to be here until I pulled into the street."

"But it's only been a few days since you gave birth. I'm surprised you're looking this good." Kiri shook her head. "Have you brought him to see his great-grandmother?"

"Do you think there's any point? I mean . . . I want her to see him, but sometimes . . ."

"You wonder if it's worth it." Kiri picked up the seat by its overhead handle. "I've no doubt it is."

As soon as she saw the little boy, Grandma began singing lullabies and rocking the seat on its shaped base. She didn't make any attempt to pick him up, but she sang the same song over again, oblivious to the girls watching her.

"Have you got any old dolls here?" Kiri asked quietly as Charise knelt down beside her grandmother. "Baby ones that she could cuddle?"

Charise looked thoughtful. "I'm sure we do. I used to have a few 'anatomically correct' ones and a couple with the soft bodies. I'm sure Mum has kept them. Do you want me to check?" She stood up as Kiri nodded. "Do you think she'll know the difference . . . between a doll and the real thing?"

"We can try." Kiri smiled and pointed to herself. "I'm still her baby, so anything has got to be an improvement on that."

Charise was away a long time, and after a few minutes the baby began to be disturbed, then let out a husky, desperate bellow. Emily began to frown and reached into the seat, so Kiri quickly unbuckled the seat straps and cradled him in her arms until he stopped crying. As he began to push his head against her arm and open and shut his tiny, puckered mouth, Kiri chuckled softly.

"Oh sweetheart, I can't help you at all. Mummy will be here soon," she said as she rocked him gently.

His tiny lips began to work again, and she cuddled him even more closely against her neck, inhaling his sweet, baby-clean smell. The feel of his tiny body against her chest and his jerky, involuntary movements seemed to create an emotional well deep in her stomach, and she held him closer as her lips trembled.

"Will this one do?" Charise came in the door with a bald, plastic baby wrapped in a pale, blue blanket. "He's got a few ink marks—courtesy of Daniel—and he smells a bit musty . . . but shall we try?"

Kiri nodded as Charise bent down beside her grandmother again and held out the doll.

"Look, Grandma . . . here's a baby for you."

There was only the slightest hesitation before Emily reached out and began to cradle the doll in her arms, murmuring the lullaby again in a broken melody.

"It seems it does work." Charise smiled as she took her baby from Kiri and gave him a tight squeeze. "And I guess the feeling never dies."

* * *

Winnie and Ted came to Christchurch several days later, and Kiri was surprised at how excited she was the morning they were expected to arrive. It was obvious they felt the same way when Winnie greeted her with a warm hug and kept hold of her hand as she led her around to Ted.

"It's good to see you, lass." He gave her a shy peck on the cheek. "The place hasn't been the same without you. Winnie keeps talking to me and expecting me to answer."

"He tries hard, but he just doesn't get as excited about quilting as you do," Winnie laughed as she took a small overnight bag from her husband's hand. "And Dan can't sit still for a moment . . . no, I lie . . . he started reading another very large book the other day."

"At least the cabin is getting finished quicker," Ted chuckled. "He's working like a man possessed. We got all the internal work finished, and he's putting landscaping in now. It's looking right cozy."

Kiri stood by the car just enjoying listening to them. Somehow their conversation seemed to invoke a feeling of hominess . . . of belonging as she imagined the cabin and the places and the people they talked about.

"And Dan sends his love." Winnie watched Kiri's reaction out of the corner of her eye as she walked inside, and she wasn't disappointed as Kiri hesitated and a warm glow heightened the color in her cheeks. "He said he tried to call the other night but you were out."

"The other night?" Kiri responded quickly. "Oh . . . I went to Enrichment night at the chapel. I've been in every other night."

She failed badly at disguising the disappointment in her voice, and Winnie smiled happily. "Well, dear, I'm sure he'll try again soon."

The Harveys greeted Winnie and Ted with their usual hospitable friendliness, having already moved furniture to create more bedroom space to house the new arrivals.

"I'm so excited to see Mackenzie," Winnie confided at the dinner table that evening. "When I spoke to her on the phone the other night, I swear she had a tiny bit of an American accent, and she sounded really . . . bouncy . . . didn't she, Ted?"

"Mmm . . . bouncy," Ted nodded as he tackled another lamb chop, then wiped his lips carefully. "I'm not sure what to expect . . . she's been gone nearly four months."

"I imagine she'll have changed quite a bit, from what Charise was saying." Sheryl handed him a plate with more food on it. "Apparently, Wade's sisters have been taking her shopping and all over the place while he's been working. They've even given her a new hairstyle."

"So which sisters are coming out for the wedding?" Winnie looked up as she tried to remember.

"Only one sister is coming, and I'm sure it's the youngest one—Mandy." Sheryl nodded. "Yes, I'm sure she's the one that just finished college, so she's coming down for a holiday before she begins a new job. She's an interior designer . . . or something like that. She's a lovely looking girl. Very tall and blond. Anna said she was interested in having a look at the cabin Dan is building, because she's going to be working for a company that does something similar."

For some reason Kiri felt a cold weight form in her stomach at Sheryl's words, and the food on her plate seemed to lose its appeal. She carefully placed her knife and fork together and sat quietly as the conversation continued about the Fenton family and all the experiences they'd shared with the Harveys over the last few years.

Kiri seemed unable to brush away the image of a younger Daniel concentrating on a miniature log-cabin construction, and a girl with long, blond curls handing him the logs.

"Doesn't she, Kiri?" She heard Rob's voice from a distance and she looked at him blankly.

"I'm sorry?" She glanced up to find them all looking at her.

"I was saying that Grandma is responding well to having you around." He pointed at her. "This young lady has made such a difference in our family. Mum is happy, and we're all enjoying just being with her now." He smiled to cover up a swift show of emotion. "Can't thank you enough, Kiri."

"Well, if we had some sparkling grape juice we could make a toast." James Harvey nodded happily. "To our Kiri . . . our angel."

Everybody around the table laughed and smiled in agreement as they raised their glasses of water. They didn't seem to notice her silence or the way her jaw clamped together and her brown eyes glistened as she fought to hide her emotions. Then Grandpa reached over and patted her hand. The sight and feel of his hand, softly wrinkled and speckled with darkened age spots, was the last straw. She stood up quickly.

"Umm . . . I don't think you all realize how much you've done for me." She tried to look at them, but her vision blurred. "This is the first real family I've . . . ever been with and . . . nothing I could do for you could express how I feel about that," she finished in a rush and pushed her chair back. "Please excuse me . . . I need to check on Grandma."

Emily was sleeping peacefully, and she knew she would be, but it provided the diversion she needed to slip away to her room, where for the first time she really let her feelings take control. She lay crying quietly, letting the tears wash away the physical pain that she was feeling around her heart.

Even the shaking of her body developed into a soothing, rhythmic release of pent-up thoughts and fears. Her thoughts became a silent movie of past experiences . . . her childhood . . . university . . . church . . . people and places blurred together as they ran in sequence. Then it was Queenstown and Glenorchy and the cabin and Winnie and Ted . . . and Dan.

For a moment the movie stopped as if she'd willed it to, then she let it go forward, and many of the painful feelings became dimmer as she recalled the "activity binge"—the jet boat ride, fishing, riding . . . kissing.

Again she began to shut it out, then a feeling of peace washed over her.

"It happened . . . and I don't have to forget it." She talked to the wall, and her fists unclenched where she'd tucked them under her pillow.

* * *

Next morning she arose early for her walk, but as she tied the laces on her sneakers in the small, back veranda, the door opened behind her and Winnie peeked around the glass-paneled door.

"Do you walk too fast for old ladies to keep up?" She looked hopeful and Kiri smiled.

"Actually I was looking for an excuse to take my time today." She finished tying the lace and stood up. "Are you interested?"

"Absolutely." Winnie smiled and stepped out, dressed in a pale pink sweat top and gray track pants and sneakers.

"I didn't know you were into walking." Kiri looked surprised. "You never said anything when I went out in Queenstown."

"Ah . . . that's because I really didn't have any desire, and then I watched a program on television about old people losing their fitness and being candidates for heart attacks and . . . well, I thought this must be a message for me." She grinned and did a brief pirouette. "So I got myself some gear . . . and poor Ted's still in shock. He's hardly ever seen me in anything but a dress and apron, but Dan said I looked stunning."

"Dan has a way with words," Kiri commented wryly as she began to walk down the three steps off the veranda. "But I think it's a great idea. Would you like to go down by the river?"

"Wherever you usually go, but probably not as far." Winnie followed close behind her. "I've only done this three times so far. Ted wants to know when I'm actually going to get my shoes dirty."

"He gives you a hard time sometimes, doesn't he?"

Winnie laughed. "He does . . . but only when he knows it's safe."

They were both laughing as they began to make their way down the road. Even at six thirty in the morning there were quite a few people out exercising.

"I've never really thought about people doing this sort of thing." Winnie turned her head to watch a woman of similar age jog by. "Working on the station . . . you just work . . . and that keeps you fit and you go to bed tired. I've begun to feel so lazy in Queenstown. It's been lovely, but I'll be glad to get back home."

"It's funny, but I can't imagine you anywhere else but Queenstown." Kiri bent her head to avoid an overhanging branch heavy with new green leaves. "Tell me more about Glencameron."

"Oh . . . it's just your normal high-country sheep station with rugged pastures and rugged weather and the most beautiful mountain scenery. Then there're flocks of Merino sheep and gardens full of flowers, courtesy of Ted. And once you've lived there you wonder why anybody would want to live anywhere else." Winnie shook her head. "Then you travel away for a while, and you realize that the world is doing other things . . . like jogging."

"It sounds wonderful." Kiri pointed to the west. "I've only ever seen that sort of place on calendars."

"Well, you'd better be planning on coming to visit us soon." Winnie wagged her finger. "Don't think you're just going to disappear out of our lives once you go away to university."

"But . . ." Kiri began to protest, but Winnie put her hand up to stop her.

"I'm serious, Kiri . . . you've become like a daughter to us and you said yourself, last night, that you've never known family, so we can be that for you." She glanced sideways. "That's if you want us to."

Kiri couldn't look at her, but she nodded her head vigorously. "I'd really like that, Winnie."

They walked for nearly forty minutes with Winnie providing a running commentary on the types of houses and the people they passed and the different types of flowers that were growing in the gardens. As they turned back, the pockets of her sweatshirt were getting full of small clippings of shrubs.

"Oh, by the way . . ." Winnie tapped her head with her hand as they turned down a street near the house. "I forgot to tell you that Dan called again last night after you went to bed. He said he was sorry he missed you."

"Oh?" Kiri stared straight ahead. "How's he doing?"

"Just fine . . . he's nearly finished his book . . . the second one."

"He must be a very fast reader." She deliberately kept her voice steady.

"Kiri?" Winnie stopped by a large oak tree that spread its branches wide over the footpath and created a darkened sanctuary on the street. "Why do you keep avoiding Dan? He really cares for you."

"I'm his friend, Winnie . . . his mate." Kiri spread her hands out at her sides. "That's all he wants . . . all I want."

"Is it . . . really?" Winnie was quietly persistent. "I thought I detected . . . something more."

"Then you're not a very good detective," Kiri responded wearily. "We just had fun together and now Dan will get himself established and then he'll marry someone like Carl's sister and all the families will live happily ever after."

"Well . . . you have got everything worked out." Winnie nodded and folded her arms. "Does Dan know that his future's all mapped out with Carl's sister . . . what was her name . . . Mandy?"

Winnie's tone made Kiri look at her quickly, then she gave a low sigh as she plucked a leaf off the tree above her head. "Oh, Winnie . . . I don't know about anything." She tore a tiny piece off the leaf. "Except that there's no future in thinking about Dan . . . except as a good friend."

"Can I ask why?" Winnie watched the muscle working in Kiri's cheek.

"He's made it completely clear that he's not interested in a commitment." Another piece of leaf fluttered to the ground.

"Would you have gone out with him if he said he was interested?"

"Winnie!"

"Would you?"

"Probably not." Kiri screwed up the rest of the leaf.

"Why not?"

"Because Dan and his family don't want a girl like me joining the ranks, so even if I did feel anything for Dan, I'd only be setting myself up for the letdown. Okay?" Kiri shook her head. "Mackenzie may have had a happy ending, but it doesn't happen every time, Winnie. Some people are just too, too different."

"What's wrong with a girl like you?"

"Winnie!" Kiri rolled her eyes in frustration.

"I'm serious," Winnie persisted. "Tell me."

"All right . . . I'm from the wrong background, I'm the wrong color, I—"

"Can we substitute *wrong* with *different,* and can I suggest that the size of those differences exists mainly in your mind?" Winnie held her arm out beside Kiri's, the warm, pale brown tone of their skin almost identical in color. "Ted once told me that he never really saw me as being a different color . . . only that it made a really appealing package."

Kiri spontaneously laughed, then grimaced as she stamped her foot. "How can you be so lovely and so annoying all at once?"

"I don't know . . . but tell Ted when you figure it out," Winnie answered complacently and began to walk ahead. "Did you notice that Dan has the same traits?"

They were just about at the driveway when Kiri stopped and pointed toward the house.

"Winnie . . . I know Sheryl mentioned Grandma's situation . . . about the baby girl she lost . . ."

Winnie nodded. "That's so sad. She must be reliving it now."

"I think she might be," Kiri hesitated. "The Harveys seemed to have taken that news . . . quite well . . . don't you think?"

"Mmm . . ." Winnie frowned. "But why wouldn't they? It happened a long time ago, and it doesn't change the fact that she's their grandmother and they love her dearly and she loves them. Besides, you never know what the circumstances were and it's not for us to judge."

Kiri seemed to ponder that as she stared at the house, then she turned to Winnie and opened the gate for her.

"Winnie . . . do you think it's ever possible to get over bad circumstances . . . like, forget them?"

"Do you mean, did Emily forget until she saw you?"

"I . . . I guess so." Kiri frowned. "I just wonder if . . . people can ever completely overcome bad things . . . or whether those things will stay with them . . . forever."

A car horn sounded loudly nearby, and they both turned quickly with a start. The distraction gave Winnie a moment to watch Kiri's face, then she moved so that she was looking straight in the girl's eyes.

"I know from experience that it always helps to talk about whatever the problem is." She kept looking at Kiri. "I was very bitter about some things that happened when I was young. It wasn't until I met Ted and he helped me work through it that I let go of the anger. The pain didn't go away, but I learned to cope with it."

Kiri lifted her head slightly to stare over Winnie's shoulder.

"Ted helped you?"

"I think he helped me to help myself." Winnie smiled. "My Ted may not say much, but he doesn't miss much either. Sometimes I think he's wasted on those sheep."

Kiri rubbed her hands down her legs and stretched her shoulders as she smiled wanly.

"So you think that I should talk to Ted?"

"Are we talking about you?" Winnie asked innocently. "I thought we were talking about Emily."

There was a long silence while Kiri traced the outline of moss on the wooden gate post. "Before . . . I said that I was from the wrong background, the wrong color. Do you think Dan and his family would want me around if they knew I'd come from a violent background as well? Do you think they would trust me with their grandmother?"

"I think the question is whether you were violent . . . or were you violated?" Winnie responded quietly.

"What if you don't know if you mightn't be violent if the situation arose?"

"So you're worrying about what might happen . . . or what did happen?"

Kiri swallowed hard. "Probably both."

"Oh, my dear." Kiri felt Winnie's hand over hers on the post. "What have people done to you that you have to live with those sort of questions?"

Kiri hesitated, then she raised her head wearily. "Definitely not the sort of things you want to talk about."

"Maybe that's the problem." Winnie patted her hand. "Maybe it's time you did talk about them . . . not to me, but to somebody who can really help you." She paused. "What about Rob Harvey?"

Kiri rolled her eyes. "That's a bit too close for comfort." She shivered and turned toward the house. "Anyway, I shouldn't have said anything. It's not like I can ever change what happened." She paused. "But thanks for listening, Winnie. I've never really had anyone do that before."

Chapter 14

"There . . . she's all set for visitors. Doesn't she look lovely, now?" Kiri made the finishing strokes with the hair brush and stood back for Grandpa to look at his wife. Emily seemed to sense that she was on show, and she fluttered her eyelashes and pursed her lips together, exposing the pale apricot lipstick that Kiri had painted on earlier. Her fine, white hair, although sparse in places, framed her face like a halo.

"She's always looked lovely." James Harvey studied her from his seat on the couch. "Now she looks angelic . . . as if she'll float away any second."

Kiri smiled as Emily reached up and patted her hair with a trembling hand.

"It's wonderful that you can talk about her that way. She must feel very special." She glanced at him. "Wasn't it lovely when she kept telling you that she loved you yesterday?"

"It was . . . but I can't help wondering if she was actually talking to me." He played with the tapestry cover on the arm of his chair. "I want to think she means me."

"And I'm sure she does." Kiri placed the hairbrush on the table.

"But . . . you know how she keeps talking about her baby that she lost . . . what if she thinks I'm him . . . the father of that child. What if . . . in her mind . . . she's back there?"

The thought had obviously been troubling him, and Kiri read the torment in his eyes as he looked up at her. Instinctively she moved to his side and knelt down by his chair.

"You know . . . that could be happening but . . ." She took his hand in hers. "I've got the advantage of being the spectator here . . .

and I see how her face lights up when you speak to her and how her eyes lose that blankness when she says that she loves you." She squeezed his hand. "I have no doubt at all that she's talking to you."

He actually looked a little embarrassed as Kiri reassured him, then he stared at his wife again. "It's not something she said a lot when she . . . in the early years," he amended. "But then . . . neither did I."

"Then maybe she's making up for lost time." Kiri smiled as she stood up. "Maybe you both can. She can still hear even if she doesn't show it all the time."

"You're a wise young woman, aren't you?" James chuckled quietly as he began to get up off the couch. "Dan's a lucky man."

His words seemed to trigger an electric shock that coursed through her whole body and made her hold onto the top of the couch. But it was a completely innocent statement, and James obviously didn't seem to register that he said anything untoward; he simply moved slowly over to his wife and tapped her on the shoulder so that she looked up at him. He reached out and gently touched her cheek.

"You look beautiful, my Emily," his voice trembled. "Do you know how much I love you?"

* * *

There was instant noise and commotion as soon as the front door opened, and suddenly the hallway seemed full of people and suitcases.

"We made it finally." Rob hung his coat on the hall stand and turned to the silvery-haired man behind him. "That traffic from the airport is diabolical."

"You're kidding . . . that was like a Sunday drive," the man responded as he stacked the bags neatly. "There were only two lanes. That's what I love about Christchurch . . . it's so peaceful."

"The only traffic congestion is right here." A slightly-built woman with similar colored hair stepped over another small bag. "Is it okay to leave everything here, Sheryl?"

"Perfectly, Anna." Sheryl Harvey pointed toward the kitchen. "Just head this way and clear the traffic jam. Winnie has lunch all ready for us . . . haven't you Winnie?"

Kiri stood in the entrance to the grandparents' apartment and waited as the melee of bodies dispersed into the lounge. Nobody had even noticed her in the alcove, so she waited until they'd moved, then walked out.

"And you must be Kiri," a pleasant voice came from behind her, and Kiri turned. A young woman, slightly taller than her, stood in the side of the hallway with a small photo album in her hand. "I'm Mackenzie Cameron. I've heard a lot about you."

Her coppery-brown hair was styled to fall around her face in generous waves, and the golden highlights accentuated the shine of amazing turquoise-colored eyes. She was wearing slim-fitting black trousers and boots and a shirt that was almost identical to the color of her eyes. She looked stunning.

"I . . . I'm pleased to meet you." Kiri automatically thrust her hand out to shake the other girl's hand, then hesitated, unsure of the reaction.

She felt her hand immediately taken in a firm grip as Mackenzie responded with a genuine smile.

"I wasn't sure what I was going to do when I met you." She gave a sheepish grin. "Winnie and Ted kept singing your praises . . . my Winnie and Ted."

There was a wealth of meaning in the last phrase, and Kiri recognized the implication of Mackenzie's words. The other girl had been the sole focus of Winnie and Ted's lives for so long . . . their little girl . . . and now she sensed that Kiri had taken some of their attention away.

"Oh, believe me . . . they're definitely your Winnie and Ted." She smiled back and sensed Mackenzie relaxing. "They absolutely dote on you. In fact . . . I was scared about meeting you."

They both laughed, and Kiri felt a lifting of her spirits as Mackenzie held up the photo album.

"Well, let's go meet the rest of the clan. Apparently Dan has always been a favorite of Joe and Anna's. They'll be thrilled to meet you."

The next few minutes were a confusing round of introductions to first Joe and Anna Fenton, and then Mackenzie reached out and took a tall, blond man by the hand.

"And this is my fiancé, Wade Fenton." Her voice softened even as she said his name, and Kiri felt the warmth of the loving glance they exchanged.

"Pleased to meet you, Kiri." His American accent was less pronounced than his parents', and he sounded and looked very much like his brother, although shorter and broader across the shoulders. "I hear you helped bring my nephew safely into the world."

Kiri pressed her hand to her throat and looked round the room at the Fentons and the Harveys.

"Um . . . not exactly. I think the story has improved with the telling. I just followed instructions on how to get to the hospital. But it is good to meet you, Wade. I've heard a lot about you and Mackenzie as well."

"So who wants to see their grandson and nephew all rolled into one handsome bundle?" Carl walked into the room carrying his son in one arm. The other arm was wrapped around his wife's shoulders. Within seconds, amid screams and hugs and handshakes, the little family were enveloped by adoring relatives with the baby being cuddled by each one in rapid succession. Miraculously he stayed asleep through it all.

"Well, he's definitely got his Grandpa Joe's genes . . . can't wake him up." Anna Fenton tried to slip her little finger under the baby's fingers, but they remained tightly curled.

"And Papa Rob's," Charise giggled happily. "He has a huge appetite."

"Enough of that." Rob rocked his grandson proudly. "Does 'he' have a name yet?"

"Theodore," Charise and Carl spoke in unison, then laughed at the universal expression of dismay.

"Actually, we thought of Robert Joseph," Charise started.

"Then Joseph Robert," Carl shrugged.

"And then, last night, we both started calling him James and it just seemed right."

There was a brief silence, then Rob took the baby over to his father who had walked into the lounge when Charise and Carl had arrived.

"What do you reckon, Dad . . . You want to have a cuddle with your namesake?"

Grandpa's hands trembled as he took hold of his great-grandson, and then he smiled as the baby suddenly yawned widely, forcing his eyes open with the effort.

"And good morning to you, young James. How would you like to come and see your great-grandmother Emily? She'll much prefer you to the old model."

As Rob and Sheryl led him carefully through to the other room, Charise finally voiced the thought that had just occurred to Kiri.

"Hang on . . . where's Mandy?" she glanced around the room. "Is she upstairs?"

"Oh, no." Anna waved a hand. "There have been all sorts of dramas in the last few days. Mandy broke her leg when she was skiing the other day, so we had to leave her with her sister . . . in plaster up to her thigh."

"Ouch!" Charise said, then pointed at Mackenzie. "But isn't she meant to be your bridesmaid?"

"Bingo." Wade shook his head. "Trust my scatterbrained little sister to pull a stunt like this. She tried to look apologetic when we left, but there were too many guys waiting to see her. I've never seen so many hearts and kooky expressions written on one plaster cast."

"No, she was pretty upset." Mackenzie nudged him in the ribs. "But it doesn't really matter . . . as long as the groom turns up on the day."

As they kept talking, Kiri began to slip away to her room. The intimacy of the family gathering was good to be a part of, yet it also created a feeling of total emptiness. She reached the hallway just as the phone rang, and a quick glance back showed that nobody had heard to answer it.

"Harvey home," she answered, quoting Rob's usual greeting. Immediately she shivered as Dan spoke on the other end.

"How nice to hear you say that. It just made the phone call worthwhile. How are you, Kiri?"

She could hear the smile in his voice, and although her instinct was to respond briefly, she found herself matching the tone of his voice. After all, he was far away.

"I'm very, very good, Dan." She sounded flippant even to her own ears. "The Fentons and Mackenzie have just arrived and the whole family is here. It's a bit of a madhouse . . . and the star of the show is totally bored with the whole proceedings."

"How is my nephew? Have they named him yet?" He paused. "It isn't Theodore, is it?"

"No." She shook her head. "He is now James Fenton . . . after his great-grandfather."

There was another pause, and then he spoke more softly. "James Fenton . . . very distinguished. I'll bet Grandpa is happy with that."

"He's busy showing him to Grandma right now." Kiri smiled. "Everybody is pretty happy around here right now. Winnie and Ted are smiling all over themselves, although Ted keeps looking at Mackenzie and shaking his head."

"Why?"

"Apparently she has a different hairstyle and a slight accent that he can't get used to. She's a beautiful girl, though. It's easy to see why they're so proud of her."

"I miss you, Kiri."

The sudden comment came as a complete surprise, and Kiri swallowed hard as she struggled to think of a response.

"Kiri?"

"Yes."

"Did you hear me?"

"Yes." She bit her lip. "Mandy broke her leg. She couldn't come down."

"What?"

"Mandy . . . Fenton. She broke her leg skiing." Kiri stared up at the ceiling. "So now she can't be Mackenzie's bridesmaid."

"That's a shame." Dan only sounded vaguely interested. "She's probably lapping up the attention, though."

"That's what Wade said," she responded in a tiny voice, unsure what to say next. Had Dan really said that he missed her?

"So . . . did you hear what I said?" he persisted, and she tried to breathe normally.

"Um . . . you missed me?"

"That's right. Have you missed me?"

"I've been very busy." Her jaw tightened. "Grandma needs a lot of attention."

"And I'm sure you're giving her the best . . . but that doesn't answer my question. Kiri?"

"Yes?"

"Have you? I need to know."

Suddenly there was no distance between them. There was no Mandy. There wasn't a past to worry about. Dan was on the line and he missed her!

"Yes." Her voice was so husky he could hardly hear her.

"Kiri?"

"Yes." She spoke more confidently and her smile began to grow.

"Yes, you're there, or yes, you miss me?" Dan's voice sounded mildly exasperated.

"Yes, I miss you." She said this loudly into the phone just as Winnie walked into the hallway. Kiri groaned and sagged at the knees as she saw the delighted look on the older woman's face. "I'm not . . ." she began to speak to Winnie, but Dan's voice responded.

"You're not what? Are you or aren't you missing me . . . because I can't get you out of my mind."

She could visualize him leaning against the kitchen wall of the house in Queenstown, with the phone in one hand and the other hand in his jeans pocket. One foot would be crossed over the other at the ankle, but occasionally he would use the toe of his shoe to play with the bottom corner of the refrigerator that stood beside him.

She smiled at the vividness of the image and knew that she could repeat the process for many situations. In the truck . . . at the cabin . . . conducting in church . . . watching television . . .

"Yes, Daniel Harvey . . . I do miss you . . . very much." She looked straight at Winnie, then she tried to think of a joking remark to follow what she'd just revealed, but no words came . . . only a sense of release. "Very much," she repeated softly, cradling the phone close to her ear with both hands as Winnie deliberately tiptoed back into the lounge.

"That's . . . oh, wow . . . now I don't know what to say."

She could imagine him standing up and running his hand through his thick hair.

"I think we just said it all." Kiri cleared her throat and managed a nervous laugh. "Shall we hang up now?"

She was rewarded by Dan's deep chuckle, then a moment's silence.

"Did you feel that?" He spoke quietly.

"What?" She looked around the hallway.

"I just gave you a hug."

"What?" She smiled and frowned at the same time.

"I just gave you a hug . . . over the phone," Dan sighed. "It's definitely not like the real thing."

She thought of the breadth of his chest and the way she would fit under his arm. "No . . . it's not."

"Kiri . . . I want to talk to you . . ." He hesitated again. "I mean . . . I know I made it pretty clear that I didn't want any commitment, but . . . I really don't want to be just friends anymore."

She swallowed hard and gripped the phone. "I realize that."

"And you're all right with that?"

"I am when we're this far apart." Her lip trembled. "I'm just not sure about when I wake up tomorrow morning . . . or when I see you again."

She almost went straight to her room after they finished talking, just to savor the whole experience. Their conversation had reverted to topical things about Grandma's progress, and young James, and his parents, and what Christchurch looked like with its spring clothing . . . all neutral things, but there was a difference in the way they asked questions and listened to each other's answers. By the time Kiri reluctantly hung up the phone, she felt warm from head to toe. She glanced at her watch. They'd only been talking for fifteen minutes, but it seemed like a lifetime had just come and gone.

She hesitated in the hallway just as Rob and Sheryl walked out of Grandma and Grandpa's room with young James.

"Come and have lunch, Kiri. Mum is fine and Dad just wants to sit and hold her hand." Rob grinned as he put his hand on his wife's shoulder. "I can't get used to Mum telling him that she loves him. I never heard it when I was growing up."

"But you never doubted that she did." Sheryl looked up at him, then down at the baby lying in her arms. "People feel love."

"They do . . ." He nodded. "But it does make a difference hearing it. I really like it."

"Good . . . I love you." Sheryl reached up and pecked him on the cheek, then winked at Kiri. "We could be onto a good thing here."

Winnie had everything laid out on the table for a salad buffet, and everyone helped themselves then sat around the long, Rimu dining table. The conversation never lapsed, and Kiri almost forgot to eat as she listened to the blend of New Zealand and American accents interspersed with the occasional deep tone of Ted's Irish brogue.

One of the main topics of conversation seemed to be the wedding and the lack of a bridesmaid. Charise typically had everyone laughing as she patted her still-rounded stomach and acted out various ways of holding a bouquet that would camouflage her size.

"I'll just have to face it . . . I'm no Mandy Fenton, and there's no way I can get rid of eight inches around the middle and gain twelve inches in height in a week." She made a face at her husband. "You married the wrong gene pool."

Carl grinned as he rocked baby James. "I married the perfect gene pool. I was looking for a wife, not a bridesmaid."

Charise leaned over to kiss his cheek. "You are so good at saying the right thing." She suddenly held up her hand. "I know . . . we could hire a bridesmaid!"

"And now I know I had to marry you . . . to keep control of the crazy ideas." Carl put out a restraining hand. "I think James needs a feed."

The laughter continued around the table, and Kiri found herself caught up in conversations on both sides—first with Anna Fenton asking about her occupational therapy work, and then Joe began asking about her time teaching in Korea.

Suddenly, Mackenzie looked up from being deep in conversation with Wade and Anna and looked directly at Kiri. She turned and called quietly across the table.

"Kiri . . ." She waited as the conversation around the table died down. "Kiri . . . we just had a thought . . ."

"We tend to think alike my nearly-wife and I." Wade grinned and covered Mackenzie's hand with his. "And we think this is a good one."

"And?" Anna rotated her hand to hurry them up.

"Well, seeing as Mandy can't be here to be my bridesmaid," she grinned at Charise, "and seeing as I don't really want to hire a brides-maid . . . I was thinking that Mandy and you would be about the same dress size, Kiri. She's just a bit taller . . ." Mackenzie glanced at her fiancé, then back at Kiri. "This is a huge ask, but . . . we just thought it would be lovely . . . only if you want to, that is . . . but we thought . . . seeing as how I'd really like to have a bridesmaid and Charise isn't quite ready for it yet . . ."

"My nearly-wife is trying to ask if you'd consider being her bridesmaid, Kiri," Wade interrupted Mackenzie with a laugh and squeezed her hand. "We'd both really like it if you would."

Kiri could feel the blood draining from her face and then rushing right back up to her hairline as all talking stopped and every eye at the table turned and focused on her. She tried to swallow the lump that instantly lodged in her throat, and then the fork she was holding began to tremble.

"I . . ." No words would come, and she instinctively looked across at Winnie and Ted. Of one accord, they gave one subtle nod of their heads, then Winnie beamed at Kiri, then at Mackenzie.

"Oh . . . that would be so wonderful." She turned and patted her husband's knee. "Wouldn't it, Ted? Both our girls together . . . what a wonderful idea."

Both our girls. Kiri gave Mackenzie a bewildered look, and the other girl immediately stood up and walked around the table to stand beside her. Kiri slowly stood up.

"I think it's a great idea." Mackenzie clasped her hands in front of her. "And we wouldn't want to let Winnie down now, would we?"

Kiri couldn't look at Winnie, and she found it hard to look straight at Mackenzie. She blew a quick breath for courage, then smiled weakly at the girl before her, a girl who had been a complete stranger just a short while before.

"I'd hate to let Winnie down . . . and if you're sure it's what you want, I'd be honored to." She looked around, then shrugged. "But Mackenzie . . . I thought bridesmaids were meant to help the bride and . . . I'm not sure who's going to be helping who here."

* * *

Dan sat down and leaned back against the wall above the window seat. The slightly amber sunscreen tint on the windows lent a golden hue to the scene that stretched before him. The hills and mountains seemed to be scorched to varying shades of copper-brown, and the sky reflected itself in the smooth maize-gold expanse of the lake. There didn't appear to be any movement at all, and Dan found himself holding his breath as if breathing would disturb the magnificence of it all.

He finally inhaled deeply, then slowly released it in a long sigh and looked at his watch. It was six hours since he'd spoken to Kiri, and he still kept stopping to recall the conversation. She'd definitely said that she missed him and her voice had changed . . . although it had taken awhile. He closed his eyes, wishing he'd been able to see her in person when he'd told her that he didn't want to be "just" friends anymore.

He smiled and picked up the cell phone beside him and pressed the "contacts" button a few times. The tiny screen lit up with "Kiri" printed on it and his finger hovered over "call," then he switched it off again.

"Don't push it, Daniel." He laid the phone back down on the seat. "Baby steps . . . just take baby steps."

* * *

It turned into an exhausting day . . . physically and emotionally. Once Kiri had agreed to be Mackenzie's bridesmaid, the women caught wedding fever and their talk had been of little else. Lunch was cleared quickly, and Mackenzie had unpacked the gown that Kiri would wear. There was an awed silence when she tried the dress on and nervously did a turn in front of Sheryl, Anna, Mackenzie, Winnie, and Charise.

"Oh, my dear . . . I do think it was made for you." Anna folded her arms and nodded happily. "And your olive complexion just works beautifully with the color. So much better than Mandy's pale skin did."

"It does . . . it's great." Charise screwed up her nose and rubbed her waistline. "I'll confess to total jealousy."

Mackenzie stood up and gently touched the sleeve, then looked at Kiri again.

"I think the dress and you will be perfect. As long as you don't outshine me on the wedding day . . ."

They all laughed, then Kiri reached down and held the dress out slightly from her sides with both hands. The style of the gown was very simple: a wide princess neckline, fitting snugly in the bodice, then flaring out from a curved seam at the hip. The main impact lay in the deep turquoise color and in the fabric itself, which draped like heavy silk but clung when she moved. She extended her arms and touched the fabric on one wrist.

"It feels like it's been poured onto me." She swayed slightly. "The fabric is just beautiful . . . and it makes me feel so . . . elegant."

"You'll have to tell Joe that." Anna smiled. "It's a new fabric they just developed at the mill. Mackenzie's gown is in the same fabric, and Wade had this piece dyed especially."

"I love it." Mackenzie clapped her hands. "I was trying not to be disappointed when Mandy broke her leg, but now . . . you've made it all perfect, Kiri. Thank you so much."

Once more Kiri felt incapable of anything but a trembling smile. Just being part of this group of strong and secure women was a new and slightly confusing experience. Here she was dressed in the first long gown she'd ever worn, and they were thanking her for doing it.

"Dan is going to flip when he sees you in it." Sheryl nodded thoughtfully, and Kiri felt her stomach tighten into a knot. In all the excitement of the last hour, she had actually forgotten her conversation with Dan.

"Dan has already flipped." Charise grinned knowingly. "Some men just take awhile to realize it."

After the excitement of trying on the gown, Kiri became an integral part of the wedding discussion and preparations. It almost came as a surprise when it was dinnertime and Rob called them together for family prayers.

Even in the large lounge it was a tight fit as they all knelt in a circle, then just before Rob began the prayer, he took hold of his wife's hand and looked slowly around the room.

"A few years ago a young American missionary sat in our lounge for the first time. He was pretty green, and we grilled him about his family as we do with all the missionaries, but . . . he was different, because at the end he asked if he could bear his testimony and he thanked his Father in Heaven for his family." He looked across the room. "I'll never forget that, Wade. You really made an impact on us as a family, and then when we had the opportunity to meet your parents in America, I could understand why you felt that way about them."

He coughed, then nodded toward Charise and Carl. "It seemed more than just a coincidence that Charise and Carl should be called to the same mission in Italy, as the seeds were already planted, and now they've united our families for eternity. Now Wade has come back and found Mackenzie, and through her, Winnie and Ted have become part of our family. And now Kiri has joined us through them and made a huge difference in our lives with the way she's caring for Grandma and Grandpa." He paused for an exaggerated breath, then smiled. "Tonight, I really want to express my appreciation to Heavenly Father for all that He has blessed us with. Any doubts I might ever have about the gospel—" He held up his other hand quickly. "Not that I have any—but they would surely be put to rest when I see us all gathered here and feel His spirit with us."

There wasn't one person who didn't have tears in their eyes as Rob finished the prayer, and after the noise and commotion of the day, there was suddenly a serenity that was almost tangible as many hugs were exchanged.

After settling Grandma for the night, Kiri found herself alone in her own room, strangely reluctant to go to sleep, as if sleeping would steal away the dreamlike quality of the whole day. She walked over to touch the turquoise gown hanging on the wardrobe, and just for a brief moment held it out quickly by the hem so the fabric flowed across in front of her. Suddenly she let the fabric drop and ran her fingers through her hair, then covered her lips. "This is crazy," she murmured against her fingertips. "I'm an orphan from a bad background and I have no right to be here enjoying myself like this. Something is bound to ruin it all if I let myself embrace it."

"Kiri?" Winnie tapped on her bedroom door and held out the phone. "It's Dan."

Kiri hesitated slightly, then she took the phone from Winnie's outstretched hand.

"Hello?"

"Good night."

"Pardon me?" She gave in to a small, nervous smile.

"I just called to say good night," Dan chuckled. "I thought it might help me get to sleep. Sweet dreams, Kiri."

"Same to you, Dan. Good night." She barely whispered, but she knew he could hear her, and then she heard the phone click as he hung up.

"Has he gone already?" Winnie hadn't even reached the door and she turned around with a quizzical look as Kiri held out the phone.

"Mmm . . . he just wanted to say good night." Kiri tried to look nonchalant and failed completely. "And sweet dreams."

"And that's all right with you?" Winnie tapped the phone on her hand.

"Very all right . . . and yet so wrong all at once." Kiri sat down on the edge of the bed and stared at the floor. "Winnie . . . is it okay to be so happy? I feel like all this can't possibly be happening to me."

"Well . . . as a key witness . . . I'd say it's definitely happening and that you have every right to be happy." Winnie sat down beside her and put her hand over Kiri's. It was warm and soft, and Kiri turned her hand over to link her fingers through Winnie's.

"I'm scared, Winnie."

"I know," the older woman responded simply, then squeezed her hand. "I still don't know why, exactly, but the way I see it . . . you've been waiting a long time for happiness, and now it's your turn. You've just got to have the courage to accept it."

Kiri shook her head. "It sounds so simple when you put it like that . . ."

"It's meant to be." Winnie shrugged. "Isn't it like that lady said in church the other day . . . that Heavenly Father has put us here on earth to find joy?"

"Winnie . . ." Kiri squeezed her hand back. "Why aren't you a member of the Church? You'd make an excellent Latter-day Saint."

She said it in a joking way, but Winnie sat very still.

"Actually, Ted and I were talking about that just a few minutes ago."

"About what?"

"The Church." Winnie clasped her hands in her lap. "It's been on my mind for a while, and when I spoke to Ted, he said that he's been having the same thoughts."

"What sort of thoughts?" Kiri was almost afraid to ask the question.

"Oh, you know . . . how the Church does good things and the whole idea of families . . ." She hesitated. "We were a bit afraid when

Mackenzie wanted to join the Church, but it's only been a good thing, and then since we started coming with you and Dan . . . it's just felt good."

"So . . . ?" Kiri prompted.

"So we were just saying we should learn more about it . . . officially . . . like Mackenzie did."

"Like have the discussions?"

"I think so." Winnie nodded, then she put her head on one side. "I'm a bit like you at the moment . . . I'm a bit scared at even thinking about it, but something really hit me tonight when Rob started talking about their families uniting for eternity and then about Mackenzie and Wade being sealed for eternity." She hesitated. "Did I ever tell you that we lost our son when he was a baby?"

"Ted mentioned it," Kiri answered quietly. "That must have been so hard."

"It was, and it's still as hard as it was then, but I always lived in hope that we'd see him again somehow . . . someday." Winnie took a deep breath. "Then Dan talked about it one night . . . about how we could be with him again . . . through the temple. I'm afraid I was a bit abrupt with him because I just didn't want to be disappointed, I guess. But after tonight . . . well, I would just hate to think that I'd missed the opportunity to be with my baby again. We both think it's worth it to find out more."

"Oh, Winnie . . . that's wonderful." Kiri smiled. "Mackenzie is going to be so happy."

"Would you be as well?"

"Me . . . why, of course I would." Kiri nodded. "Actually . . . it would mean a great deal to me."

"So it looks like we need to give each other encouragement." Winnie stood up and began to walk to the door. "I'm going to tell Ted right now."

"Umm, Winnie?" Kiri moved her scriptures which were lying on the bed.

"Yes, dear?"

"I think . . . when I hear you say those things . . ." Kiri frowned and turned back the cover of the Book of Mormon. "I think I've taken the Church a bit for granted, or at least I haven't really understood it properly. My grandfather was a member but not a good one, and I only really started going to church when a missionary couple took me. I've always felt . . . secure there, but I would sort of shut out all the 'happy family' concepts because I couldn't relate to them. Tonight is the first time that I've ever thought that . . . joy . . . actually can happen . . . for all of us."

Winnie studied her for a moment. "My mother always used to say, *'Hiki ake ki tou ake mana. Ka haere mua.'* Do you know what that means?"

Kiri nodded. "Lift yourself . . . realize your strength." She faltered. "Move on."

"In a positive direction," Winnie added quietly. "That's what is happening for you, Kiri, and the joy is part of it. Don't let it escape you."

Chapter 15

She tried not to think about him, but the next two days seemed a lot longer as Kiri expected to hear from Dan again but the phone never rang. She went for a long walk each morning, but without Winnie, who had developed a mild head cold. The other hours in the days were busy with keeping Grandma occupied, helping wherever possible with the wedding preparations, or just helping prepare meals for a houseful of people.

The Fentons had originally planned to go back to Glencameron with Mackenzie and the Morrises for a brief stay before the wedding, but on Friday, Carl and Charise asked if they could all stay and participate in young James's blessing on Sunday.

The plans were quickly changed, and on Sunday morning, Kiri waited outside the house as everybody filled seats in all the cars before going to church.

"This feels like an army maneuver," Joe laughed heartily as he tried to shepherd his wife into the Harveys' car. He had to wait as Anna gave her grandson another kiss before Carl buckled James into his car seat. "Although I think I could move a whole platoon faster than this woman," he added.

"Oh, shoosh." Anna waved her hand happily. "I just had to get a little peck before you grab him at the other end. Is everybody ready?"

"All ready and waiting for you." Joe held the car door open for her. "Maybe we should just leave for Hamilton now," he joked with Rob, then pretended pain as his wife gave him a neat jab in the ribs. "Or maybe I'll be quiet."

They took up nearly two entire rows in the chapel and Kiri deliberately sat on the end of the row beside Grandma so she could take her out if necessary. She watched as Rob took his place on the stand with the bishopric and Sheryl sat close by him ready to conduct the music for the meeting.

As the notes for the first hymn began to swell from the organ, she noticed the expressions on Sheryl's face as she connected with the congregation and silently entreated them to sing with feeling. By the end of the second verse she found herself quickly reading ahead and anticipating the emotion with which the words could be sung.

She watched Sheryl as the end of the song approached, and just before the final words, her face seemed to radiate and she brought the song to a conclusion with a brilliant smile before sitting down.

"Excuse me . . . is this seat taken?"

Kiri jumped as someone spoke behind her, and then Grandma turned around.

"Danny!"

"Hi, Grandma." Dan leaned across behind Kiri and gave his grandmother a quick kiss on the cheek. Then he sat down beside Kiri. "That's a treat. That's the first time she's recognized me since I got home from my mission," he whispered in her ear. "It was worth coming."

Kiri couldn't think straight. Her heart was pounding so hard she could hear it in her own ears, and because of the cramped seating, she could feel the warmth of Dan's body all down her right side as he squeezed in beside her. She started again as he laid his arm along the seat behind her and gave his grandmother a gentle rub on her shoulders. Grandma turned and gave him a beautiful smile, then reached over and patted his knee and then Kiri's.

"Danny . . . Kiri's here." She wasn't aware of the loudness of her voice, and several people, including the families, turned around to look.

"I know, Grandma," Dan whispered and leaned his head close to Kiri's. "Although she hasn't said hello to me yet."

"Hello, Danny," Kiri tried to whisper as the bishop stood up at the pulpit, but her voice caught in her throat and she began to choke. Her body started shaking and tears were forming in her eyes as she battled to draw a breath, then it stopped suddenly as Dan gave her a swift thump on the back. She gave a few weak gasps, then put her hand over her face to cover her embarrassment and take a deeper breath.

"Okay?" She felt his hand rubbing between her shoulder blades and could only nod. "Just relax."

She almost laughed when he said it but immediately felt the choking sensation begin again, so she took another long breath through her nose. *Just relax . . . this is joyful!*

A few minutes later the bishop announced that Carl was going to bless young James and all the Fenton men and Dan and his father stood up. As they gathered in a circle by the pulpit, each one of them dressed in a suit and white shirt and tie, Kiri had an overwhelming sense of the power of the priesthood they represented. It was a totally new experience, as if it lit up her body and mind, and she shivered and held the hymnbook tightly in her lap.

They all cradled baby James in their hands as Carl began to pronounce the blessing on him . . . good health and strength, love for his parents and brothers and sisters and extended family, and a testimony of his Savior Jesus Christ and of his Father in Heaven. As the blessing continued, Kiri could imagine young James growing up with his parents and grandparents and uncles nurturing him. She could almost see what he would be like . . . and it was thrilling.

The men stood aside to let Carl precede them from the stand and then Wade and his father followed. Dan hesitated as his father briefly shook his hand in welcome, both men smiling, both so similar in build and appearance, then Dan walked down from the pulpit, his eyes firmly on Kiri.

It was the first time she had looked directly at him, and she had to look away and looked straight at Winnie who was leaning back to watch her reaction. Again, Winnie gave the briefest nod, then held two fingers up to the corners of her mouth and forced a comical smile. The hint brought the desired smile to Kiri's face, and she looked up as Dan reached their seat. Neither spoke, but as he sat down he put his arm along the back of the seat and she relaxed against him.

She was almost afraid to move too much and sat very still through the sacrament and then as the first speaker gave her talk. Every now and then she would look down, and just the sight of Dan next to her with his hand lightly clenched and resting on his leg gave her small shivers. She was grateful for having the hymnbook to hold onto, but as her hands lay on top of the hard, green cover, Dan reached forward and began to trace the veins on the back of her hand very lightly with his finger. He seemed preoccupied, and she wasn't sure if it was with her hands or if he was concentrating on what the speaker was saying.

"You have very nice veins," he whispered as the speakers changed.

It was so unexpected that she struggled not to laugh and tried to scowl instead.

"Focus!" She clenched her fist on the book.

"I am . . . and I keep seeing you," he whispered closer, then left her alone until she went to stand up after the closing prayer and he held her firmly in place with his hand around her upper arm. He meant it kindly, but in an instant she felt a mounting sense of panic as the all-too-familiar pressure increased on her arm and she fought to control the urge to pull away from him. Her throat seemed to constrict and she took a few shallow breaths.

"It's time for Sunday School," she whispered as she tried to lean forward, but he still held her and again the panic mounted as his hand seemed to burn around her arm. "Dan, please!"

He instantly became aware of the desperate tone of her voice and let go, but couldn't ask what was wrong as several people moved toward them and he stood to greet them. Kiri subsided against the pew and her hands shook as she picked up her scripture bag.

"I need to look after Grandma. She tried to walk home last week." She stood up quickly as he made to sit down again.

"Then let's do it together." He greeted another couple, then stepped out into the aisle to let his grandparents and Kiri past him.

"Good to see you, Danny." Grandpa helped his wife out of the row, then gave his grandson a very firm hug. "This young lady of yours has been a real blessing to us."

"She's a real winner, isn't she, Grandpa?" He touched Kiri lightly across the small of her back, then leaned forward to cuddle his grand-mother as she held her arms up to him.

There was such a contrast between them as Grandma rested her head against his chest, and he leaned down and kissed her on the forehead, his dark, wavy hair the complete opposite of the fine whiteness of hers, his strong muscular frame enveloping her frailness.

As he released her, she reached up and touched his cheek, then smiled at her husband.

"James . . . Danny's here. We're at The Church of Jesus Christ of Latter-day Saints."

There was a stunned silence as her words seemed to fall on all the family members in the row. Even Rob had just joined them from off the stand, and his eyes immediately misted over.

"She hasn't recognized anything for so long." James's voice was barely audible, and his hand trembled as he held onto the back of the seat. The whole family seemed to have come to a standstill, then Emily began to walk away, seemingly oblivious of the distraction she had caused. "Maybe it's having all the family around again."

As Rob moved quickly to his mother's side, Dan reached for Kiri's hand. "Something tells me it's more than just having the family around that's making her happy." He squeezed her hand. "It seems like having you around has made everyone happy."

"Don't be silly." Kiri refused to look at him and pointed with her other hand at the Harvey and Fenton families filing out of the chapel. "She can't help but feel all the happiness of everybody around her. It's very catching."

"So you're happy too . . . being with my family?"

There seemed to be more to the question than he was actually saying, and Kiri hesitated.

"Like I said . . . it's very catching."

"Okay." Dan stopped in the foyer. "So are you happy I'm here?"

"I'm working on it." She couldn't look at him and tried to ease her hand away as her pulse began to beat in her wrist. He tightened his grip on her hand and pulled her closer as he glanced at the clock on the wall.

"We've got three minutes to get into Sunday School, and I'm not going to sit through another forty-five minutes without knowing. Now tell me that you're glad I'm here, or I'll have to kiss you right here in the foyer to find out for certain."

She felt genuine panic race through her whole body as she looked quickly at the families who were taking their time moving into the next classroom.

"Daniel!" She pressed her hand against his chest. "You can't . . . !"

"Try me," he challenged quietly with the same broad smile she'd seen when she fell in the water on their fishing trip.

Suddenly the tension went out of her and she relaxed against him with a sweet smile.

"Force me and you'll never know for certain." She knew she was teasing and it felt wonderful. "Besides . . . it's good to have something to look forward to."

She slipped her hand away and began to walk into the classroom.

By the end of the three-hour block she could watch him without feeling breathless, and after her initial apprehension she found that the way he would reach for her hand was oddly comforting. He even did it in public as he was greeted by the many ward members he had known since he was a child. She began to relax and just enjoy the sense of belonging.

"All right, I've waited patiently for three hours." Dan faced her as they reached his truck in the church car park.

"And you must be so hungry." Kiri smiled indulgently as she opened the door. "Good thing lunch is ready at home."

"Kiri!" His tone was a mix of exasperation and firmness. "I've spent the whole time driving up here trying to imagine what it would be like when I saw you. Frankly it alternated between our running into each other's arms and you totally ignoring me." He rested his hand on top of the door she'd opened. "Now I get the sense that you're pleased I'm here but that you're also avoiding the . . . issue."

"Issue?" The word stuck in her throat.

"Yes . . . the issue." He gently took her hand. "The issue of whether it's okay between us. The issue of our not just being friends. The issue of whether you really are pleased to see me."

"That's three issues." She swallowed hard, suddenly finding it difficult to look straight at him.

"Kiri!" he almost moaned as he put his finger under her chin and gently tipped her face up till she was looking right at him. "Please."

She had to clench her hands into fists to stop their shaking as the inevitability of the situation overwhelmed her, then she closed her eyes.

"Yes . . . yes . . . yes." It was almost a resigned sigh.

"I take it you mean yes?" Dan leaned closer. "It just doesn't sound very enthusiastic."

"What do you want . . . blood?" Kiri suddenly stamped her foot and stared at the ground. "This is very, very different from saying things over the phone!"

She didn't dare look up, even when he put his hands on his hips and started laughing out loud.

"Oh, Kiri . . . you are a gem." He rubbed his eyes, still grinning as she folded her arms and leaned back against the truck. "I knew I made the right choice."

"I don't know what you find so funny." She frowned and in an instant she felt his finger on her brow smoothing out the frown line.

"They say laughter is the closest thing to tears," Dan answered softly. "And my emotions are running pretty high at the moment. I've been feeling worse than a cat in a clothes dryer."

She finally looked up with her mouth open. "That is a really disgusting image."

"Sorry." He shrugged with an apologetic smile. "You'll have to blame Grandma for that one . . . old family story."

Kiri finally began to smile and shake her head until she put her hands over her face and leaned weakly against his chest. His arms were around her in a second, holding her close.

"I take it this is a *yes*." He rested his chin on top of her head.

"Yes, yes, yes." Her response was muffled but definite.

"Once is enough," he teased as he loosened his hold and held her at arm's length. For the first time she looked back at him confidently, but it only lasted a second as he suddenly kissed her full on the mouth.

"Dan!" she gasped and looked quickly around the car park as he lifted his head. "You promised you wouldn't!"

"No . . . I promised I would . . . if you didn't tell me you were pleased to see me." He didn't look at all repentant.

"But I just did!"

"Then that was your reward."

Chapter 16

"Kiri," Dan's head appeared around the door of his grandparents' apartment. "I've checked with Mum, and she'll look out for Grandma so we can go out."

"Oh . . . all right." Kiri looked up from the album she was holding. "Right now?"

"Soon as you're ready." He walked in and sat down on the other side of his grandmother on the couch. "Hi, Grandma. Do you like looking at all the family photos?"

Emily stared at him blankly, then looked back at the photos, studying each one intently.

"She's hardly responded since Sunday." He frowned, then shrugged. "Then again . . . I wasn't expecting her to recognize me at all, so I'll have to take that as a bonus."

"She recognizes you in your baby photos." Kiri gently reached across and turned back a few pages of the album, then pointed to some photos of a small, chubby baby with fair hair sitting in a paddle pool. "Who's this?"

Without hesitation, Grandma smiled and pointed as well. "Danny swimming."

Another photo showed him at about four years of age, again in swimming trunks and striking a Mr. Universe pose with both arms raised out to his sides. This one brought a chuckle from his grandmother as she touched the photo where his face was screwed up with the effort of posing.

"She appreciates me in my prime," Dan nodded. "That's a good thing."

Kiri laughed as she stood up.

"You were a total exhibitionist." She shook her head. "No wonder she's laughing."

"Wait till I see your baby photos." Dan kissed his grandmother quickly and stood up as Kiri turned away.

"You can't." She walked out the door without looking at him. "There aren't any."

The sun was beginning to lose its warmth as they drove out of the city and through the Lyttelton Tunnel, then they followed the road farther west toward the Port Hills. Conversation flowed easily between them as they discussed first his grandparents and his new nephew, then the wedding, then Kiri asked about his work at the cabin.

"It's all done." Dan slowed to maneuver the truck into a lookout area higher up on the hills. Below them to the east, the first evening lights were beginning to glow in among the cluster of tiny geometric shapes that were Christchurch City.

"You've finished . . . completely?" Kiri looked surprised. "I thought you'd just come over for James's blessing."

"Well . . . I didn't have much else to distract me, so I finished quite quickly." He let the windows down a fraction and switched the engine off. "But a few things have come up . . . as well as young James. That's what I wanted to talk to you about."

"Talk to me?" She felt immediate apprehension but tried to sound calm. "That sounds formal."

Since Sunday when they'd broken down the final barriers and he'd kissed her, they had settled into an easy relationship of teasing and talking that had been encouraged by the other family members who all seemed delighted to see them together. Dan had openly preferred to be by her side even when his father suggested that the men get together and plan a trout-fishing trip for after the wedding.

It wasn't until the other women had insisted she try on the bridesmaid dress and parade for them all on Tuesday night that he'd become quieter and more withdrawn. Kiri had felt anguish building in her stomach as she had twirled gracefully in the turquoise gown only to see his smile fading. Even his comments on how beautiful she looked had seemed almost perfunctory and at his mother's insistence.

This morning, after a sleepless night, she had dreaded seeing him at breakfast, but he appeared to be his normal self once again, greeting her with a smile and offering to help with Grandma until lunchtime. At noon he had gone out, leaving Kiri to try and concentrate on her work and control her own thoughts.

Now her heart began to beat faster once more and she stared out at the darkening sky as she played with the CTR ring on her right hand.

"I love it up here." Dan spoke quietly as he pointed toward the city. "Mum and Dad would bring us up here when I was little and I could never understand how those little lights could possibly be the city. I think that was the first time I ever questioned them."

"The first time?" She tried to relax in her seat.

"Mmm . . . the first of many." He nodded. "I questioned a lot of things growing up . . . even the Church as I got older. That's why I was such an old missionary going out . . . I had to be completely convinced that what I was doing was right."

"But it was all right when you went?"

"Oh, absolutely." He looked sheepish. "I regretted, after, that I hadn't gone sooner, but it was an amazing experience all the same . . . maybe even better for me because I was a bit more mature by then."

"Your mother said you served a wonderful mission." Kiri glanced sideways.

"It was good." He nodded. "And I fully expected that I would be blessed when I came home for serving faithfully. You know . . . marry a good woman and settle down." He rubbed both hands on the steering wheel. "I was convinced Sarah was 'the one' . . . except that she had different ideas and it never happened. It made me doubt . . . really doubt again . . . that I could receive inspiration."

Kiri sat silently but he didn't seem to need any response as he kept talking.

"I was really pleased to be able to help you when you were sick in Queenstown, and I honestly didn't think that I would be . . . could be . . . attracted to you so soon after breaking up with Sarah. In fact, I just welcomed you as a distraction and I rationalized that I was helping you like a good member of the Church should. You didn't seem to have much fun in your life . . . so it was a good excuse to . . . do stuff together."

"And I appreciated that," Kiri murmured as the ring dug into her finger. "You were a good friend when I really needed one."

"My mate," Dan sighed. "I was happy with that as well . . . until you came back here and . . . I had to face the fact that I didn't want to just be your mate anymore." He reached out for her hand. "I've had all sorts of battles with myself over the last few days because I feel so great when I'm with you, but then I start to doubt myself again because I know that you weren't wanting a relationship and that I might be just wanting something to happen." He hesitated. "Then when you came out in that dress last night and you looked so amazing . . . it just shut me down because I realized that I had to make a decision . . . but I already knew the answer."

Kiri felt the pressure of his hand increase on hers, and the distant lights blurred into a bright haze as he kept talking.

"The thing is, Kiri . . . I know you've had your sights set on your career and you've said all along that you preferred to just be friends but . . ." He hesitated. "Mitch Savage called me just before I came back to Christchurch and he wants me to go up to Canada for a few weeks." He rushed on. "I know . . . I hope . . . things are different between us now . . . so I just wanted to lay everything on the table before I left . . . so that we understand each other completely."

The tears began to flow freely down her cheeks as she rested her head back against the headrest. She drew a deep breath and reached down to pick up her handbag off the floor. Her hands were shaking as she reached inside and pulled out a small journal, then flicked slowly through the pages. Somewhere near the middle she stopped and took out a photo.

"You're right, Dan." Her bottom lip quivered. "I was avoiding a relationship and I have been set on continuing my education . . . but I have my reasons." She bit her lip hard and swallowed. "I wasn't expecting it, but things have changed between us . . . and you're so right about needing to lay everything on the table." She shook the small photo gently. "But this is something you probably weren't expecting."

He had to squint in the twilight to see it properly, then the features of a child began to focus. Even as his eyes adjusted he found it difficult to tell if it was a boy or a girl or how old they were, as the black hair was cut short over the ears. The disturbing part was the badly swollen features and dark bruising over one side of the child's face. A faded sleeveless shirt revealed the same deep bruising on the left arm and shoulder.

"Kiri?" He found it hard to even say her name.

"You asked about seeing my childhood photos," her voice was flat and toneless. "That's about the only one I have . . . courtesy of Social Welfare. I was twelve years old."

Suddenly there were no more tears, as if her words had dried up the well inside of her and there was nothing left. She placed the photo onto the seat between them and clasped her hands loosely in her lap. After a long silence, Dan picked up the photo and studied it for a long time.

"Who did this? Was it someone in your family?" He could feel the anger rising inside his chest.

She could only nod as a sense of hopelessness drained through her body.

"How long ago?" Dan's voice was flat as he laid the photo back on the seat.

"Eight years ago they stopped." She looked out the side window. "I was sixteen when I left home."

"Sixteen." He drew a long, deep breath. "You've been on your own since then?"

"I've always been on my own." She twisted the ring again. "The last eight years I haven't been hurting . . . at least not so much."

They sat in silence until there was nothing but a black void in front of them lit in tiny parts by a few stars and the city lights. Finally, Dan stretched both arms out in front of him, gripping his fingers around the steering wheel.

"When did it start?"

She answered immediately, her head down.

"Soon after my mother died . . . I think."

"You think . . ." He frowned, unable to comprehend what she was saying.

"I was nearly five when my mother died. Apparently it was a combination of alcohol and drug overdose and physical abuse, but I don't really remember anything except standing up on the hill behind our house where she was buried at the family grave. I never knew who my father was or anything about him . . . except that he'd been *Pakeha* and so I was really the only light-skinned one in the family . . . just enough to be a bit of an outcast." Her voice quivered. "I really only remember missing her cuddling me at night and . . . sitting by her grave waiting for her to come back . . . but she never did."

"So who looked after you?" Dan felt his heart tighten at the thought of a tiny girl waiting beside a mound of cold dirt.

Once again she shook her head.

"I'm not sure. As far back as I can remember I got meals ready and cleaned the house. My grandfather and my uncles just expected it of me."

"But . . . who abused you?" He suddenly hated himself for the curious fascination he felt in wanting to know. "Who could possibly hurt you like that?"

Kiri shook her head as she touched the photo with her fingertip.

"They actually didn't beat me often at all. That was just the time my aunt was sober enough to take me to the hospital. She thought I was dead. I don't think my uncles would have bothered."

"So it was your uncles . . ." Dan stopped as she nodded.

"My uncles . . . and sometimes their friends." She turned her face away and began to rub her left shoulder as if to get rid of an old pain. "I was the girl factor." She hesitated, and there seemed to be a wealth of meaning in the last statement. "When I began . . . when I was old enough to realize what they were doing . . ." Her voice broke in a choked sob. "When I began to resist, they would beat me. They hurt my auntie so much after we got back from the hospital that I just used to hide after that . . . until the bruises went away."

"Did they . . . how did they hurt you before that?" Dan suddenly loathed himself for asking. He knew the answer.

Kiri took a long time to answer, then she began to make small circles in the frosted surface of the car window.

"I missed my mother telling me stories. She used to cuddle me in bed and tell me stories." Her finger traced one circle repeatedly. "After she died . . . my uncles started telling me stories . . . and they'd . . . cuddle me as well. I liked it. I even looked forward to it." There was a long silence as she drew a line through the circle. "I was quite old when I realized they only told me stories after my grandfather went to bed and . . ." She struggled with the words. "And that they weren't just cuddling me."

"So he didn't know?" Dan could barely breathe.

"I really don't know." Kiri hung her head. "I think he'd do anything to keep his sons close to him . . ."

"Even ignore what they were doing to you?" He shook his head in disbelief. "Kiri . . . why didn't you tell him?"

"I tried . . . a few times . . . as I got older . . . when I realized what they were doing." She couldn't look at him as she raised her head. "He just told me I was worse than my good-for-nothing mother." She hesitated and gave a wry smile. "He'd tell them off for getting drunk, but not for what they did when they were drunk."

Kiri wiped the tears off her cheeks with the back of her hand.

"As I got older the only place I felt safe was at church. My grandfather had me baptized when I was eight. He thought it was the right thing to do, but we didn't go very often. He used to get into arguments. One day the Jensons . . . a missionary couple . . . noticed some bruises and they really helped me." She made a feeble attempt at a smile. "They told me I had to talk to my grandfather. I tried again and he only repeated that it was my mother's fault."

She turned her head away and let the tears flow freely and silently for several minutes. It was as if the years of pain were washing out of her body, and it brought a feeling of release.

"It was like something died inside me right then. I packed the few things I owned into a plastic bag and walked to town, and I've never been back since."

Dan struggled with the image of Kiri, young and abused, fending for herself in a completely unknown world. He took a deep breath.

"Where did you stay after you left?"

"I went to the Jensons and they arranged for me to stay with members from the branch for a few days . . . but the family were a bit scared of my uncles so I left as soon as I got a job in another town. I stayed with another Church family there and that was good . . . but as soon as I had enough money I moved up to Hamilton." She smiled, remembering. "I decided I would go to university, but then I realized I didn't have a clue what to do. Then I remembered that Sister Jenson was an occupational therapist—she represented everything that I wanted to be, so . . . I managed to get a loan and went down to university in Dunedin to train." She tilted her chin almost defiantly. "I also made up my mind that I would fend for myself financially so I would never, ever have to go back. That's why I have to work," she finished quietly.

"Oh, Kiri . . ." Dan reached out to touch her hand, but she instantly pulled away toward the door of the car.

"I told you before, Dan . . . we come from such different backgrounds." She sighed. "And now that I'm telling you about it . . . it only makes me realize just how different we are . . . and how impossible it is to even think about anything . . . between us."

She picked up the photo and slipped it back between the journal pages.

"I've kept this photo . . . not to feel sorry for myself but as a reminder . . . so I would never hurt anyone else." Her voice caught. "Either physically by passing it on, or emotionally with my issues. But I could never guarantee that . . . so I'll never risk it."

"Just because they did terrible things doesn't mean you will!" Dan protested immediately, but she was shaking her head as he spoke.

"But it might . . . don't you see? It's in my blood, Dan! It's bad blood!"

"But you're good . . ." He stopped as she held up her hand, then answered him quietly.

"Dan, please don't . . . I can see this is not what you'd been anticipating, so I completely understand how this . . . changes things now . . ." She knew she was babbling, but she didn't want a response. "So let's just go home now and you can go to Canada without any complications and I'll be off to university and we'll have a few great memories of a good holiday."

"Tell me, Kiri . . . how can I help?" Dan interrupted her quietly but he didn't look at her.

Again it took a long time for her to speak. She longed to feel the touch of his hand on hers, but she knew she was alone even though they were only inches apart.

"You have helped." She tried to smile but her lip was quivering, so she clamped her jaw tightly then stared at the bright, digital numbers of the clock on the dashboard.

"You . . . Winnie and Ted . . . your family. You've all helped me see what life can be like."

"But you still want to walk away from it?" Dan's question was almost hurtful in its bluntness, and she winced slightly. If he were to take her into his arms now, would her resolve disappear? Wasn't that where she wanted to be more than anything she'd ever let herself contemplate? And yet she was telling him to go away . . .

Dan stared out into the blackness. Even though he knew that he wanted to reach out and hold her, there was something stopping him . . . a feeling of revulsion that gnawed at the pit of his stomach . . . and he couldn't distinguish whether it was just about the way she'd been treated or . . . about her too. Everything she had told him was so difficult for him to comprehend. Would that sort of knowledge always be between them?

"I don't really expect you to understand," she voiced his thoughts. "But you can see why I only wanted to be friends. We're just too different . . . I'm just not worthy of . . ." She hesitated and folded her arms. "I'll always be grateful for your helping me when I was sick, and our fun times together were wonderful . . . but now I think it's time you went to Canada, and by the time you get back, I'll be gone. We can just put this behind us."

Her voice was quietly calm and didn't ask for a response, so Dan didn't say a word as he reached down to turn the key in the ignition. The roar of the truck engine was a welcome respite, and on the way home he turned the car stereo up loudly enough that neither spoke until they reached the driveway of the Harvey home. Kiri jumped out immediately, and he watched as she pushed the front door open. He could see her go straight down the hallway to her room before the door swung closed behind her.

"Kiri," he murmured as he shook his head and reached into his pocket. "I thought I knew." He clenched his fist around the small, burgundy velvet box, then opened it up and stared at the glittering diamond set onto a slim gold band. "I thought I knew."

* * *

There was an early morning business flight from Christchurch to Auckland the next day, and Dan quickly made arrangements to be on it. It only preempted his plans by a day and a half, but his family all sensed the change in him as he and Kiri both went their separate ways in the evening. Even his mother couldn't get any response from her questions except that he just needed to leave earlier.

As Rob Harvey sat beside his son on the way to the airport, he took one quick glance at Dan's normally smiling profile and could almost feel the pain he saw on his son's face. His son obviously hadn't slept, nor had he bothered to shave, and the growth of dark stubble only accentuated the deep shadows under his eyes.

They were nearly at the airport buildings when Rob finally spoke. "Are you sure you're doing the right thing, son?"

"At the moment it's the only thing to do, Dad." Dan's response was quiet but immediate, as if he'd anticipated what his father was going to say.

"Well, I like to think that you make reasoned decisions, Dan," Rob chose his words carefully. "It just seems like you're leaving very suddenly . . . too suddenly."

"It's only a bit earlier." Dan slowed the truck to enter the car park and pulled into a space. "I was leaving anyway."

"But not like this." Rob undid his seat belt and faced his son. "We haven't had time to go on a fishing trip, Dan . . . but I think we need to talk a bit more. It seemed that things were pretty good between you and Kiri . . . what happened to change that so fast?"

A few more cars drew into the spaces alongside them, and the sky began to transform itself from a deep purple into the pinkish hues of sunrise as the airport came to life. Dan watched the increasing activity without seeing any of it.

"We took a ride up to the hills last night." He clasped both hands around his seat belt strap. "I wanted to tell Kiri that I had to go away for a few weeks, and I wanted to just clear away any doubts before I left." He gripped the strap. "Before I proposed to her."

Rob nodded slowly. "So what happened?" he prompted gently.

Dan stared ahead, the muscle working in the side of his jaw.

"Kiri showed me a photo . . . of when she was young." He looked down. "She was badly beaten in it. Then she told me how she was abused since she was little." His voice broke and he looked across at his father. "Dad . . . I've heard about abuse and I've even counseled some people about it . . . but suddenly . . . it was Kiri and she was just a kid . . . and I just felt sick about it." He slammed his fist against the steering wheel. "I wanted to find everybody that had ever hurt her and just beat them to a pulp."

Rob watched the emotions raging in his son and felt helpless. He waited as Dan gained control, then he reached out and rested his hand on his son's shoulder.

"Did you tell Kiri that was how you felt?"

"No . . . I couldn't say anything." Dan shook his head. "I just felt sick, and at first . . . I couldn't decide if it was for her . . ." He bit his lip. "Or about her. I don't know if I could deal with that the rest of my life."

Rob tightened his grip as he realized his son's torment.

"Then Kiri said that she understood that this changed things between us and that's why she'd only ever wanted to just be friends . . . that we were just too different." Dan's voice shook. "I wanted to tell her it was all right and that nothing has changed . . . but I couldn't."

"Because it has changed." Rob nodded as he lowered his arm. "Your relationship has moved to a whole new level."

"What do you mean by that?" Dan glanced sideways.

"I think that up till now your feelings about Kiri have been . . . on a physical level." Rob smiled. "You've been attracted to each other, and you've realized how much you want to be with her . . . but now you're facing a much bigger challenge . . . and you don't know how you feel . . . because of her past."

"I trust Kiri." Dan frowned. "I just don't know that I trust myself . . . to feel the same way anymore."

"Well, that's a step in the right direction . . . at least you're not making her accountable for her past . . . or are you?" Rob waited a moment. "Have you prayed about this yet, Dan?"

His son slowly shook his head. "I tried last night. I got down on my knees and nothing happened . . . no words . . . no feelings . . . nothing."

"So you decided to run away?"

Dan recognized the tone of his father's voice . . . the same chiding tone he'd always used whenever Dan had done something wrong as a child and tried to avoid being found out. He looked up and managed a slight smile.

"How do you always manage to say the right thing at the right time?"

"I just say very fast prayers." Rob grinned. "And I must have a good connection because it works most times." He hesitated. "Dan . . . do you remember when we took that vacation on the West Coast and we went to the old gold-mining town? You and Charise had a race to find the first piece of gold."

Dan nodded while he frowned. "I remember . . . but I don't see the point right now."

His father held up his hand. "Just think about the process you went through. There was a lot of muck and rubbish in the stream, and you'd swill the pan around and empty it and try again."

"And again, and again . . . even when Charise found hers first."

"Exactly . . . and then you saw your gold . . . it just shone amongst all that rubbish . . . and you were so excited." Rob smiled, remembering. "They put it into a little bottle for you, and you thought you were the richest person on the planet."

"I was six, Dad."

"It's the thought that counts." His father tapped the dashboard to make the point. "Age has nothing to do with it."

Dan stared out at the buildings that were beginning to brighten with the early morning sun. Suddenly the yellow rays struck a pane of glass and it shone brilliantly, creating a golden glare. He slowly turned to his father.

"I think I see how that relates to my emotions." He swallowed hard. "I don't know how it can possibly change anything . . . but I can see what you mean." He held out his hand. "Thanks, Dad . . . maybe when I get back from Canada we can do that fishing trip."

Rob grunted as he reached over to embrace his son.

"I'm going to hold you to that, Danny."

Half an hour later, Rob Harvey shielded his eyes from the early morning sun as he watched Dan's plane lift above the airport buildings and quickly become a small dot in the brightening blue sky. As he slowly lowered his arm he thought about the conversation he'd had with Kiri just a few days ago—a conversation where he'd counseled her to talk to Dan about her past and assured her the Lord would help her find the right words.

Afterward, Rob had sat with his mother and wondered how such good people could come from such harsh backgrounds.

"They do it with the Lord's help, Dan. But they need our understanding as well." He switched on the car engine. "She's a gem, my son . . . just like your grandmother, but you've got to find that out for yourself."

* * *

"Are you going to sleep all day?" Winnie tapped on Kiri's bedroom door and walked in with a tray set with some toast and juice. "I noticed you didn't go for your walk, so I thought you might need a little sustenance."

Kiri rolled over on her stomach and buried her face in her pillow so Winnie couldn't see the heavy rings under her eyes. When she hadn't been crying, she had lain awake most of the night, and sleep had only rescued her less than two hours ago.

"What time is it?" She spoke into the pillow.

"Nearly nine o'clock." Winnie set the tray down beside the bed. "Dan left nearly four hours ago."

The only response was the total stillness of Kiri's body . . . as if she'd stopped breathing completely.

"He must have left early," her voice was still muffled.

Winnie snorted. "I know they've stepped up security at the airport . . . but I thought it was supposed to be two hours early . . . not thirty-two." She folded her arms and waited by the bed. "So are you going to tell me what happened?"

The boldness of her statement was enough to finally make Kiri raise her head. She turned to look at Winnie, then dropped back down onto the pillow with a low groan.

"My life happened, Winnie, and it came back to haunt me . . . just like I always knew it would." She cradled her head on her arms. "I tried to fool myself for a while that dreams could come true . . . but then there's reality."

"Are you going to tell me about reality?" Winnie asked softly as she sat down on the edge of the bed.

She waited for a long time as Kiri didn't move or answer. The only sounds were outside as Sheryl turned on the garden hose and the water sprayed finely over the window pane above the flower garden.

"Dan told me that he was going to Canada for a few weeks." She finally rolled over and stared at the ceiling. "He wanted to get everything cleared up before he went . . . so I told him that I was abused when I was a child . . . physically and sexually." She tried to sound flippant. "The usual things that a boyfriend wants to hear."

Winnie's hand went to her throat as she struggled to think of something to say, but Kiri shook her head.

"There's nothing to say, Winnie . . . nothing that can change things. I told Dan that I was from too different a place and that I was grateful for the good times we've had . . . end of story."

"Did you give him a chance to say anything?"

"There wasn't anything he could say," Kiri answered abruptly, then looked at Winnie. "I'm sorry . . . but it's just better that he's gone now, and I'll be gone before he gets back."

"Why?"

"Why?" Kiri couldn't disguise the disbelief in her voice. "Oh, Winnie . . . it's so obvious."

"The only thing that's obvious to me is that you gave the man a total shock, then pretty much made up his mind for him before he has a chance to understand . . . how you feel or how he feels."

"But . . ." Kiri clenched her fingers on the bed cover, then shook her head. "No, Winnie . . . it's better this way. I'm not worth . . . it just wouldn't work."

"You're not worth . . . ?" Winnie raised one eyebrow so high that Ted would have recognized the warning sign. "That's really what this is all about, isn't it?"

"I don't know what you mean." Kiri's tone was weary and resigned.

"You just don't see your own worth, young woman," Winnie scolded. "I don't know the whole story about what has happened to you in the past . . . I only see a young woman who has done very, very well to rise above something terrible. What really gets up my nose is that I see that she's prepared to give something wonderful away . . . because of pride."

"Pride!" Kiri finally reacted. "What have I got to be proud of?"

"Oh, my dear," Winnie's voice dropped and she reached out and stroked Kiri's cheek. "Some people have everything handed to them.

You've had to fight for everything you have . . . but now you're giving up the prize." She held up her hand as Kiri shook her head. "And I'm not just talking about Dan . . . it could be any man . . . any good situation. You've earned your place in the world through hard work and sheer goodness . . . but you're letting the past catch up and take over every time you reach a better place."

"But, Winnie . . ." Kiri moaned and closed her eyes. "It's better that I just make my own way . . . it avoids any complications."

"You know, my girl," Winnie snorted. "I've sat with you a few times in church now, and I think I listen way better than you. Didn't they talk in that Sunday School class about opposition . . . and that it makes you a better person?"

"I don't remember . . ."

"Well, I do," Winnie interrupted. "And it seems to me like you've had a whole heap more opposition than most people—that you've overcome—and that should make you a much better person. Correct me if I'm wrong!"

Her voice was sharp and decisive, and Kiri opened her eyes and stared as if she'd been spanked. She opened her mouth to retaliate, then the tiniest hint of a smile lifted the corners of her mouth and she sat up in bed and flung her arms around Winnie, squeezing her tightly. For a second it was hard to distinguish whether she was laughing or crying as she buried her face against Winnie's shoulder and her whole body shook.

"I hope you're laughing, my girl," Winnie tentatively patted her on the back. "But I'm not sure why."

Kiri finally leaned back and wiped her eyes. They were still swollen, but there was more light in them than there had been.

"Did you ever tell Mackenzie off like that?"

"Mmm . . . a few times." Winnie pursed her lips. "Don't know what it is about my girls that you can't see what wonderful people you are. I keep asking myself if they're blind."

"Oh, Winnie . . . where would your girls be without you?" She leaned over and hugged her again. "I don't know if it'll ever make any difference with Dan, but at least I feel better knowing I have you and Ted."

"You better believe it." Winnie coughed and looked away. "And don't let me ever catch you being negative like that again."

"Yes, ma'am." Kiri saluted with two fingers, then smiled. "I wonder if anyone else has ever been told off for being good."

"Knock, knock. Can I come in?" Mackenzie's head appeared tentatively around the edge of the door. "Kiri, have you seen . . . Winnie! I've been looking for you." She glanced at Kiri's swollen eyes. "Oh, I'm sorry . . . I'll come back . . ."

"No, no . . . come on in." Kiri rubbed her face briskly with her hands. "Winnie has been telling me off, so I need some moral support."

Winnie shook her head as Mackenzie came and sat down on the bed beside her.

"You two will start ganging up on me if I don't watch out. Heaven knows, I can only handle one of you at a time." She patted Mackenzie's hand. "I've been trying to convince Kiri that she needs Dan."

"But . . ." Mackenzie frowned. "I thought . . ."

Winnie smiled. "You missed a bit while you were getting your beauty sleep. Dan has gone off to Canada because he thinks Kiri doesn't want him around."

"But you were cuddling yesterday!" Mackenzie looked genuinely confused. "What happened?"

Kiri glanced at Winnie, then took a deep breath. "I shared a few things from my past . . . which made me realize . . ."

"Which made you think . . ." Winnie interrupted swiftly.

"Which made me think . . ." Kiri hesitated. "That our relationship shouldn't continue."

"Oh, dear." Mackenzie looked at Winnie, then she smiled. "And Winnie's been telling you off. Has she offered any solutions yet? She had mine all worked out for me." Winnie raised her hand in protest, and Mackenzie caught it and held it tightly. "For which I'll be eternally grateful." She winked at Kiri. "Does she have your plan worked out yet?"

"Give me time, girls," Winnie chuckled and reached out for Kiri's hand as well. Then she was suddenly serious. "Kiri, you love Dan, don't you?" She kept Kiri's hand firmly in hers, then squeezed a bit more tightly as she hesitated. "I'm not usually wrong, my girl, but I need to hear it from you."

"Yes, I . . . love . . . Dan." Kiri glanced at Mackenzie. "Did she make you do this?"

"Oh, yes." Mackenzie nodded knowingly. "And it works."

"And now you have to tell Dan," Winnie stated simply.

"But Dan's on his way to Canada!" Kiri shook her head. "It's always so much easier to say these things when he's not around."

"Well, how long is he gone for?" Winnie insisted quietly.

"About two weeks . . . maybe more," Kiri sounded despondent. "Just enough time to lose my resolve."

"Or gain a lot more." Mackenzie smiled as she placed her hand on Kiri's. "Maybe we could have a prayer together . . . to give us all a bit more courage, eh Winnie?"

Winnie nodded slowly and her face puckered for a moment before she squeezed both of their hands tightly.

"Say a prayer with my girls? That sounds just perfect."

* * *

Dan stood at the check-in desk at the Auckland terminal. He had already tried to transfer his connecting flight to Canada and fly straight on through in a few hours, but the only seat available was the next day. He glanced at his watch. Another twenty-four hours to wait. He went and sat down in one of the long rows of cushioned seats and set his computer case on his lap, but even before he undid the zipper he knew it was a pointless exercise . . . just as it had been on the plane when he'd tried to read for nearly an hour.

He looked at his watch again, then pulled out his cell phone, contemplated the blank screen for another few seconds, then dialed.

"Hello . . . Mitch? Dan here." He set the case on the floor. "Actually, no . . . I'm not in Christchurch . . . I'm here at Auckland Airport . . . no, I'm early." He ran his hand through his hair. "Mitch . . . something's come up and I'm really not sure what to do. Can I meet with you?"

He only waited half an hour before a burgundy four-wheel drive pulled up in front of the airport and a broad-shouldered man with short, sandy-colored hair jumped out.

"Dan . . . good to see you again!" Mitch shook his hand firmly. "I'm glad you came up early . . . it'll give us a chance to catch up." He picked up a large sports bag and put it in the back of the truck. "I've called Meredith's boyfriend, Grant, and he's coming over for dinner this evening."

"Wow . . . I'm impressed." Dan looked genuinely surprised as he lifted his other suitcase. "I didn't even think to call him . . . I mean, I didn't actually get to meet him before Meredith left on her mission, so I wasn't thinking of him being here. Have you heard from her?"

"She wrote the other day, and of course she writes to Grant regularly. She's doing really well and especially happy now that Grant is seriously investigating the Church. He's a good man . . . I'm sure you'll like him." Mitch thumped him on the back. "And between us all we should be able to sort out your problems."

"Who said I had problems?" Dan frowned, then grinned ruefully as Mitch looked skeptical. "Oh . . . the unshaved look is a dead give-away, I guess. I thought it might look fashionable."

"It might . . . without the sunken eyes." Mitch smiled. "Or the fact that Grant mentioned that your mother had told your Aunt Nan that you were very happy with a certain young lady . . . and now you turn up not looking very happy at all and wanting to get away to Canada."

"Ah." Dan shook his head. "The good old family network going overtime."

"You can't beat it." Mitch laughed as he went round to his door. "At least you know they've got your best interests at heart. In fact, it sounds like they're pretty fond of your young lady as well."

"They love her." Dan climbed into the passenger seat. "She's kind and pretty and hardworking. She's great at looking after my grand-mother, she helped my sister in labor, and everyone thinks she's wonderful . . . but she's not my young lady anymore."

"Why?" Mitch checked for traffic, then swung out onto the road. "What's the problem?"

Dan hesitated, then he reached out and played with the lock on the dashboard. "Oh . . . just the usual. I wanted to ask her to marry me before I went up to Canada, then, before I could, she told me that there are issues from her past and that she doesn't think she should commit to a relationship because of it."

Mitch nodded slowly. "That must have been hard to take. Should I ask what the issues are?"

"Um, things that no woman should have to suffer . . . let alone a child. I didn't know what to say." Dan shrugged. "I just never expected . . . I mean, she's such an amazing woman . . . but . . ."

"But the picture is spoiled?"

"Not spoiled . . . more like confused, because I'm trying to figure out what it means, but then she's not allowing me to make a decision anyway." Dan hesitated. "What would you have done?"

"I'm not sure I'm the right person to ask," Mitch grimaced. "It was probably harder for Sharon to take me on because I'd had the non-LDS background."

"How did she handle that?"

"She loves me in spite of it," Mitch grinned. "She says it gives me character, but you can be sure I had to do the hard yards to prove I was going to live the gospel properly before she would marry me. She says she needed a lot of faith . . . in herself and in me."

"Kiri already lives the gospel . . . which is amazing considering her upbringing." Dan drummed his fingers on the dashboard. "She's already done the hard yards, and she's a gem."

"So what exactly is the problem, then?"

They were traveling through an area of sprawling parkland at the foot of a large hill, and Dan looked out at the crest of the hill and the puffy, white clouds suspended motionlessly in the bright aqua sky.

"The problem is . . . we agreed to be just good friends right from the beginning . . . because it suited us both." He paused, remembering. "She was set on going back to university, and I'd come from a failed relationship and I really didn't want to get into anything serious. Neither of us wanted commitment, so it was easy to have fun together. It seemed to be a good situation . . . until Kiri went to Christchurch to help look after my grandmother. It only took a few days to realize how much I missed her company . . . and that I didn't want to be 'just friends' anymore. When I told her, it seemed like she felt the same way and we were really happy. Then all of a sudden, when I knew I was going up to Canada, I wanted to know that she . . . wanted me . . . before I left. Then all the past came out, and . . . I basically left because she insisted it was better for both of us."

"So you took the easy option?" Mitch kept his eyes on the road.

Dan opened his mouth then shut it again, clenching his jaw.

"Have I read it wrong?" Mitch arched one eyebrow.

"No . . . you read it pretty well." Dan took a deep breath and laid his arm along the window edge, resting his head on his hand. "You don't happen to know the ending, do you?"

"Well . . . the way I see it," Mitch held up one finger, "you can go to Canada and just tell yourself it's all over with . . . ?"

"Kiri," Dan said her name softly.

"With Kiri, or you can go back down to Christchurch and try and sort things out with her."

"You know you just stated the absolutely obvious?" Dan glanced sideways.

Mitch touched the side of his nose knowingly. "Aah . . . it's the Irish in me," he laughed. "But it seems to me that you should go down and talk to her again . . . tell her exactly how you feel. She'll either say yes or no, but at least you'll know you laid it on the line."

"But what about Canada?"

"What about Canada?" Mitch grunted. "I don't think it's going to move much in the next week or so."

Dan actually laughed as he suddenly felt new resolve, tinged with apprehension, grip somewhere around his heart and leave him breathless.

He thumped his chest. "Part of me says that you're right. And part of me says that you shouldn't give up your day job as a property developer to be a counselor."

"And it seems to me like my success in either of them depends largely on you . . . so you better not let me down." Mitch grinned as he swung the car out onto the highway. "Now you'd better get ready for a grilling from my Sharon. She's got a woman's instinct for things like this, and besides . . . she's so happy with me she thinks everybody else should be happy as well. You can guarantee she'll give you a hard time."

Mitch was right, and Dan felt as if he'd met a Canadian version of his sister Charise when he met Sharon Savage a short while later. She welcomed him as if he was a long-lost brother, and after serving him up a cooked breakfast she settled down on the small couch beside the dining room table and discreetly fed her baby while she plied Dan with questions about Glenorchy . . . and Kiri.

"It sounds absolutely beautiful," she commented after he described the newly completed log cabin. "Almost idyllic."

"It is," Dan nodded as he toyed with a glass of orange juice. "I was sitting in the window seat the other night, looking out over the lake, and everything was in shades of bronze and gold in the sunset . . . even the lake. It was magic."

"So we shouldn't have any problem selling them?" Mitch sat down on the couch beside his wife and rested his arm behind her. He absently stroked the fine sandy-colored down on the top of his daughter's head. "I had a hard time convincing Dad about these cabins, but in light of all this movie-making interest down there in Glenorchy, and judging by your descriptions . . . I think we've done the right thing."

Dan nodded. "We had a number of people come and look around . . . mainly looking at buying investment properties to rent out, but they were all really interested."

"So, should we set up this cabin as a display home . . . with furniture?" Mitch stared at the ceiling, visualizing. "How are you at interior decorating, Dan?"

"Reasonable . . . although Kiri came up with some great ideas while she was working up there. She seems to have a good sense of color coordination, especially with so much exposed timber."

"Log cabin with a New Zealand flavor?" Sharon moved and passed her daughter to her father. "Lots of natural fibers?"

"Combinations of native wood furniture and handcrafted quilts, pottery, and wool products," Dan agreed quietly. "She and Ted Morris's wife, Winnie, did some quilts that would really give the place a homey feel. Not the same ones, of course," he amended quickly. "But something like it."

"Maybe we could get them to do some for us," Mitch suggested as he gently raised the baby to his shoulder and rubbed the tiny back. "It could give you a reason to go back and talk to her."

* * *

They spent the rest of the day in Mitch's office going over new cabin designs and discussing the projects that Dan would inspect in

Canada. By six o'clock, when Grant Bascombe arrived for dinner, they had determined plans for several new projects based on Dan's knowledge of the real estate potential around Queenstown and especially Glenorchy.

Even dinnertime turned into a discussion of property development as Grant expressed a lively interest in the development plans and also a keen knowledge of the legal implications involved in the projects.

"Enough!" Sharon finally laid down her dessert spoon and wiped the remains of a banana cream pie from her lips. "I'm just sitting here listening and getting fatter. Would you three men please leave the log cabins alone and finish your dinner?"

"Yes, Mother," Mitch was immediately contrite and grinned as he leaned across to serve himself up some pie and ice cream. "It's just so good to be able to talk with these guys."

"Talking with Dan has made it all so much more a reality," Grant agreed as he held out his plate. "I can see real potential for investment. I'm sure my father will be interested as well."

Dan sat back, watching the other men and feeling a sense of gratitude . . . not just at having his mind diverted from Kiri, but at being able to talk about his work and his passion for building with other men who understood and could build on his own dreams.

"It's great to be able to report some good things back." He nodded toward Mitch. "Especially when you took me on board pretty much sight unseen."

"Hey," he shrugged, "Meredith recommended you and I've always trusted her judgement completely." Mitch motioned toward Grant. "Even with this guy . . . he's a bit dodgy but basically good, I reckon."

"Thanks for the vote of confidence." Grant smiled, then he rested his elbows on his knees and looked around. "Actually . . . we're all here because of Meredith, aren't we? Mitch was Meredith's friend at the Surf Club, and she taught him about the gospel . . . then Sharon was only interested in Mitch because he knew about the Church through Meredith . . . Dan is here because Meredith recommended him to Mitch . . . and I saw her potential as a lawyer . . ."

"Your father saw her potential as a lawyer," Mitch immediately corrected with a chuckle. "You just fell in love with her."

Dan noted the easy camaraderie between the two men. "You know, it's kind of hard to believe that you're talking about my cousin, Meredith," he commented. "I mean, I've never actually seen you all together, and it's been nearly four years since I saw Meredith and now she's on her mission."

"She's a powerful woman." Grant nodded. "Even when she's not here."

"And it's a powerful gospel that also brings us all together," Sharon added quietly. "That's what really unites us . . . the gospel . . . and trust. Meredith was the vehicle to bring us unity in that."

They were all quiet for a moment, then Mitch reached over to squeeze his wife's shoulder. "I love the way you do that . . . sum it all up in a simple statement."

"She'd make a great lawyer," Grant grinned.

"And an even better wife and mother," Mitch added easily, then glanced at Dan. "And speaking of unifying . . . we need to get Dan sorted out in the love department."

Sharon folded a tiny pair of trousers on her lap. "Is there a problem?"

"Mitch doesn't seem to think so." Dan shifted his weight on the stool. "I'm just trying to figure a few things out."

"That's where we need your womanly intuition, love." Mitch patted his wife's knee. "What do you do when you plan to be good friends because it suits both parties and you have a great time, but then after awhile both want to be a bit more than just friends, but then the lady suddenly says she doesn't want a relationship?" He paused for effect. "Does she really mean it, and what should he do about it?"

Sharon glanced at Dan. "It sounds like there's been too much fun and not enough talking. Real talking."

"That's my girl. Straight to the point." Mitch grinned and nodded toward Grant. "And this guy can probably give you some good advice. He knows what it's like to nearly lose his true love."

They all laughed as the color rose in Dan's cheeks, but he appreciated the relaxed way Mitch dealt with the issue. Suddenly he had a genuinely comfortable feeling in his chest as Grant leaned back in his chair and raised an eyebrow at Mitch.

"Talk about summing up . . . you just reduced months of anguish to half a sentence."

"Not to belittle your romantic endeavors." Mitch held up his hand. "It was more to introduce you as the expert on such things."

"Well recovered." Grant grinned and looked at Dan. "I assure you that if Mitch decides that your relationship is right, then he will proceed to shovel you onto the right track with all the finesse of one of his bulldozer drivers."

"For which you will be eternally grateful," Mitch grunted, then glanced at Dan with a suddenly serious look. "I guess I'll take a leaf from Sharon's book here and ask . . . what is Kiri's testimony like? Grant and I have both had to prove ourselves in the gospel before our wives . . . sorry," he corrected himself as Grant looked up quickly, "girlfriends . . . would consider any commitment."

"And I'm still working on it," Grant added and looked at his watch. "And I've got about twelve months to get it right."

"Twelve months," Dan barely breathed the words. "I've known Kiri about two months . . ."

"So . . ." Mitch encouraged him gently. "Why don't you tell Sharon and Grant the whole story?"

"Yes, let me recapture the romance." Sharon smiled encouragingly.

They all sat quietly as Dan finished speaking some time later. It was a relief to share how he felt about Kiri, but even knowing how objective they would be, he had still been reluctant to discuss her earlier ordeals in any detail.

"She's an amazing woman, but she's determined to make it on her own." He shook his head. "I don't know if I can break down that barrier . . . or if she even wants me to."

"I'm sure she wants you to." Sharon curled her fingers through her husband's and he gave them a firm squeeze. "I get the feeling there's a lot you're not telling us, but . . . it must have been traumatic for Kiri to actually talk about terrible things that have happened to her. She must trust you a lot even if she thinks you won't want her."

"Maybe both of you are thinking too much about each other." Mitch nodded thoughtfully. "You know, Dan, it does show that she trusts you . . . to have shared her past like that. I think she's really put the ball in your court even though she's said she wants to break up."

"But how do I show her that . . . that knowing about her past only makes me admire her more?" He studied the pattern in the carpet. "She won't let me near."

"Perhaps she's scared of her own feelings," Grant offered quietly. "I've had divorce cases where clients have suffered early abuse and their marriages have suffered a lot as a result. They haven't been able to let themselves have a proper physical connection with their spouse because of memories or feelings of guilt. Maybe she's scared of that."

Dan sat quietly until Mitch laid his hand on his shoulder. "Do you think you're the one to help her through all that?"

"I want to be." Dan nodded as he took a deep breath. "I finally think I'm ready to learn how, but how do I convince her of that?"

"Just be there," Sharon smiled. "Two months is not long . . . waiting and helping may take a little longer, but she needs you now. You have the priesthood to comfort her and the faith that she needs to move on."

There was a long silence, then Grant leaned forward. "You know, Dan . . . I don't know if any of these guys have mentioned it but . . . several years ago I couldn't even see the point in living." He hesitated and shook his head. "I had a car accident . . . a very bad accident . . . I was driving . . . and my wife and my little baby girl were both killed." He stopped for a long moment, and Dan felt a coldness run the length of his spine as he waited for Grant to speak. "For years I felt like I was in the worst situation in the world after losing the two people I loved most. I even tried to block them out of my mind . . . just forget them. Then Meredith came along and helped me see that they could always be a part of my life if I let them. I was shutting them out because I didn't want to hurt."

He toyed with the edge of the couch cushion. "Now I look forward to the future with Meredith while I can still appreciate what I had before. The gospel has helped me realize that." He looked at Dan for a long time. "I guess I'm saying don't let Kiri go. You've helped her come this far . . . but be prepared for the long haul. She's got a lot to overcome."

* * *

Dan settled his bags into the backseat of the truck, then turned to Sharon and Mitch as they waited behind him.

"Thanks for the use of the truck . . . and all the advice." He rubbed his hand through his hair. "I guess you got a bit more than you bargained for when you took me on as a builder."

"Hey, what are friends for?" Mitch shook Dan's hand firmly, then gave his wife's shoulder a squeeze. "Just make sure you keep us up-to-date with what happens down in Hamilton."

"Hoping that something does happen." Dan shrugged. "The last few days I've fluctuated between getting really excited at seeing Kiri again and then imagining she just ignores me . . . which she's totally entitled to."

"At least you have the opportunity." Sharon smiled. "Your mother did say Kiri was still being the bridesmaid?"

"Oh, yes." Dan nodded, then he gave a rueful grin. "Mum was pretty surprised when I called from Auckland instead of Canada, but she assured me that all the plans were going on whether I was there or not."

"The wedding goes on," Mitch grunted. "It's good to know that nothing will stop the course of true love."

"Except true stupidity." Dan took a deep breath. "Let's hope I wasn't too stupid."

Chapter 17

The sun was putting finishing touches of burnt orange on the ivory walls of the temple spire when Kiri walked out onto the balcony of the motel. The metal handrail was cold to the touch as she rested against it and watched as the color slid away with the sunset. The incoming twilight brought with it an almost instant chill, and she shivered and pulled her jacket more tightly around her body.

"Isn't it amazing how different the temple looks when the sky changes color?"

She turned her head as Wade walked up beside her and leaned against the railing.

"It's beautiful." She looked back at the temple. "I've only been here a couple of times before, but it does make you feel peaceful, doesn't it?"

"Peaceful . . . hopeful about things to come." He pointed up to where the temple sat on the crown of the hill overlooking a broad expanse of farmland. "I love the way it sits up there . . . like we're on top of the world."

"And aren't you . . . on top of the world?" Kiri smiled. "You get married there tomorrow, so you have every reason to be."

"I think I've left the world way behind." Wade grinned. "I'm right up there on cloud nine. It's been a long year."

"But well worth the wait." Kiri nodded back toward the motel room behind them. "You have one very beautiful bride in there."

"Ah . . . my nearly-wife." He looked smug as he folded his arms. "I'm so glad we decided to come back to New Zealand to get married. It's a year ago tomorrow that I baptized Mackenzie at the chapel up the road . . . the day of Charise and Carl's wedding." He shook his head. "I'll never forget that. I came down here dreading the thought of going through the whole wedding process because I thought I'd lost her . . . and there she was waiting for me in her white gown all ready for me to baptize her."

"So dreams can come true," Kiri murmured softly.

"I'd even given up the dream." Wade frowned. "When I met her again after my mission I thought my dreams had come true. She was real . . . incredible eyes and all . . . and I thought that I had been led back to her and that I just had to teach her about the gospel and everything would be all right."

"But?" Kiri already knew Mackenzie's version of their courtship, but she found herself wanting to hear Wade's thoughts.

"But it wasn't that easy." Wade shook his head. "Apart from a pretty pathetic inability to teach her about the gospel, I found that I was second-guessing her all the time . . . making her decisions in my own mind and cutting myself down in the process."

"But you made it," Kiri commented quietly.

"Only with the help of resourceful friends and family." Wade smiled. "Sometimes you can't see what's best for yourself . . . or the person you love. I only ever wanted the best for Mackenzie, but I didn't realize that I was actually taking away her right to choose when I ran away . . . I just assumed that I knew best."

There was a long pause while Kiri stared at the temple, then she gripped her hands around the railing.

"Has Winnie been talking to you, Wade?"

"No, but I imagine she's been talking to you. Winnie is one of those people who assumes she knows what's best for everyone." He chuckled. "Thankfully she gets it right. We just have to learn to listen."

"I think I listened too late."

"Oh . . . I don't think it's ever too late," Wade responded. "Anyway, I have to go and find Carl now. I'll see you tomorrow morning. I'll be the nervous-looking bridegroom."

She stayed on the balcony, appreciating the stillness. There was no sound for a long time except a car moving slowly up the hill beside the motel. Two birds played a swinging game of tag in the sky overhead as she fixed her gaze on the stark lines of the temple.

"Or maybe I listened but didn't believe the answers," she murmured and closed her eyes, feeling the despair settle on her shoulders like the darkness that was dropping inevitably out of the sky.

She heard a door open and shut farther down the balcony, and as footsteps sounded close behind her, she partially turned, fixing a bright smile on her face.

"Good eve . . ." The smile froze as she gasped. "What . . . ?"

"I couldn't go to Canada." Dan spoke quietly. The number of opening lines he'd practiced on the drive down from Auckland suddenly seemed inadequate as he watched the range of emotions crossing her face.

"I . . . I thought you had to go." She tried to make her voice sound normal.

"I did . . . but I got to Auckland and I didn't want to go any farther."

"Does Mitch know?" It seemed an inane question, but her mind wouldn't register anything else.

"He picked me up from the airport, and I've been staying with him and Sharon the last few days."

Kiri hugged her arms and stared at the ground. "What did you tell him?"

The twilight seemed to feel darker and closer as she waited for him to answer.

"Initially, I didn't have to tell him anything. He took one look at me at the airport and asked me if I needed help in the Kiri department."

She looked up quickly then. "But he doesn't even know . . ." She stopped to try and make her heart slow down. Then she actually looked at him again. He was wearing the pale blue denim shirt and jeans that she always visualized him in . . . and his hands were thrust deep into his pockets.

"Maybe he didn't exactly say your name . . . but at least it got you to look at me." Dan shrugged and looked past her as if concentrating on the temple. "And now that you are looking at me . . . I feel like turning around and walking away again."

"Why?" Her voice was barely a whisper.

"Why?" He attempted a smile. "Because when I saw you standing here I just wanted to hold you and . . ." He coughed. "You may not feel the same way."

"And what if I do feel the same way?" Her hand gripped the rail tightly beside her, and she stared at his shoulder as Winnie's words of encouragement sounded clearly in her mind.

Dan swallowed hard and bit his lip. Kiri looked so defenseless with her eyes wide, and he could see the white of her knuckles as she held onto the rail. He still wanted to hold her.

"Let's take a walk."

It wasn't a request, and as he held out his hand, she timidly reached out and felt hers taken in a firm grip, fingers interlacing. For a second he just held her hand, then he turned and pulled her gently after him. "I think the temple grounds are a good place to walk."

They walked in silence up the short hill slope, each busy with their own thoughts, then as they walked around the front of the building, Dan drew her over to one of the seats that overlooked the visitors' center, and the Church College campus, and the surrounding acres of lush, green farmland.

In the deepening dusk the palm trees and buildings below them took on a darkened silhouette, and as the final pink tones disappeared from the sky, Kiri shivered. Dan immediately put his arm around her shoulders and drew her closer beside him on the bench seat. She didn't resist, and he gave her a firmer hug as she settled neatly under his arm.

Suddenly the lights came on inside the visitors' center and lit up the statue of the *Christus*, illuminating its whiteness and the density of the deep, blue wall behind.

"Oh . . ." Kiri put her hand to her lips. "It looks so beautiful."

"It does." Dan nodded. "I had them turn the lights on for us."

"You what?" She gasped, then saw his smile. "Oh . . . you're . . ."

"Thoughtful? I just thought it would make it more special."

"You did not . . . they must be turned on every night." She pointed down at the buildings.

"Well . . . if they didn't, then I would have arranged it just for you." Dan grinned as she nudged him in the ribs, and suddenly they were back to their familiar relationship. "Just for my mate."

Tiny prickles tickled Kiri's spine and she shivered again.

"Are you really cold?" Dan rubbed her arm. "We can keep walking."

"No . . . I'm fine . . . it's not cold goose bumps." Kiri smiled at the view, feeling comfortable being close to him but still uncertain what to say and still unable to look directly at him.

They sat in silence for a while longer, then Dan cleared his throat. "So . . . I guess I'd better explain what happened after I left Christchurch."

Kiri nodded. "I thought this trip was urgent."

"It was . . . very urgent . . . which should make you realize that I must consider you even urgenter." Dan grinned as she glanced at him. "I love it when you look at me like that . . . you get a tiny little trench between your eyebrows."

Her stomach tightened as he gently touched the small frown line on her brow, then ran his finger down to the tip of her nose. It was the smallest movement, but it seemed to break down a wall of misunderstanding in Kiri's mind and she finally looked him straight in the eye.

"I've been praying that I would see you again." She gripped her hands together in her lap. "I know I didn't deserve to, but . . . I just kept hoping . . . and praying."

"Why didn't you deserve to?" Dan asked quietly.

"I . . . I just . . ." She shrugged. "I didn't think I deserved . . ." Her voice broke as she closed her eyes to stop the tears from coming. Then she felt herself gathered against his chest, his arms tightly around her body. It was easy to cry when she felt so safe, and the tears began to flow, releasing years of fear and self-inflicted punishment.

Dan kept his eyes focused on the *Christus* as he gently rocked her in his arms, willing his spirit to give her the comfort and strength she needed. Maybe, later on, she would tell him the details of her experiences as a child, but for now, he only wanted to be part of the healing. The darkness continued to close around them, and it seemed as if the *Christus* shone brighter with each moment.

As her body stopped shaking, Kiri leaned her head back against Dan's shoulder and took a long, shuddering breath.

"I'm sorry." She stared up at the sky. "I'm a bit hopeless when someone is nice to me."

"Would you rather I was nasty?" Dan spoke against her forehead.

"No . . ." She smiled as she wiped her eyes with her hand. "I just can't believe I'm here . . . that you're here."

"Don't you believe prayers can be answered?"

Kiri frowned. "I guess I didn't . . . I mean, I've always said prayers since I found out about them. I used to pray that I could get away from home . . . then that I could find a home . . . a real home . . . but I don't think I ever recognized the answers as actual . . . answers . . . from Heavenly Father."

"Then who were you praying to?" Dan eased her back against him.

"I'm not sure I ever thought about it that hard . . . in case there wasn't anyone listening," she admitted, shaking her head. "I guess it's that independent streak in me."

"So what made the difference this time?"

Kiri stared down at the *Christus* then out at the ebony expanse of fields.

"I think Winnie gave me the courage to believe that I was worthy of being helped . . . of having my prayers answered." She shook her head. "She told me off for not letting myself reach a better place."

"Thank goodness for Winnie." Dan smiled. "And my Dad . . . and Mitch and Sharon . . . for telling me off as well . . . and Wade and Mackenzie . . . for getting married here so I could see you again in just the right place . . ."

"And your grandmother for getting old . . . and Charise and your mum for trusting me to look after her . . ." Kiri nodded in agreement.

"And Ted . . . for finding you at the bus stop," Dan chuckled.

"And my landlady for helping me get pneumonia in that terrible flat." She giggled and put her hand up to his mouth before he could say anything else. "We must be a bit hopeless that we needed that much help?"

"And I still nearly blew it."

"We nearly blew it." She frowned. "And I'm still scared, Dan."

"I know . . . and you're not alone in that." He stood up and held out his hands to her. "Let's walk down to the bottom of the stairs."

They made their way slowly down the concrete steps that flanked the temple gardens, Dan keeping his arm firmly around her waist. Near the base of the stairs, they passed another couple walking hand in hand as they made their way up to the front of the temple. Both couples smiled at each other, then passed on.

"Do you think they've had problems?" Dan looked back briefly. "I grew up thinking that once you decided to get married in the temple then everything would work perfectly and you'd live happily ever after."

"I didn't even think about it," Kiri admitted honestly. "As much as I loved being at church . . . I just couldn't relate to those ideas."

They had reached the front of the visitors' center, and the *Christus* statue was now standing regally in front of them, the Savior's arms outstretched and His head slightly bowed.

"I've actually been down here in Hamilton since yesterday." Dan looked up at the face of the Savior. "I spent a long time in the temple, and then I came down here last night and I just sat here, trying to understand what I wanted . . . what I could do to convince you that I wanted to be with you—to tell you that what's happened in the past is in the past."

"But it doesn't go away." Kiri shook her head. "And I let those things happen . . . which makes me as bad as them."

"No, Kiri . . . you're not!" Dan took a deep breath, then pointed up at the Savior. "Look, what I realized last night was that . . . He died for us. The Savior suffered and died for our sins and our sorrows so that we could repent and move on . . . to a better place, just like Winnie said." His voice dropped to a whisper. "He died so that each of us could find peace. If we refuse to let ourselves move on, then His dying was pointless. If you can't forgive the people who did those things to you, or especially, if you can't forgive yourself . . . then the Atonement was for nothing. Kiri, you've got to see yourself as worth loving . . . so that I can love you the way I want to."

Kiri stood silently as she thought about his words, but she was instinctively shaking her head, as if denying the possibility.

Dan waited for a moment, then he kept talking.

"My father reminded me about a vacation we took when I was about six." He hesitated, but she was still staring at the *Christus*. "We went panning for gold, and I spent ages sifting through all this muck and stones until I found this one tiny piece of gold shining all on its own amongst all the dark stuff around it. I nearly missed it, but Dad saw it and pointed it out to me before I let it wash away." He waited, but she didn't respond. "I think he saved me from losing my treasure again."

Kiri finally looked up, and her eyes glistened in the light from the building.

"I don't know if I can get used to this." She shuddered. "It's hard to think of yourself as gold when you've only floundered in muck and sludge for so long."

"Then the sooner you start, the sooner you'll get used to it." Dan stood behind her, putting his arm around her and taking hold of her hands. "Speaking of precious materials, you're an example of that diamond-under-pressure metaphor. You've gone through the fire and the pressure and come out the strongest and most brilliant gem of all."

Kiri found it hard to breathe as her emotions played havoc with her heart. Part of her wanted to deny everything she was hearing, while her heart wanted to believe that he meant what he was saying.

"If I'm a gem, I still need lots of cutting and polishing," she tried to joke, but as she leaned back she could feel his heart beating behind her shoulder blades and it all seemed too close . . . too unreal. She pulled away and put her hand over her eyes. "I don't know if I can handle this, Dan . . . what if the pressure builds up and I'm not a diamond? What if I turn out to be just like my family?"

He could hear the genuine fear in her voice. "Kiri . . . you don't have to change. You are you . . . and you just have to accept that you're a wonderful person . . . not what everyone in the past has convinced you that you are. You are a true diamond." He reached into his pocket. "Look, I want you to wear this forever, and every time you look at it, you'll hear me reminding you of that and you'll know that it's true."

He held the diamond ring between his fingers for a long moment before she finally turned around. The facets caught the light from behind, and the single stone glittered brilliantly as he held it toward her.

"I know that didn't sound like it . . . but that was actually a proposal." He ran his other hand through his hair, then deliberately knelt down on one knee in front of her. "Kiri Karaitiana . . . through you I've learned about love and charity . . . and I've discovered what hope really is, and now I'm taking a giant leap of faith. Will you please, please marry me?"

A thousand negative thoughts seemed to race through her mind at once, and she even turned her head away from him . . . but she'd turned straight toward the Savior. The faintest moan escaped as she covered her face with her hands, then dropped her hands to her sides and looked directly at Dan. She could actually see herself reflected in his eyes, and it brought a strange comfort that enveloped her from head to foot like a warm cocoon.

"I will marry you, Daniel Harvey," she barely whispered, but she could tell he heard as he stood up and gently took her left hand and slid the ring onto her finger.

"Repeat after me . . . I'm a true diamond." He held her hand tightly until she formed the words.

"I'm a diamond." She shook her head.

"No . . . I'm a *true* diamond." He squeezed her hand.

"I'm a true diamond." She could feel the laugh forming in her throat, but it was a bubble of total happiness.

"And I love Daniel Harvey." He took her other hand.

"I love . . ." She hesitated.

"I love . . ." He coaxed her again.

"I love Daniel Harvey." She ducked her head, but he put his finger under her chin and tipped her head up.

"And I love Kiri Karaitiana . . . Say it," he prompted gently as she looked confused.

"And I love . . . Kiri Karaitiana." The tears began to flow down her cheeks as he gathered her against him.

"Me too."

* * *

The morning was quite cool and overcast, but by the time Mackenzie walked up the stairs to the temple holding onto Ted's arm, the sun was emerging from behind gray clouds that were fast turning white. Kiri bent down to pick up the short train on Mackenzie's wedding gown and followed carefully behind.

Wade's sister had made the dress, and the whole design had been based on a small, gold pendant that Wade had given Mackenzie . . . a tiny scroll shape with its two ends twisted upwards together. Two lives as one . . . for eternity. Kiri stared at the design repeated around the hem and neckline of the finely draped, white wool crepe gown. Even the little jacket Mackenzie had for wearing in the temple had the design worked along its edge.

Kiri stayed a few steps back as they reached the foot of the temple stairs where Wade waited with Carl and his parents beside him, both brothers dressed in dark navy suits with white shirts and deep, terra-cotta–colored ties. She watched as Mackenzie suddenly had eyes for nobody but Wade, her cheeks tinged pink as she saw his face light up with a combination of admiration and adoration.

Kiri glanced quickly down at the ring on her finger and ran her thumb over the solidness of the band to test its reality. Would Dan look at her like Wade was looking at Mackenzie? Was this really going to happen to her one day?

Soon, Dan had said. She touched her hand to her throat as she glanced around to see if he was there, then forced herself to concentrate as Mackenzie turned to hand her the bouquet before she went into the temple.

"I can't believe we're here at this temple again, and it's our girl that's the bride," Winnie spoke beside her, and Kiri smiled as the older woman wiped tears from her eyes. "I told Ted last night that it's time we stopped being left outside."

"You did? What did Ted say?"

"He agreed, actually." Winnie folded both hands over the handle of her handbag. "We're going to do something about it when we get back to Christchurch."

"Oh, Winnie . . . that makes me so, so happy." Kiri held both bouquets carefully as she gave Winnie an enthusiastic kiss on the cheek. "That just makes a perfect day."

"I'm glad to oblige." Winnie smiled happily, then pointed at the bouquet. "Now show me that ring again."

Kiri juggled the bouquets and held out her hand just as the front door of the temple opened and Dan stood in the opening, holding the door for the bride and groom to enter. As he closed the door behind them he turned to look directly at Kiri, his gaze fixed on her as a slight smile tipped the corner of his mouth. She suddenly remembered that she was dressed up as well in the turquoise bridesmaid's gown with her hair and makeup carefully done . . . quite unlike her usual casual dress. She made an unsuccessful attempt at nonchalance as Dan walked down the stairs.

"You look amazing." He bent forward and kissed her gently on the lips. "Would you marry me?"

"Get away with you." Winnie nudged him as Kiri fought to keep her composure.

"Um . . . I can't right now . . . I'm busy." She rolled her lips together to stop smiling.

"Someday soon, then?" He put his hand in his pocket and leaned forward. "A few weeks all right?"

"A few weeks?" Winnie's mouth dropped just as Ted walked over.

Kiri blushed thoroughly this time and lifted the bouquet to her nose to hide the telltale color.

"It's okay, Winnie." Dan grinned and looked totally relaxed as he rested his hand on the back of Kiri's neck. It felt warm and comforting . . . and right. "I'm just testing the waters. I know you girls like to do lots of planning."

Kiri smiled at Dan. "Winnie and Ted are going to have the discussions soon . . ." She hesitated. It even felt strange to talk about future events with him. "Maybe we should wait . . ."

"I don't know," Dan teased. "What is it they say about opposition . . . ?"

Winnie reached out and patted his cheek. "It's all right, love. We understand enough about the temple to know it'll be awhile for us . . . we wouldn't expect you to wait that long."

"Thanks, Winnie." Dan was suddenly serious. "That means a lot to even have you think of that. I'd happily wait, because if it hadn't been for you two we wouldn't even be at this point." He slipped his arm around Kiri. "You two have been our guardian angels."

"Well then, you two and Mackenzie and Wade had just better make sure you're here when it's our turn." Winnie nudged Ted. "It'll be just like a reunion, won't it? All of our children together . . . in the temple."

There was silence as they all realized she was also talking about their son who had died as a baby. Ted coughed and looked up at the spire. "That's the way it should be . . . everyone together. I'm just sorry it took us this long to find out."

"But at least you did," Dan said. He'd heard the emotion in Ted's voice, and he felt an overwhelming sense of love for the older man who had been a complete stranger just a few months before. "And you listened."

"Seems like we've all done a bit of listening, lately." Winnie reverted back to her usual briskness and patted Kiri's arm. "And see how well things work out when you do?"

They had a luncheon at a lovely restaurant that overlooked a lake in botanical gardens. It wasn't far from the temple, and after the meal Kiri wandered out onto the balcony. As she quietly watched some black swans performing a ritual of gliding and swaying on the water below her, the noise from the group inside filtered out to her. Without looking, she could discern the different voices and imagine the looks on the faces, even the mannerisms, of all the people there. All the people who would soon be her family.

"Finding some peace and quiet?" Sheryl Harvey spoke quietly beside her.

Kiri turned quickly, then moved over to make room at the balcony.

"Not so much peace and quiet as time out to really appreciate everything. It's been so busy all day . . . and last night," she added self-consciously.

"Oh my, yes. Last night was a treat, wasn't it?" Sheryl smiled as Kiri nodded shyly. "I'll never forget the look of pride on Dan's face when he brought you into our motel unit. He didn't even have to tell us."

"I still can't quite believe it's happened." Kiri played with her diamond ring hesitantly. "Are you . . . are you sure you and Brother Harvey are . . . all right with it?"

Sheryl looked genuinely surprised. "Of course we are, dear. Why ever wouldn't we be?"

"I . . . I just thought . . . I mean . . . has Dan talked to you at all?"

"Oh . . . you mean about when you were young?" Sheryl asked matter-of-factly. "Yes. He did tell us. At least he told Rob before he left Christchurch, and then Rob told me . . . and we did talk with Dan again last night after you went to bed."

"But that was after midnight!" Kiri sounded surprised.

"Yes, I guess it was . . . but time doesn't really matter when your children need you." She smiled. "And this was one of those very special times. Dan hasn't always been the easiest person to communicate with, so it was a double blessing last night."

"So . . . you don't mind . . . about Dan marrying me?" Kiri stared at some ducks diving nearby.

"Kiri." Sheryl touched her on the elbow to turn her to face her. "You were there when we found out about Grandma Emily's baby, and you saw that it took us by surprise. What I hope you saw, as well, was that we still love her dearly, regardless."

"I did see that," Kiri answered quickly. "And it made me realize for the first time that maybe I wasn't as bad as I feel . . . that maybe I could be loved by . . . someone. I know how much I've come to love Grandma."

"And we all do," Sheryl agreed. "So many people have sad or bad things happen to them that aren't of their own making and unfortunately, they allow it to ruin their lives forever."

"Dan said that unless I forgive myself . . . that I'm not really letting the Atonement work for me."

"He's a wise man." Sheryl smiled. "Dan hasn't ever been a bad person, but he has learnt the principle of repentance through some of the things he chose to do in the past. He's learnt wisdom in his youth."

"I guess I'm learning it now," Kiri whispered. "Loving Dan is the wisest thing I've ever done . . . I'm just scared I'll wake up—that I've been dreaming."

The ducks suddenly sent up a cacophony of squawking and wing beating, protesting at an intruder in their space. Kiri waited until the noise died away and the birds resumed their seemingly effortless movement on the lake.

"Lately, I sometimes feel like those ducks." She smiled. "I'm trying to appear all calm on the surface, but underneath I'm paddling like crazy just trying to keep up with everything that's happening. So much is changing."

"But it's all good, isn't it?" Sheryl patted Kiri's arm. "Dan mentioned something last night . . . that you felt inadequate because of your background . . . being very different from ours. I couldn't sleep for thinking about it, and then I thought about something that happened while you were out with Grandma during the week."

"On Wednesday?"

"Mmm," Sheryl nodded. "Dan's old girlfriend came over." She paused and shook her head. "She'd just come back from overseas, and apparently her parents went home after church full of news about Dan being with you. It obviously triggered something and she came over to 'renew their friendship.' She's been missing him."

"Oh." Kiri felt a coldness in her stomach. "Does Dan know?"

"He does. I told him and he was about as unimpressed as we were."

"Unimpressed?" She felt her heart begin to beat faster.

Sheryl glanced back behind her as Dan's laugh rang out from the room behind.

"I think the point I'm trying to make is that your background is not really the issue." Sheryl frowned. "That girl comes from a diligent Church family, but she's caused them many problems and cost them a lot of money in the process . . . basically through selfishness. She only tried to get back with Dan because you suddenly became a threat."

"Me . . . a threat?" Kiri laughed weakly. "That's definitely a new concept."

"You underestimate yourself," Sheryl smiled. "As far as we see it, you're a beautiful young woman who has had some dreadful things happen to you. You didn't ask to be born into that situation. But more importantly, you chose to lift yourself out of it through living the gospel properly—and our family has benefited already because of your decisions. Having you marry Dan is a bonus for us. We're just delighted with the way things have turned out, and I know you love Dan and you'll make him very happy. That's all we ask as parents," she finished simply.

"My goodness," Kiri could barely whisper as the tears began to well in her eyes. "I never thought of myself as bringing the love. I feel like I've been the one receiving it all." She quickly turned her head away, but in a second she was gathered up in a warm embrace.

"You're a true daughter of God, Kiri, and we love you for that."

It seemed as if years disintegrated as Kiri felt the strength of a mother's love . . . as if she was a small girl again, being reassured and comforted. Her shoulders shook, but she felt more relief than embarrassment.

"Mum . . . what are you doing to make my fiancée cry?" Dan spoke quietly behind them.

"I've just been telling her a few true stories about you." Sheryl gave Kiri a firm hug, then turned her gently toward Dan. "She's in shock, poor child. She may need therapy."

"As long as I'm the one providing it." Dan put his arm around Kiri's shoulders and peered down into her face. She looked up to see real concern in his eyes and gave him a crooked smile as she wiped away the tears with her hand.

"I may need a lot." She attempted a grin. "They were pretty bad stories. I think I may be having second thoughts."

"Okay . . . joke's over." Dan gently prodded his mother's shoulder. "I don't want anything said that may change this woman's mind."

"I don't think you need worry about that." Sheryl caught his finger in her hand and squeezed it lovingly. "She's come through my best mother's interrogation with flying colors. It makes it easier when we all want the same result."

She left them alone to go back into the reception room, and Dan watched her quietly, then he tightened his grip around Kiri.

"I've always loved my mum so much that I didn't think it was possible to love somebody else." He rested his cheek against her head. "When I saw the two of you out here I wanted to come out straightaway, but then I realized you were probably having 'girl talk.'"

Kiri nodded. "She's a wonderful lady."

Dan bit his bottom lip. "When I saw her hug you . . . it made me realize how much I loved her for doing that, but then I also realized that I was loving you as well." His surprised tone made Kiri giggle happily, and she turned toward him, laying her hands against his chest. "Now you're beginning to realize how I feel. For so long there hasn't been anyone, and now there're so many people to love and enjoy . . . it's all a bit overwhelming."

"As long as you love me most." Dan scowled as he covered her hand with his.

"Oh . . . you may have to work on that," she laughed. "I mean . . . Grandpa is so refined and lovable, and Grandma is adorable, and your parents are so wise and—"

"And so I'm going to need eternity to prove that I can love you best." Dan sighed dramatically. "That's a long time, but I think it can be arranged."

* * *

The green paddocks surrounding the temple were all lying limply under a low blanket of pale silver fog when Kiri stepped out onto the balcony. She shivered and blew a small breath of icy air.

"You'd better put that jacket on." Dan walked down the concrete walkway from his room at the other end of the building. "It's really cold this morning."

Kiri nodded as she pulled the apricot sweatshirt she was carrying over her arms then up over her head. As her face emerged through the opening, Dan kissed her nose lightly.

"I like that sweater." He helped pull it into place. "It reminds me of the first day you came out to help at the cabin."

"That seems so long ago." Kiri shook her head. "I wasn't much use to you either."

"You didn't need to be." Dan took her hand and led the way down the concrete stairwell. "You increased my work rate considerably because I wanted to show off."

"Show off?" She looked sideways.

"My cabin . . . my building prowess . . ." Dan nodded seriously. "I wanted to impress you."

"Well, I had no idea." Kiri rolled her eyes. "I was trying to impress you with my work skills . . . after being a burden for so long."

They walked along the silent road running along the base of the temple hill, nodding occasionally to other people out jogging or walking. The sun began to move upward, gently melting the wisps of mist and creating a sparkling carpet of the acres of dew-laden grass. The birds began to chatter in the heavy concealing arms of the palm trees that lined the road as they turned to walk toward the visitors' center.

Kiri breathed deeply and swung her free arm out wide.

"I don't think I ever want to leave here. This feels just perfect."

Dan tightened his grip on her hand as if to agree, but he was staring up at the temple as they reached the paved area in front of the *Christus*.

"Kiri . . . I think we should go and visit your grandfather." He kept his gaze on the temple spire as she stopped walking, and for a long moment she stared at him, then turned away.

"Are we about to have our first disagreement?" she asked quietly.

"It depends." He felt her fingers slipping out of his and tightened his hold again. "I was thinking about it a lot last night, and it's not something I've even considered before, so . . . I figured the Spirit was trying to tell me something."

"Then why didn't the Spirit tell me the same thing?" She toed the ridge between the paving stones. "I haven't had any feeling to go and see him again."

"Maybe that's why I got the impression," Dan answered simply, "because you wouldn't be open to it. I'm feeling more like it is a good idea."

"But, Dan . . . everything is right finally." She gave a low moan of frustration. "If I go back it will only stir up old, bad memories."

"Or lay them to rest," he responded quietly, then drew her toward him until she rested against his chest. After several minutes she shook her head wearily.

"What would it really achieve, though?"

He detected a tone of acquiescence, although she was still resisting.

"I'm really not sure," he answered truthfully. "Except that this time you'll go back on your own terms knowing you've conquered what you came from. Maybe your grandfather needs to see you as much as you need to see him."

"But I don't need to see him," she protested immediately.

"Then maybe it's for his benefit . . . or to show what you became in spite of him."

"I just don't know, Dan." She looked up at the temple. "I can handle the idea of forgiving myself, but . . . I think it's better I just leave Koro out of it. I don't know if I can forgive him or the others."

"Well, it's up to you of course, but maybe that's why you need to go back." Dan rested his hands on her shoulders and turned her toward the *Christus* behind them. "Maybe that's what you need to make the break from your past complete."

"Oh, Dan." Her shoulders slumped. "I just don't know if I can."

He was silent for a moment, then he gripped her shoulders supportively. "If you do choose to go back, I'll be with you this time, and I'll never let anything or anyone ever hurt you again."

They walked slowly back up the steps to the temple, and as they neared the top they were greeted by Winnie, Ted, and Joe and Anna Fenton coming around the top path beside the temple.

"Hey, you two," Joe greeted them enthusiastically. "We thought *we* were up early—you must have been up with the sun."

"Just making the most of being at the temple, Joe." Dan raised his hand in greeting.

Kiri looked at her friends, realizing how much they'd changed her life for the better. She cleared her throat. "Dan thinks we should take the car Mitch is letting us borrow and go see my . . . my . . ."

"Folks," Dan supplied.

Winnie's brow furrowed in concern as she watched the expression on Kiri's face, then she saw Dan's hand squeeze Kiri's, and she nodded.

"That sounds like a good idea, Kiri. You need to go back and clear the air."

It was as if Winnie's words were confirmation of Dan's thoughts, and suddenly Kiri felt a weight release from around her heart like an iron band snapping. She knew Dan was right, and she felt maybe she could face Koro. She looked up at Dan's profile, then back at Winnie. "I feel a bit like a pawn being moved on a chessboard these last couple months . . . and I like it," she joked. "For once I have somebody to help me with decisions."

"That's what family are for, dear." Anna Fenton reached for her husband's hand. "Decisions are always a lot easier to make when you have support."

"And easier to follow through with." Joe nodded and raised an eyebrow at Dan. "You've got a good man beside you. You'll be fine."

In that instant Kiri realized that they all knew her situation and they were all supporting her. Dan was going to be by her side, and she knew that the others would be praying for her . . . even Winnie and Ted.

Again, as if in response to her thoughts, Winnie nodded.

"We'll all be praying for you, Kiri." She nudged her husband. "Won't we, Ted?"

"Yeah . . . yeah, I guess we will." He shook his head in disbelief. "Not that I ever thought I'd hear myself say that."

They all laughed as he scratched his head, and Kiri felt her spirits rising as literally as the sun that lifted in the sky above them.

"So when are you all going back?" She looked at the Fentons. "You're going back to see young James, aren't you?"

Anna glanced at Winnie. "We are, and then we've arranged to go back to Glencameron with Winnie and Ted for a couple of weeks until Wade and Mackenzie get back from their honeymoon."

"Aye," Ted chuckled. "We're going to put them to work."

"You're going to try sheep farming?" Dan grinned at Joe.

"Maybe a bit," Joe laughed. "The main work is going to be teaching these two about the gospel. I've been honing my skills as the ward mission leader, so now I can put them into practice."

"I don't want you practicing on us," Ted grunted good-naturedly. "I want the real thing now that I've made a commitment."

"Oh, believe me . . . you'll get the real thing all right, and if you believe everything we tell you, then we'll talk with the mission president about actually baptizing you."

"Whew." Ted pretended to wipe his brow. "Things were a lot less complicated when it was just me and my dogs to worry about."

"Thanks," Winnie prodded him quickly. "Where does that leave me and our son?"

She was smiling as she spoke, and Kiri watched the love that seemed to flow between them as Ted self-consciously took Winnie's hand and tucked it into the crook of his arm.

"A man can change, love." His voice was rough. "And I'd only change for you . . . not my dogs, even though I miss them."

"Well, then." Joe coughed. "The sooner we get back and get things started, the better. It only seems like yesterday that we were doing the same thing for Mackenzie."

"Then maybe we should just stay here awhile and make ourselves really useful." Anna raised her shoulders. "You're always complaining that you and Rob don't get to do enough fishing, and I'm rather enjoying being around our new grandson."

Joe nodded slowly and folded his arms. "Maybe you're right, love. Maybe it is time we took a bit of time to ourselves."

He was still nodding thoughtfully as Dan and Kiri excused themselves and walked back down to the motel.

"It seems like everybody's life is going through some sort of change." Dan glanced at Kiri. "How do you feel about your decision?"

"I feel fine . . . now." Kiri nodded. "When you suggested going back at first . . . I didn't like you very much . . . but now I realize I have so much support from wiser people who love me, I feel like I could do almost anything."

"Like marry me?" Dan stopped outside her motel unit.

"*Almost* anything." She teased him with her eyes. "Now you're pushing it."

"When, Kiri?" He lifted a strand of hair off her face. "When will you marry me?"

She felt a delicious warmth spreading through her body at his question. Dan loved her and he wanted to be with her . . . forever. She just had to say when. Suddenly the future seemed positive and precious.

"I've always liked the number ten." She looked down shyly.

"Ten months?" His voice was dangerously near a squeak, and she burst out laughing.

"Not ten months." She shook her head.

"Oh . . . ten days . . . that's all right, then." Dan shrugged. "I can handle that."

"Not ten days!" It was Kiri's turn to look alarmed. Then she looked at his face and smiled happily. "Ten weeks sounds good."

"Then ten weeks it is." Dan took both of her hands and held them firmly. "And I want you to remember that whatever happens over the next few days, in ten weeks we're together forever . . . no going back."

She closed her eyes as he raised her hands to his lips and kissed them gently.

"No going back, Dan." Her sentence was a promise.

Chapter 18

They stopped the car on the hillcrest just off the shoulder of a winding, gravel road. Beyond a steep embankment of native fern and low bush, the ground below leveled out to roughly grazed pasture, dissected by occasional dry gullies and patches of yellow-flowered prickly gorse. Post and wire fences divided the paddocks but sagged in most places in a sad state of disrepair. A group of houses sat in an unplanned cluster a few hundred yards away from the surf that rolled onto a rock-strewn beach.

"And there's my home . . . or where I came from," Kiri amended quietly. "I don't think anything has changed in eight years."

Dan rested his forearms on the top of the steering wheel and stared out at the scene. "It looks like a beautiful place. Wake up with the sunrise and fall asleep to the sound of the surf."

"It has potential, but I didn't like waking up because it meant a new day. Going to sleep was even worse." She folded her arms across her stomach as if in physical pain. "And right now, I'd rather be far, far away."

Dan reached out and covered her hands with his. Suddenly his inspiration at the temple seemed to diminish as he realized the depth of the pain she must be feeling. It was all right for him to insist that she confront her past, but he hadn't had to live it and he had no idea what she was going to have to contend with just a few miles down the road.

He stared at the small cluster of run-down houses and the remains of old cars lying in long grass that reached past the windows. There didn't seem to be any sign of people actually living there.

"You don't have to go down there," Dan said, regretting his insistence for a moment.

"Yes, I do." Kiri nodded. "You're right . . . and Winnie's right . . . I need to put the past to rest. Besides . . . that would be a six-hour drive for nothing."

"Not for nothing." Dan smiled. "I couldn't think of anything better than being alone with you for six hours . . ."

"I slept for a long time," she protested, but she knew what he meant. Even the silences between them had a comforting feeling, and she had felt completely relaxed . . . until they entered the valley.

"You know . . . I have another story." Dan grinned. "I've got lots of stories, but this one seems appropriate."

"Right now a story would be great." She turned away from the scene below.

"Okay . . . we were at a youth camp once, and there was another group using the cabins as well. They were obviously kids from really bad backgrounds who had trouble with authority."

"I know the type," Kiri put in quietly.

"They had a woman in charge of them, and one day they were at the swimming hole with us and she made them go up on this really high ledge—way higher than we were allowed. The idea was that in order to jump they had to conquer their fear. She called it 'slaying their dragons,' and that once they conquered that they could . . ."

"Move on," she finished for him. "Do you think it worked?"

"Well, they sure made a lot of noise and really big splashes, and I really don't know if it worked for their fears, but the impression stayed with me. Since then I've often thought about slaying dragons when I've been uncertain about things."

Kiri looked down at the houses below them. "There are a lot of dragons down there . . . and I'm not very brave."

"Then we'll slay them together." Dan switched on the car engine, paused, then turned it off again. "But how about we have a prayer first . . . so that we know the best way to handle it?"

The road down was bumpy and stony, and the car rocked from side to side on some of the deeper ruts, but they finally parked beside a small weatherboard house that had paint peeling and hanging off in places. The long grass around the wrecked cars swayed as they drove up, and two hens jumped from one car, protesting loudly at being disturbed, their red combs wobbling with indignation as they fluffed their multi-colored feathers.

"That was one of my jobs." Kiri pointed at the hens and the car. "I was the chief egg collector . . . and that's the henhouse."

Another three hens suddenly leapt from the rear of the old car and strutted around toward the visitors, their necks extending and receding in abrupt movements as their tiny black eyes darted back and forth in a quest for food. They stalked through the grass, then wandered onto the dusty driveway, pecking pointlessly at the dry soil until a fight erupted over some tiny scrap.

"I used to get scared they would attack me when I was little." Kiri rested her hand on the door handle. "They seemed so big and threatening, and they'd run at me." She smiled. "I'd use a basket of food to defend myself—drop the food and run for the eggs while they were fighting over the food."

"Survival of the fittest," Dan commented as he watched the hens and waited for Kiri to make the first move toward the house.

"No . . . survival of the fastest." She squeezed the handle. "A lot of times I wasn't fast enough and I'd get hurt."

He wondered if she was referring to the hens or her family, and he felt a gnawing discomfort in his stomach. How was he going to react when he met these people who'd hurt her? He'd been preoccupied with helping Kiri confront her past, but he suddenly realized that he was going to have to deal with his own feelings as well.

"Kiri . . . what do you want to do? Do you want to go in alone, first?" He bent his head slightly to look at the house beside them. "Or shall I come with you?"

There was a long silence as she contemplated the ocean, then gazed back at the sightless windows with faded pieces of fabric draping from sagging curtain wire.

"Can you come with me, please?" She took a deep breath and straightened her shoulders, then shivered. "I don't think I could handle it on my own."

Her finger looped through the door handle, and she clenched her fist around it and pushed the door open with firm resolve. "Let's go."

Dan was close behind her as she paused a moment outside the car, then led the way up the three wooden stairs at the side of the house, carefully stepping over the top one where it sagged brokenly in the middle. "I think they'd probably hurt themselves if they ever fixed that."

She tapped hesitantly on the door, but when there was no reply for several moments, she tried again, with louder, more decisive knocks. The second time they could hear sounds of movement from inside, but nobody came to the door.

"He must be home . . . he just doesn't like answering the door." Kiri turned the handle and pushed at the door. It gave way and creaked loudly as she stepped inside into a tiny kitchen. Dan followed closely behind as a swarm of flies lifted off a plate that sat on a bench piled with dishes. Even at midday, it seemed as if all the curtains were drawn and the house was dark and humid.

"Koro! Are you here?" Kiri checked round the door and walked into a small room that contained a well-worn floral couch, a fold-out table with one leg slightly bent under so that it sat crookedly, and a wicker chair that had most of the back missing. An old television sat on top of a wooden trolley, but papers piled on top seemed to indicate that it wasn't used much.

She led the way into an even tinier bedroom, then shrugged as she looked back at Dan.

"There's no one here." She glanced around. "He must be down at the beach."

As she spoke, the door behind them opened.

"Herewini . . . is that you? Did you get the meat for dinner?"

He wasn't much taller than Kiri, but from the way his shoulders stooped, he would have stood much taller as a younger man. His hair was thick and snowy white, curling onto the collar of a thick, plaid shirt. His beard and moustache were also white, but around his mouth there was a slight creamy-yellow staining from pipe tobacco. Brown corduroy trousers that would have fit him as a younger person were gathered around the waist with an old leather belt, and his shuffling walk was accentuated by loose carpet slippers. A walking stick with an ornate carved handle served as a stick to find his way through the room.

"Koro?" Her voice caught and Dan reached for her hand. "Herewini isn't here. It's . . . it's Kiri."

Her grandfather stopped and lifted his head in her direction, then he shook it stubbornly as his lips tightened. "Kiri's gone . . . just like her mother." He shuffled farther into the room and reached out for the arm of the couch, feeling his way through the air till he touched the worn wood. Instead of sitting down, however, he stood facing the wall with his head bent.

Dan watched as Kiri took a deep breath. It had obviously taken her by surprise to see that her grandfather was blind, and he could see the battle that was going on inside her as she studied the old man's back. Now he appeared to be the vulnerable one in the room. She exhaled slowly, then walked deliberately over to her grandfather's side.

"I said Herewini's not here, Koro. It's me, Kiri, and I've come back to visit you all." She made her voice sound light and matter-of-fact, but Dan knew what it was taking to keep her voice from faltering. He offered a silent prayer, willing her to have strength to finish what she'd come for.

The old man still didn't answer, although they could tell he'd heard. He sat down heavily on the couch and placed both hands on the top of his walking stick and stared toward the ocean.

"Kiri's gone . . . just like her mother," he repeated with a determined tilt to his chin, and Dan saw a family resemblance for the first time between Koro and his granddaughter. In that instant he could also see the deliberate blindness that would have kept the old man from seeing what was being done to his granddaughter for many years. He waited as Kiri stared at the ceiling, then knelt down beside her grandfather.

"It is me, Koro. You know it's me and you know I'm not dead like my mother. I've come to see you, and I've brought the man I'm going to marry to meet you."

Once more they felt his silent comprehension of what she was saying, then he turned away from her voice as if she hadn't spoken. But in the next second he was lifting his head as if to sense where Dan was in the room.

"Where are you?" They both knew he was speaking to Dan.

"I'm here, Bro . . . Mr. Karaitiana." Dan held up his hand to stop Kiri as she went to speak. "My name is Daniel Harvey and I'm glad I could meet you. I wanted you to know that I think Kiri is a wonderful girl and I'm very proud to be marrying her. I really wanted you to know that."

The silence seemed even longer this time, and Kiri folded her arms around her body and shivered, as if the past was gradually seeping back into her bones the longer she stayed in the house. She glanced toward a tiny curtained porch behind her, then quickly averted her gaze from the narrow bunk bed that sat against the wall and stared at the curled edge of the carpet square on the floor.

Until now she had been preoccupied with seeing her grandfather, but as she stood quietly, the room suddenly seemed to speak volumes. She closed her eyes as a rapid succession of memories ran vividly through her thoughts, and suddenly she was nine years old again and sitting on her uncle's knee . . . then he was laying her on the bunk bed . . . and then she was older and it was a different face, then two faces.

She felt the blood drain from her face as she forced herself to work through the memories; a low moan escaped her lips as she shook her head then opened her eyes to stare blindly at the wall behind the bed.

Dan watched the blank stare and felt his fists clench as Kiri swayed slightly, then braced her shoulders and swallowed hard. She knew he was watching her, but she couldn't look at him.

It had been hard to convince herself that she could be happy with Dan, and being with him at the temple had made anything seem possible. Now she stood in the very room where so much of her past had happened, and she felt physically ill even contemplating a future . . . let alone with Dan. Her head fell forward and Dan could see the despair. He moved toward her, but then, in an instant, knew to stay back.

He glanced at the old man and gritted his teeth.

"As I said, Mr. Karaitiana . . . I'm glad I could meet you and tell you what a wonderful person Kiri has become. She's finished her degree and is excellent at her job . . . and she's an amazing person." He couldn't stop himself from his last words, "Despite everything she's had to overcome."

"She was a good girl when she was little." Koro nodded slowly, his voice rasping as his breath caught and he gave way to a fit of rattling coughing. "She ran away."

"She *is* a good girl," Dan corrected him, and felt anger rising in his throat as the old man refused to acknowledge his granddaughter's presence. "She's a wonderful girl and she's standing right beside you. She wanted me to meet you."

Dan waited, fighting the impulse to tell the old man exactly what he thought. Then he looked at Kiri and knew to say nothing. He could almost see the agony stripping away and being replaced by a calmness that could only come from within her. When she finally spoke there was a quiet dignity that he could feel and see.

"I left because there was no life for me here . . . only misery." Her chin quivered and she stopped till it was still. "I left because my own family hurt me and used me."

Dan watched the old man's jaw set, and again he visualized Kiri's life. It was as if her story was unfolding in his mind and he felt the pain she would have lived with. How could this man be a member of the Church and yet resist everything that was loving or kind? He shook his head and stared at Kiri, but she was watching her grandfather and her face only registered pity.

"Then I'm glad I came today, Koro." She kept talking as if he were listening. "I'm glad because now I know that I did the right thing in leaving . . . I'm even glad my mother died so she didn't have to live here either. I just can't believe that I was the one who has felt guilty all this time."

"You must never feel guilty, Kiri."

Dan turned as a soft voice spoke behind him, and Kiri stared, her face registering disbelief mingled with happiness.

"Herewini!" Kiri's lip trembled and her hands lifted at her sides. "You're still here."

A tall man, broad shouldered and heavily built, stood in the doorway. His black T-shirt and jeans were damp against his body, and his black hair hung down his back in a long, matted ponytail.

"Some of us never got away." His voice was incredibly soft considering his size. "Koro is blind now . . . the others are all gone or just useless. Nothing much has changed." His lips parted in a brief smile as he noted the neat beige trousers and black shirt and sandals she was wearing, and the way her hair was styled into a neat, short cut. "You look good, cousin. The years away have agreed with you."

Kiri nodded slowly. "It was a good move. I enjoy my work."

There didn't seem to be anything to say, and yet a thousand questions were going through her mind as she stood there. She couldn't look straight at her cousin, and as she glanced away she held out her hand toward Dan. He moved to her side immediately.

"Herewini . . . this is Dan Harvey." She felt the color touch her cheeks as she felt Dan's hand, warm and firm, on the small of her back. "We're going to be married soon."

"Married? Little Kiri getting married . . . and to a Pakeha." Herewini grunted, but it wasn't intimidating, and he held out a large, calloused hand toward Dan. "*Kia ora*, Dan. You'd better be good to her . . . no one else was."

The simple sentence said it all, and for the first time, Dan saw Kiri's face crumple with emotion. She crossed the room quickly and threw her arms around her cousin. Neither spoke, but much was said in their embrace. Only the two of them understood what the other had been through. Their grandfather sat stoically on the couch, staring straight ahead, the only movement his hand clenching and unclenching on the head of his walking stick.

"Do you want to go for a walk down the beach?" Herewini gestured toward the door. "I just brought in a netfull." He grinned slightly as he turned round. "You haven't forgotten how to gut fish, have you, little one?"

"She wants to forget here . . . where she began," Koro's voice trembled. There was another long silence as Kiri took a deep, trembling breath. She suddenly felt like yelling at her grandfather and describing in detail all the things that had ever been done to her under his roof . . . all the times he had ignored her suffering or the suffering of her mother. All the times that death would have been a pleasant reprieve.

She felt Herewini's hand on her arm and looked straight at him. She knew, in that instant, that he had suffered as well . . . but she had escaped.

"Let's go to the beach." He nodded toward the door, and suddenly she remembered the times when her uncles had been drinking and Herewini had quietly taken her down to the beach and out in the old wooden dinghy . . . rowing across the bay, sometimes for hours. She realized that he had saved her from so much more, and had, no doubt, suffered the consequences afterward.

"Yes . . . yes, let's go to the beach." She shook her head vaguely as if getting rid of the images. "The beach is the best place to go," she repeated the words she had often heard him say as she followed him out the door.

But as she went to leave the room, Kiri hesitated, and both Dan and Herewini watched as she stopped to look back at her grandfather. For a long time she studied the old man as her hands gripped into fists, then they released and she turned back and stood in front of him. She could tell he knew she was there, but his sightless eyes stared straight ahead, refusing to acknowledge her until she bent and kissed him gently on the forehead.

"Thank you for life, Koro . . . without it I couldn't find happiness."

This time, as she left the room, she didn't look back. If she had, she would have seen the continuous tears that began to flow down his wrinkled, brown cheeks to wet the yellowed beard. She would have seen his head lift to follow the sound of their footsteps on the wooden boards outside and his hand lifting in silent, trembling farewell.

"*Haere ra, taku mokopuna. Mate atua koe e manaki.* God be with you."

Kiri stood on the tiny porch outside as the wind began to blow from the sea, stirring the leaves and branches of the Pohutukawa trees on the hill behind the house. Herewini stood by her side as she raised her hand to shade her eyes.

"Are the graves still there?"

"Ai . . . the grass has just about overgrown them . . . but I try to clean it up when I can." Herewini folded his arms, and the movement emphasized the width of his chest and upper arms. "Your mother would be pleased to see you . . . and your man, here. When are you getting married?"

Dan waited quietly at the bottom of the stairs, and as Herewini spoke, Dan received an impression of a man large in stature . . . spiritual as well as physical.

Kiri smiled. "Soon . . . about ten weeks."

"And are you a member of the Church?" Herewini walked down the stairs and faced Dan squarely. "Kiri needs to marry a good member of the Church."

Although the question was a surprise, Dan felt a sense of relief.

"I am a member. I serve in the branch presidency in Queenstown."

He found himself being studied from head to foot, then Herewini smiled and shook his hand again with a strong grip.

"I can tell you'll look after my little cousin. I'm glad of that." He nodded and turned back to Kiri. "And I meant what I said back there. I'm glad you left . . . it was the best thing for you to do."

He finished speaking and began to walk down a well-worn track to the lighter, dry sand at the top of the beach. Long strands of grass growing sparingly in the sand whispered at his bare feet as he strode ahead and Kiri and Dan followed behind.

The strong smell of fish wafted up the beach as they walked down to the aluminum dinghy that was pulled up high onto the sand above the tide. Kiri wrinkled her nose as she stopped to slip her sandals off and wriggle her toes into the sand.

"I haven't been to the beach for so long." She lifted her head to the sunshine, letting its warmth soak into her skin and her soul. She closed her eyes and let her mind empty of everything except the muffled crashing of the waves onto the sand. Herewini and Dan waited quietly as she breathed deeply and ran her hand through her hair, then over her face. There was almost a ritual in her slow, deliberate movements—as if the last few minutes had set years of doubt and fear to rest and the open sky and fresh air were spiritually rejuvenating her.

"I hadn't realized what a blessing it was to have the beach to come to. We really did escape here, didn't we?" She opened her eyes and looked up at Herewini with a smile. "Some memories are good, aren't they?"

"The ones with you are mainly good." Herewini leaned down into the dinghy and hefted a large polystyrene container up onto the edge, resting it against his leg as he lifted the lid off and held up a large snapper. "Ready to get to work again, girl?"

He deliberately imitated their grandfather's gruff, rasping voice, but this time Kiri could laugh. Herewini glanced at Dan.

"She's never liked this job, but she was always obedient." He dropped the fish back into the container and sealed the lid again. "She was quick, too."

"Of course I was quick." Kiri folded her arms. "I had to find the fastest way to finish the job so I could get away."

"Except the faster you went . . ." Herewini shook his head.

"The more they gave me." Kiri shrugged and grinned. "I guess I could moan about that, but the good thing is I can go and buy filleted fish now, and when I bless it I am really and truly grateful for the hands that prepared it for me."

They were all conscious of their move to a safe topic and their attempt to reduce the severity of their upbringing with lighthearted comments. Dan leaned against the side of the boat as the cousins recalled more incidents from their past and gradually discussed the various family members who had caused them so much pain in their childhood.

"Petera was in prison down south after he molested a six-year-old girl. He was attacked by some of the inmates and died before they could get him to hospital. Then there's Henare. He was drowned last year." Herewini raised his arm and pointed out to a large rocky outcrop at the far end of the beach. "He was drunk and he took the boat out off the island when it was getting rough. The boat got washed in later without him, and we found his body on the rocks the next day."

Kiri listened as she stared out at the ocean. Those two men had been the main cause of her suffering for so many years, and she registered the details of their deaths almost with indifference. She didn't feel pleased that they were dead, and try as she might, she couldn't even visualize the faces that had haunted her in nightmares for such a long time. She felt nothing . . . as if a veil had literally been laid over the past.

"Kiri?" Dan spoke gently beside her. "Are you all right?"

She didn't realize she had been quiet for so long, and she blinked and stared up into his face.

"I'm very all right, Dan." She smiled and rested her hand against his chest. "Thank you for bringing me back . . . so I can move on."

"*Ka haere mua.*" Herewini folded his arms again. "You must move on, little cousin. You must make a new life with Dan."

"*Ka haere mua*," Kiri whispered as emotion gripped her throat at her cousin's unconscious repetition of Winnie's words. "I can do that now." She turned to Herewini. "But what about you? It's not fair that I should leave and you have to stay."

He shook his head and raised one eyebrow as he nodded his head in the direction of the house behind them.

"There's no one to look after Koro anymore and . . . he won't be here long." He looked up at the sky. "I knew he was sick, but we found out a few months ago that he's got cancer. It's right through him, and the doctor says unless he has all the treatments he's only got a few more months."

Kiri frowned as she looked up at the house. "So is he going to have any . . . treatments?"

Herewini grunted and shook his head.

"Can you imagine Koro at the hospital in one of those gowns that ties at the back and having injections?" He gave a short laugh. "That would kill him before the cancer did."

Kiri smiled weakly at his very accurate description of their grandfather. She could never remember Koro being sick, and he would never be able to stand the confines of the hospital. "So it's just a waiting game?"

"Pretty much." Herewini nodded. "I started giving him painkillers, but he wanted to use some herbs that the old woman gave him." He grunted again. "Then I realized he couldn't see what I was giving him, so I mix the two up. Apart from his cough and feeling tired, he thinks he's in good shape."

"Oh, Herewini!" Kiri's exclamation was about much more than just his comment on the medication. It was a realization of what her cousin had had to live through—and was still enduring—with such mildness and patience. She reached forward and embraced him fiercely as if the harder she hugged the more he would realize how much she loved and appreciated him.

"Take it easy, little one." He sounded gruff, but he was hugging her back just as much, and Dan could see his warm brown eyes misting with unshed tears. It had been worth the trip back if only to reunite Kiri with her cousin.

"What will you do . . . after . . ." Kiri left the sentence unfinished as she looked up at Herewini.

"After Koro goes?" He was more matter-of-fact. "I'm not sure yet." He glanced around at the hills behind them, then out to the ocean that extended to a distant, unknown horizon. "I love it here, but . . . there's not much left. They closed the local school so the children have to go away for school, and they don't come back once they're old enough to get jobs. And there's really only a few of the old people left."

"Have you still got a job in town?" Kiri asked. She knew he had been working in a construction crew occasionally when she'd left.

"Ai." He nodded. "The work is still on and off, but it's suited me . . . with looking after Koro." He kicked at the sand self-consciously. "Actually . . . I have been going into town more often. I've been going back to church lately."

Kiri's eyes opened wide as she touched his arm. "That's wonderful." She smiled as she gave him another hug. "I'm so pleased to hear that someone else in my family is going to church."

Dan noticed immediately that she'd said "my family," and warmth filled his chest as he heard her acknowledge that she had someone of her own, that she wouldn't just be absorbed into his family.

"Mmm . . . it's been good to get back, and everybody has been really friendly . . . once they stopped recalling stories about Koro." He shook his head. "He fussed when I started going back. But then the branch president came to visit him last week and Koro even let the president give him a blessing."

Kiri frowned, trying to reconcile the image of the stern old man back in the house accepting a blessing.

"He's not that bad, Kiri." Herewini read the expression on her face. "And he's gotten a lot mellower since he got sick. I think he just realizes that he doesn't really have anyone anymore. His posterity is gone."

"But it's mainly his fault," she protested immediately. "He's so stubborn."

"So proud," Herewini agreed. "And he simply doesn't know how to repent or say sorry." He raised his thumb in the direction of the house. "He has often talked about you over the last few years, but you could see the way it was when he actually had to talk to you. He doesn't know how to express love or even his feelings, and when he heard you it just came out harshly . . . about your leaving."

"At least I don't feel like I hate him anymore," she murmured and folded her arms.

"And that's what the Church does for you." Herewini nodded his head, his own experience similar. "We're taught to forgive and repent."

"But he went to church," she protested quietly.

"But he never really listened." He smiled. "We were baptized because it was the honorable thing to do in his family. He's proud of that part of our heritage . . . that his *whanau* were among the first members of the Church in New Zealand . . . but he's never really known what it's all about, and when he did come, he just wanted to tell everybody how to run things . . . the way he thought."

Kiri blushed as she remembered the arguments that had occurred the few times her grandfather had attended church with her. It was ironic that he had been so outspoken about everybody else's faults but had failed to recognize or admit to what was wrong in his own home.

"I wonder if he can repent. I mean . . . I know he knew what was going on . . . with us . . . even though he never actually did anything himself. Doesn't that still make him accountable?"

"I would think so." Herewini nodded. "But I keep telling myself that the most important thing is not whether Koro repents but whether I can forgive him . . . and myself."

Kiri stared as her cousin expressed the same fears that had worried her. If only she had stayed in contact with him instead of them both suffering alone for so long.

Herewini sensed her thoughts. "I guess we didn't have each other, so the Lord sent us help." He glanced at Dan. "You got Dan to help you through it, and . . ." Herewini grinned almost sheepishly. "I've met somebody at church who's helped me a lot."

"And?" Kiri clasped her hands together, her eyes suddenly bright.

"Her name's Mara." He nodded. "She's a good lady, and she's been through a hard time in the past. We hit it off right from the start."

"Oh, that sounds wonderful." Kiri clapped her hands. "And we're happy at the same time."

It was a childish statement, but it summed up their feelings for each other . . . and their hopes. They had survived their past, and they had hope for the future.

"So, you're going to have to keep in touch, little one." Herewini rested his hand on her shoulder. "Let me know each time you reach a better place with your man."

"I will." She automatically reached for Dan and he moved beside her. "And you'll do the same?"

"I'll do that." He nodded and held out his hand to Dan. "Look after her."

"For certain." Dan shook his hand firmly. "And you'll let us know if there's anything we can do for you . . . or Koro?"

Kiri heard him say *us* and *we* and her heart seemed to swell. It wasn't just her anymore. It was her and Dan . . . together . . . and it was all right. She felt his arm around her shoulders. It was so much better than all right.

They left Herewini at the boat and made their way back to the car. Kiri hesitated with her hand on the door handle as she looked back at the weatherboard house.

"Do you want to see him again before we go?" Dan asked quietly across the top of the car.

"No." She shook her head and opened the door slowly. "No . . . there's nothing to say right now. He wouldn't want me to know he's sick."

"At least you can keep in touch with Herewini now."

"True . . ." She tapped the door frame lightly with her fingers and lifted her head to look up the hill. "There is one thing I'd like to do before we leave."

"Your mother?" He knew immediately what she was thinking. Kiri looked back at him with a small smile of gratitude for knowing.

"I'd like to visit her . . . for the last time." She nodded.

They drove back up the hill a short distance, taking a barely discernible path through a paddock, then Dan parked where Kiri indicated beside a wire fence. Hand in hand they walked through knee-length grass to a roughly fenced area beneath a large, gnarled Pohutukawa tree. Three hand-hewn rock headstones were just visible through the grass, and Kiri knelt beside one of them for several minutes before she began to pull handfuls of grass away from it. Dan watched as she began hesitantly, then became more decisive in her movements, stripping the long shafts in clumps and throwing them over the moss-covered wooden fence beside the grave. It didn't take her long to clear the headstone, then she sat back and clasped her hands in her lap, staring at the barely legible name written on the stone. Dan waited quietly behind her until she turned to him.

"Dan, do you think it would be all right to say a prayer . . . for my mother?" She didn't look at him as she folded her arms.

"I'm sure it would be fine." He put his hand on her shoulder. "Do you want me to say it?"

Kiri hesitated, then she shook her head.

"No . . . there's some things I need to say."

They stayed by the grave for a while, then walked back to the car and drove slowly down the hill back onto the road. At the foot of the hill, where the track met the road, Herewini stood leaning against one of the main fence posts. He held up his hand to slow them as they reached him and made a gesture for Kiri to open her window.

"I've got a message from Koro." He leaned down to Kiri's level. "It's really for you, Dan, but I think Kiri will understand. He said to tell you that you must look after her." He paused and hung his head, then looked up again. "He said you must look after her . . . because he didn't."

Kiri took one last look back as they reached the brow of the hill, then she put out her arm as if to stop the car. Dan pulled to the side of the road, and she pointed down to the house where her grand-father stood on the porch, his sightless eyes following the path of their vehicle up the hill. As the sound of the engine stopped, they watched him raise his hand in a half wave.

"*Haere ra, Koro* . . . Good-bye. *Mate atua koe e manaki* . . . God be with you." Kiri touched her lips with her fingers as if to blow a kiss. "Good-bye."

Chapter 19

Dan stood quietly in the doorway to his grandparents' small lounge. He pressed himself slightly against the wall so he could watch without being seen as Kiri carefully helped Grandma Emily to hold young James. The old woman's thinly veined hands were trembling as she plucked at the baby's soft fleece blanket and tried to tuck it around him as she held him in her other arm, supported by Kiri. She made sweet, comforting noises as the baby opened his tiny mouth and yawned widely, then waved his fists in a final act of resistance before sleep overtook him.

"He wants to go to sleep, Grandma," Kiri spoke softly to Emily. "If you sit back you can cuddle him more."

She used gentle pressure with her other arm to encourage the older woman to sit back against the couch.

"My baby." Grandma moved slightly and tightened her hold, then she suddenly looked up at Kiri and her forehead creased in momentary confusion as she stared at Kiri then down at the baby again. "My baby?"

"Your baby, Grandma . . . it all started with you." She smiled, and Emily's frown disappeared and she began to croon again, leaning against Kiri, her eyes fixed on the baby.

Dan swallowed hard, watching the smile stay on Kiri's face as she reached up and stroked the baby's head in time to Grandma's tuneless humming. He rested his head against the doorjamb as he thought about the last few days. It seemed as if every day exposed a new facet of his feelings for Kiri as he watched her interact with first her own family and then his.

Their trip back from her grandfather's place had been filled with many hours of talking and sharing feelings and hopes . . . and fears, and laughter. He had deliberately recounted stories of his childhood that had made him look foolish or thoughtless, and she had laughed until she cried. Eventually, she had shared some of her own stories, but they had been mainly about Herewini, the beach and the animals and the ocean . . . good stories with a focus on the positive aspects of her childhood.

When they'd arrived back in Christchurch, Kiri had immediately been swept away into caring for Emily, and Dan had been kept busy organizing deliveries of materials for the new cabin he was going to begin building when he returned from Canada in two weeks.

"Are you getting sleepy too?" He heard Kiri questioning gently, and he looked back around the corner as Emily's head began to nod and fall against Kiri's shoulder. He watched as she carefully eased Grandma's head back against some cushions and maneuvered the sleeping baby under one arm to ease herself off the couch. Checking that Grandma was comfortable, she cradled young James against her chest as she walked over to the window.

"Got everything under control?" Dan stepped into the doorway.

"Oh, Dan." Kiri looked around quickly. "You startled me."

"You were in a world of your own in here." He walked over and tipped the baby's blanket to get a better look. "I swear he gets more handsome every day—looks more and more like his uncle."

"Shh." She muffled a giggle as he gently stroked the baby's cheek with his finger. "I've been trying to convince him that he's not hungry. Charise isn't due back for another half hour."

They stood quietly as the baby suddenly craned his neck and screwed up his face into tight wrinkles, then yawned widely again.

"He can do all that and still stay asleep?" Dan watched the contortions with a look of disbelief. "He could hurt himself."

Kiri smiled broadly and shook her head.

"He's just getting used to his body. At this age, everything they do is wonderful."

He noticed the softening of her voice as she bent her head and cradled James against her cheek, and the future opened up before him.

* * *

He called every evening from Canada, and the rest of the family knew not to answer the telephone around eight thirty. Kiri found that her whole day became centered around keeping Emily occupied and then having her happily settled by eight o'clock. As soon as Emily was asleep, she would shower while she waited for the phone to ring.

"Must be nearly eight thirty." Rob Harvey settled himself in his recliner chair opposite the couch where Kiri was sitting reading a magazine. "I don't even need to look at my watch anymore."

She looked up from her reading and pretended to look surprised. "I didn't know you were turning psychic. I'm impressed."

"Ha!" He wagged his finger at her just as the phone rang, then walked out to get it as Kiri stood up quickly. "I wonder who that'll be?" he added.

He was teasing her with the phone as he put it to his ear and dropped his voice several tones.

"Christchurch Fire Station. Can I help you?"

Kiri put her hand to her mouth as he listened to the voice on the other end, then she watched his eyebrows draw together as his voice changed to the more formal tone he used when making Church calls.

"I'm sorry . . . this is the Harveys' home. This is Dan's father. Can I help you?"

She watched as he began to frown, then he looked toward her.

"One moment . . . I'll just get her for you." He held the phone out to Kiri, then put his hand over the mouthpiece. "Herewini Karaitiana . . . for you."

"Herewini?" Kiri frowned as she automatically held her hand out for the telephone. Rob shrugged as he gave her the phone and discreetly walked back into the lounge.

"Hello . . . Herewini?" She smiled as his soft voice responded. "Are you all right?"

"I'm fine." He paused, and as soon as he stopped she felt a cold tide of realization flow through her body.

"Koro?" Her voice faltered.

"He's gone, Kiri." Herewini had never wasted time with words. "After you left he pretty much stopped eating and wouldn't take his medication." He hesitated. "I think he was trying to die."

"Trying to . . ." The pattern on the wallpaper in front of her blurred as she took in what he was saying. "But so quickly?"

"You know Koro . . . once he makes up his mind." Herewini chuckled, but she knew what he was feeling.

"When is the funeral?"

"Wednesday." He hesitated. "You don't need to come up, Kiri. You said your good-byes . . . and so did he."

"But . . ." She slowly nodded as she remembered the image of her grandfather waving from the porch. "Yes, we did, didn't we?"

"And he said to tell you . . . the last thing he said was, 'Tell Kiri, *Aroha mai . . .*'"

I'm sorry. "Oh, Koro," she barely breathed his name.

"He was trying to make it up to you, Kiri . . . he even asked me to give you some photos. I'll send them down."

"What photos?" she frowned. "There weren't any—"

"You'll see," Herewini stopped her. "I better go now, but I'll keep in touch."

* * *

The large picture, set in an oval-shaped mat, was a black-and-white of a woman of about thirty years of age. She was Maori, her features more fine than rounded, and she was gazing directly at the camera, her eyes wide and trusting. Her long, black hair fell in a wavy mass down over her shoulders, and the simple round neckline of her white dress was offset by a large, greenstone carving hanging on a black cord.

The smaller was a color photo, but slightly yellowed with the edges curling. A young woman was kneeling on the ground with her arms around a toddler. The little girl had her arms tightly wound around the woman's neck and both were laughing.

Kiri picked it up, shivering as she recognized herself as the toddler and her own mother smiling up at her.

Over the years she had tried to recall what her mother looked like, but it was always a feeling she associated with, rather than a visual image.

She reached her hand up and ran it over the encased picture first. *"Maata . . . just like my mother."* Then she traced over the second photo as if she were actually feeling the features on the woman's face and touching her hair.

Kiri sat down on the edge of the bed and looked at the two images. So her mother and grandmother had both been called *Maata*. There was a definite similarity between the two women. The same eyebrows and high cheekbones. The same neatly rounded chin and long, slim neck.

She unconsciously reached up and touched her own chin, feeling the same shape. These were her family. She had gotten her personality and her features from these women. She felt the strength of both almost emanating from the flat images, and she rubbed her finger over her similarly shaped eyebrow. Terrible things may have shaped their lives, but they were good women. There was so much that could have been said . . . so much anger and hurt that could have been expressed, but she didn't feel any of it—only an overwhelming sense of peace and gratitude that he had said anything.

"It's fine, Koro." She stroked the photos. "I'm fine . . . we're all fine."

Epilogue

"Where are we going?" Kiri turned in her seat as they passed the signpost for Lake Pukaki. "Wasn't that our turnoff?"

"It depends whether you want to go that way." Dan concentrated on the road as he pulled the visor down to dim the brightness of the final afternoon sun.

"But we do want to go that way . . . that's the road to Glencameron." She reached for some written instructions on the seat.

"Maybe we're not going to Glencameron yet . . . maybe we're taking a slight detour." He looked unconcerned. "Maybe we're eloping."

Kiri looked sideways at him and she could see the dimple forming in his cheek.

"Okay . . . so where are we going? We can't take too long or we'll miss the baptism. Winnie told me she wants it to happen quickly—before Ted changes his mind."

"Ted won't change his mind." He patted her hand. "And I've already talked to them. This won't take long, but I need to attend to it now."

As the familiar miles of landscape rolled by, she turned with a quizzical look.

"Why are we going to the cabin?"

"I need to do some finish work." Dan waved his thumb toward the back. "Urgent."

"Was that Mitch who called before we left Christchurch?"

"Mmm . . . he wanted to clear up some business."

"Are you going to build more cabins? Did his company get the go-ahead for more contracts?" Kiri tried to sound excited, but she immediately began to think of the lonely weeks without him while he would be working. After seeing each other nearly every day for the last four weeks, she found it hard to contemplate not seeing him often.

"Something like that." Dan turned the truck up the driveway to the cabin, then quickly reversed in the clearing so the front window was facing the lake. "Just wait while I get the lights turned on . . . the new path is still a bit tricky in the dark."

Kiri waited, happy just to watch the almost transparent calmness of the lake and the V-formation of a group of ducks making their way toward the farthest shore.

"Okay . . . come and see the finished product." Her door opened and Dan held out his hand to lead her up the path. Two windows shone with a subtle light, making the cabin look warm and welcoming.

A wide, cobbled path wound up to the front veranda, where the stairs were flanked by some small, dark green bushes. On the veranda, two rugged, wooden rocking chairs sat on either side of a small slatted table with a kerosene lantern flickering on top.

"It looks lovely, Dan . . . Mitch is going to be so happy with it," Kiri began enthusiastically, then she stopped suddenly and her hand went to her throat as she stared at the outside wall. "That's my quilt." She walked forward and touched the familiar fabrics. "What is it doing here? How did you . . . ?"

"I thought it needed to be here." Dan leaned against the veranda post. "Didn't you tell me a story about it . . . about the slaves or something?"

Kiri nodded. "People would hang the Log Cabin quilts with black squares . . . to show that theirs was a safe house."

"That's what I thought." He folded his arms. "That's why I had to hang it up . . . for you . . . for us."

Kiri kept rolling the fabric between her fingers as she began to realize what he was saying . . . but she wouldn't let herself comprehend it until she felt him by her side.

"It's ours, Kiri. We can move here as soon as we get married . . . if we want to. Mitch said we can have it rent-free while we build the other cabins." He hesitated as she didn't react. "I know you still want to finish school, and I think that's really important, so we could move to Dunedin after we finish here. You could go to school or set up your own clinic, and I can easily find work . . ."

He stopped as she turned to touch his face gently, loving the way he immediately rested his head against her hand and cupped her hand under his.

She couldn't answer immediately, but the words were as clear as if she'd stitched them onto the quilt herself. *You deserve a better place . . . your safe house.*

She thought about her drive to pursue her career and suddenly knew that there would be time for that in the future. There would always be opportunities to help others with the skills she had . . . especially her own family. Their family.

Kiri smiled as she slipped her arms around Dan's waist and rested her head on his shoulder before looking straight into his eyes.

"I love it, Daniel Harvey . . . I've always loved the cabin . . . but I love you. And wherever you are . . . that will always be my safe house."

About the Author

Pamela Carrington Reid loves writing romantic fiction and children's stories set in her native New Zealand and the Pacific area. She combines writing with a bridal design business, and is currently working on her master's degree in Family History Creative Writing. She is particularly interested in helping grandparents record their stories for posterity.

Pamela and her husband Paul are the parents of five children and grandparents of two. They currently reside in Auckland, New Zealand. Pamela would love to hear from you and can be contacted through Covenant Communications, P.O. Box 415, American Fork, Utah 84003-0416, or through e-mail at info@Covenant-lds.com.